SECOND CHANCE
AT THE SUGAR SHACK

SECOND CHANCE
AT THE
SUGAR SHACK

CANDIS TERRY

AVONIMPULSE

This book is a work of fiction. The characters, incidents, and dialogue are drawn from the author's imagination and are not to be construed as real. Any resemblance to actual events or persons, living or dead, is entirely coincidental.

EPub Edition July 2011 ISBN: 9780062105226

Print Edition ISBN: 9780062115720

12 11 10 9 8 7 6 5 4 3

This very first book is dedicated—finally—to my incredible husband Bill. You never gave up on me even when I wanted to give up on myself. You never complained when you had to eat frozen pizza (again). You've given me the most wonderful (and sometimes offbeat) adventures that have opened my eyes to the great big beautiful world around me. And you've made me laugh, even if its been at your expense. I love you so much.

CHAPTER ONE

Kate Silver had five minutes. Tops.

Five minutes before her fashion schizophrenic client had a meltdown.

Five minutes before her career rocketed into the bargain basement of media hell.

Behind the gates of one of the trendiest homes in the Hollywood Hills, Kate dropped to her hands and knees in a crowded bedroom *In Style* magazine had deemed "Wacky Tacky." Amid the dust bunnies and cat hair clinging for life to a faux zebra rug, she crawled toward her most current disaster—repairing the Swarovski crystals ripped from the leather pants being worn by pop music's newly crowned princess.

Gone was the hey-day of Britney, Christina, and Shakira.

Long live *Inara*.

Why women in pop music never had a last name was a bizarre phenomenon Kate didn't have time to ponder. At the end of the day, the women she claimed as clients didn't need a last name to be at the top of her V.I.P. list. They didn't need one when they thanked her—their stylist—from the red carpet.

And they certainly didn't need one when they signed all those lovely zeros on her paychecks.

Right now she sat in chaos central, earning every penny. Awards season had arrived and her adrenaline had kicked into overdrive alongside the triple-shot latte she'd sucked down for lunch. Over the years she'd become numb to the mayhem. Even so, she did enjoy the new talent—of playing Henry Higgins to the Eliza Doolittles and Huck Finns of Tinsel Town. Nothing compared to the rush she got from seeing her babies step onto a stage and sparkle. The entire process made her feel proud and accomplished.

It made her feel necessary.

Surrounded by the gifted artists who lifted their fairy dusted makeup brushes and hair extensions, Kate brushed a clump of floating cat hair from her nose. Why the star getting all the attention had yet to hire a housekeeper was anyone's guess. Regardless, Kate intended to keep the current catastrophe from turning into the Nightmare on Mulholland Drive.

Adrenaline slammed into her chest and squeezed the air from her lungs.

This was her job. She'd banked all her worth into what she did and she was damn good at it. No matter how crazy it made her. No matter how much it took over her life.

After her triumph on the Oscars red carpet three years ago, she'd become the stylist the biggest names in Hollywood demanded. Finally. She'd become an overnight sensation that had only taken her seven long years to achieve. And though there were times she wanted to stuff a feather boa down some snippy starlet's windpipe, she now had to fight to maintain her success. Other stylists, waiting for their star to shine, would die for what she had. On days like today, she would willingly hand it over.

In the distance the doorbell chimed and Kate's five minutes shrank to nada. The stretch limo had arrived to deliver Inara to the Nokia Theatre for the televised music awards. With no time to spare, Kate plunged the needle through the leather and back up again. Her fingers moved so fast blisters formed beneath the pressure.

Peggy Miller, Inara's agent, paced the floor and sidestepped the snow-white animal shelter refugee plopped in the middle of a leopard rug. Clearly the cat wasn't intimidated by the agent's nicotine-polluted voice.

"Can't you hurry that up, Kate?" Peggy tapped the Cartier on her wrist with a dragon nail. "Inara's arrival has to be timed perfectly. Not enough to dawdle in the interviews and just enough to make the media clamor for more. Sorry, darling," she said to Inara, "chatting with the media is just not your strong point."

Inara made a hand gesture that was far from the bubble gum persona everyone in the industry tried to portray with the new star. Which, in Kate's estimation, was like fitting a square peg into a round hole.

"Kate?" Peggy again. "Hurry!"

"I'm working on it," Kate mumbled around the straight pins clenched between her teeth. Just her luck their wayward client had tried to modify the design with a fingernail file and pair of tweezers an hour before showtime.

"Why do I have to wear this . . . thing." Inara tugged the embossed leather tunic away from her recently enhanced bustline. "It's hideous."

The needle jabbed Kate's thumb. She flinched and bit back the slur that threatened to shoot from her mouth. "Impossible," she said. "It's Armani." And to acquire it she'd broken two fingernails wrestling another stylist to the showroom floor. She'd be damned if she'd let the singer out the door without wearing it now.

"Inara, please hold still," the makeup artist pleaded while she attempted to dust bronzer on her moving target.

"More teasing in back?" the hair stylist asked.

Kate flicked a gaze up to Inara's blond hair extensions. "No. We want her to look sultry. Not like a streetwalker."

"My hair color is all wrong," Inara announced. "I want it more like yours, Kate. Kind of a ritzy porn queen auburn." She ran her manicured fingers through the top of Kate's hair, lifting a few strands. "And I love these honey-colored streaks."

"Thanks," Kate muttered without looking up. "I think." Her hair color had been compared to many things. A ritzy porn queen had never been one of them.

"Hmmm. I will admit, these pants seriously make my ass rock," Inara said, changing gears with a glance over her shoulder to the cheval mirror. "But this vest . . . I don't know. I really think I should wear my red sequin tube top instead."

Kate yanked the pins from her between her teeth. "You can *not* wear a *Blue Light Special* with Armani. It's a sin against God." Kate blinked hard to ward off the migraine that poked between her eyes. "Besides, the last time you made a last-minute fashion change you nearly killed my career."

"I didn't mean to. It's just . . . God, Kate, you are so freaking strict with this fashion crap. It's like having my mother threaten to lower the hem on my school uniform."

"You pay me to threaten you. Remember?"

"I pay you plenty."

"Then trust me plenty." Kate wished the star would do exactly that. "Once those lights hit these crystals, all the attention will be on you. You're up for the new artist award. You should shine. You don't want to end up a fashion tragedy like the time Sharon Stone wore a Gap turtleneck to the Oscars, do you?"

"No."

"Good. Because that pretty much ended her career."

Inara's heavily made-up eyes widened. "A shirt did that?"

"Easier to blame it on a bad garment choice than bad acting."

"Oh."

"Kate? Do you want the hazelnut lipstick?" the makeup artist asked. "Or the caramel gloss?"

Kate glanced between the tubes. "Neither. Use the Peach Shimmer. It will play up her eyes. And make sure she takes it with her. She'll need to reapply just before they announce her category and the cameras go for the close-up."

"Kate!" Peggy again. "You have got to hustle. The traffic on Sunset will be a nightmare."

Kate wished for superpowers, wished for her fingers to work faster, wished she could get the job done and Inara in the limo. She needed Inara to look breathtaking when she stepped onto that red carpet. She needed a night full of praise for the star, the outfit, *and* the stylist.

Scratch that. It was not just a need, it was absolutely critical.

Inara's past two public appearances had been disasters.

One had been Kate's own oversight—the canary and fuchsia Betsey Johnson had looked horrible under the camera lights. She should have known that before sending her client out for the fashion wolves to devour. The second calamity hadn't been her fault, but had still reflected on her. That time had been cause and effect of a pop royalty temper tantrum and Inara's fondness for discount store castoffs. It may have once worked for Madonna, but those days were locked in the fashion vault. For a reason.

Kate couldn't afford to be careless again. And she couldn't trust the bubble gum diva to ignore the thrift store temptations schlepping through her blood. Not that there was anything wrong with that for ordinary people. Inara did not fall into the *ordinary* category.

Not anymore.

Not if Kate could help it.

As soon as she tied off the last stitch, she planned to escort her newest client right into the backseat of the limo with a warning to the driver to steer clear of all second-hand clothing establishments along the way.

"This totally blows." Inara slid the shears from the table and aimed them at the modest neckline. "It's just not sexy enough."

"Stop that!" Kate's heart stopped. She grabbed the scissors and tucked them beneath her knee. "Tonight is not about selling sex. Leave that for your music videos. Tonight is about presentation. Wowing the critics. Tomorrow you want to end up on the best-dressed list. Not the *What the hell was she thinking?* list."

Inara sighed. "Whatever."

"And don't pout," Kate warned. *Or be so ungrateful.* "It will mess up your lip liner."

"How's this look?" the makeup artist asked, lifting the bronzer away from one last dusting of Inara's forehead.

Kate glanced up mid-stitch. "Perfect. Now, everybody back away and let me get this last crystal on."

"Kate!"

"I know, Peggy. I know!"

Kate grasped the leather pant leg to keep Inara from checking out the junk in her trunk again via the full-length mirror. She shifted on her knees. A collection of cat hair followed.

Once she had Inara en route, Kate planned to rush home and watch the red carpet arrivals on TV. Alone. Collapsed on her sofa with a bag of microwave popcorn and a bottle of Moët. If the night went well, the celebration cork would fly. If not, well, tomorrow morning she'd have to place a *Stylist for Hire— Cheap* ad in *Variety*.

Kate pushed the needle through the leather, ignoring the hurried, sloppy stitches. If her mother could see her now, she'd cringe at the uneven, wobbly lengths. Then she'd deliver a pithy lecture on why a career in Hollywood was not right for Kate. Neither the Girl Scout sewing badge she'd earned as a kid nor the fashion award she'd recently won would ever be enough to stop her mother from slicing and dicing her dreams.

Her chest tightened.

God, how long had it been since she'd even talked to her mother? Easter? The obligatory Mother's Day call?

In her mother's eyes, Kate would never win the daughter-of-the-year award. She'd quit trying when she hit the age of thirteen—the year she'd traded in her 4-H handbook for a *Vogue* magazine.

Her mother had never forgiven her.

For two long years after high school graduation, there had been a lull in Kate's life while she waited anxiously for acceptance and a full scholarship to the design school in Los Angeles. Two years of her mother nagging at her to get a traditional college degree. Two years of working alongside her parents in their family bakery, decorating cakes with the same boring buttercream roses, pounding out the same tasteless loaves of bread. Not that she minded the work. It gave her a creative outlet. If only her mother had let her shake things up a little with an occasional fondant design or something that tossed a challenge her way.

Then the letter of acceptance arrived.

Kate had been ecstatic to show it to her parents. She knew her mother wouldn't be happy or supportive. But she'd never expected her mother to tell her that the best thing Kate could do would be to tear up the scholarship and stop wasting time. The argument that ensued had led to tears and hateful words. That night Kate made a decision that would forever change her life.

It had been ten years since she'd left her mother's unwelcome advice and small-town life in the dust. Without a word to anyone she'd taken a bus ride and disappeared. Her anger had faded over the years, but she'd never mended the damage done by her leaving. And she'd never been able to bring herself to come home. She'd met up with her parents during those years, but it had always been on neutral ground. Never in her mother's backyard. Despite her mother's reservations, Kate had grown up and become successful.

She slipped the needle through the back of the bead cap and through the leather again. As much as she tried to ignore it, the pain caused by her mother's disapproval still hurt.

Amid the boom-boom-boom of Snoop Dog on the stereo and Peggy's non-stop bitching, Kate's cell phone rang.

"Do *not* answer that," Peggy warned.

"It might be important. I sent Josh to Malibu." Dressing country music's top male vocalist was an easy gig for her assistant. He'd survived three awards seasons by her side. He could walk the tightrope with the best of them. But as Kate well knew, trouble could brew and usually did.

Ignoring the agent's evil glare, Kate scooted toward her purse, grabbed her phone and shoved it between her ear and shoulder. Her fingers continued to stitch.

"Josh, what's up?"

"Katie?"

Whoa. Her heart did a funny flip that stole her breath. *Definitely not Josh.*

"Dad. Uh . . . hi. I . . . haven't talked to you in, uh . . ." *Forever.* "What's up?"

"Sweetheart, I . . . I don't know how to say this."

The hitch in his tone was peculiar. The sewing needle between her fingers froze midair. "Dad? Are you okay?"

"I'm . . . afraid not, honey." He released a breathy sigh. "I know it's asking a lot but . . . I wondered . . . could you come home?"

Her heart thudded to a halt. "What's wrong?"

"Katie, this morning . . . your mother died."

Chapter Two

A hundred miles of heifers, hay fields, and rolling hills zipped past while Kate stared out the passenger window of her mother's ancient Buick. The flight from L.A. hadn't been long, but from the moment she'd received her father's call the day before, the tension hadn't uncurled from her body. The hour and a half drive from the *local* airport hadn't helped.

With her sister, Kelly, behind the wheel, they eked out the final miles toward home. Or what had been her home a lifetime ago.

They traveled past the big backhoe where the Dudley Brothers Excavation sign proclaimed: We dig our job! Around the curve came the Beaver Family Dairy Farm where a familiar stench wafted through the air vents. As they cruised by, a big Holstein near the fence lifted its tail.

"Eeew." Kelly wrinkled her nose. "Gross."

Kate dropped her head back to the duct-taped seat and closed her eyes. "I'll never look at guacamole the same again."

"Yeah. Quite a welcome home." Her sister peered at her

through a pair of last season Coach sunglasses. With her ivory blond hair caught up in a haphazard ponytail, she looked more like a frivolous teen than a fierce prosecutor. "It's funny. You move away from the Wild Wild West, buy your beef in Styrofoam packages, and forget where that hamburger comes from."

"Kel, nobody eats Holsteins. They're milk cows."

"I know. I'm just saying."

Whatever she was saying, she wasn't actually saying. It wasn't the first time Kate had to guess what was going on in her big sister's beautiful head. Being a prosecutor had taught Kelly to be tight-lipped and guarded. Though they were only two years apart in age, a world of difference existed in their personalities and style. Kelly had always been on the quiet side. She'd always had her nose stuck in a book, was always the type to smooth her hand over a wrinkled cushion just to make it right. Always the type to get straight A's and still worry she hadn't studied enough.

Kate took a deep breath and let it out slowly.

It was hard to compete with perfection like that.

"I still can't believe it's been ten years since you've been home," Kelly said.

Kate frowned as they passed the McGruber farm where someone had planted yellow mums in an old toilet placed on the front lawn. "And now I get the pleasure of remembering why I left in the first place."

"I don't know." Kelly leaned forward and peered through the pitted windshield. "It's really spectacular in an unrefined kind of way. The fall colors are on parade and snow is frosting the mountain peaks. Chicago might be beautiful, but it doesn't compare to this." Lines of concern scrunched between Kelly's eyes ruined the perfection of her face. "I know how hard this is for you, Kate. But I'm glad you came."

The muscles between Kate's shoulders tightened. Right now, she didn't want to think about what might be difficult for her. Others were far more important. "I'm here for Dad," she said.

"You know, I was thinking the other day . . . we all haven't been together since we met up at the Super Bowl last year." Kelly shook her head and smiled. "God. No matter that our brother was playing, I thought you and Mom were going to root for opposing teams just so you'd have one more thing to disagree about."

"I did not purposely spill my beer on her."

Kelly laughed. "Yes, you did."

The memory came back in full color and Kate wanted to laugh too.

"That's why Dad will be really glad to see you, Kate. You've always made him smile. You know you were always his favorite."

At least she'd been *somebody's* favorite. "I've missed him." Kate fidgeted with the string attached to her hoodie. "I didn't mean to . . ."

"I know." Kelly wrapped her fingers around the steering wheel. "He knew too."

The reminder of her actions stuck in Kate's throat. If she could do it all over, she'd handle it much differently. At the time she'd been only twenty, anxious to live her dreams and get away from the mother who disapproved of everything she did.

The interior of the car fell silent, except for the wind squealing through the disintegrating window seals and the low rumble of the gas-guzzling engine. Kate knew she and her sister were delaying the obvious discussion. There was no easy way to go about it. The subject of their mother was like walking on cracked ice. No matter how lightly you tiptoed, you were bound to plunge into turbulent waters. Their mother had given birth to three children who had all moved away to different parts of the country. Each one had a completely different view of her parental skills.

Her death would bring them all together.

"After all the times we offered to buy her a new car I can't believe Mom still drove this old boat," Kate said.

"I can't believe it made it to the airport and back." Kelly tucked a stray blond lock behind her ear and let out a sigh. "Mom was funny about stuff, you know. She was the biggest 'if it ain't broke don't fix it' person I ever knew."

Was.

Knew.

As in past tense.

Kate glanced out the passenger window.

Her mother was gone.

No more worrying about what to send for Mother's Day or Christmas or her birthday. No more chatter about the temperamental oven in their family bakery, or the dysfunctional quartet that made up the Founder's Day parade committee, or the latest gnome she'd discovered to stick in her vegetable garden.

No more . . . anything.

Almost a year had passed since she'd been with her mother. But even that hadn't been the longest she'd gone without seeing her. Kate had spent tons of time with Dean and Kelly. She'd snuck in a fishing trip or two with her dad. But an entire five years had gone by before Kate had finally agreed to meet up with her mother in Chicago to celebrate Kelly's promotion with the prosecutor's office. The reunion had been awkward. And as much as Kate had wanted to hear "I'm sorry" come from her mother's lips, she'd gone back to Los Angeles disappointed.

Over the years Kate had meant to come home. She'd meant to apologize. She'd meant to do a whole lot of stuff that just didn't matter anymore. Good intentions weren't going to change a thing. A knife of pain stabbed between her eyes. The time for could have, should have, would have, was history. Making amends was a two-way street and her mother hadn't made an effort either.

She shifted to a more comfortable position and her gaze landed on the cluttered chaos in the backseat—an array of pastry cookbooks, a box of quilting fabric, and a knitting tote where super-sized needles poked from the top of a ball of red yarn. Vanilla—her mother's occupational perfume—lingered throughout the car.

Kate inhaled. The scent settled into her soul and jarred loose a long-lost memory. "Do you remember the time we all got chicken pox?" she asked.

"Oh, my God, yes." Kelly smiled. "We were playing tag. Mom broke up the game and stuck us all in one bedroom."

"I'd broken out with blisters first," Kate remembered, scratching her arm at the reminder. "Mom said if one of us got the pox, we'd all get the pox. And we might as well get it done and over with all at once."

"So *you* were the culprit," Kelly said.

"I don't even know where I got them." Kate shook her head. "All I know is I was miserable. The fever and itching were bad enough. But then you and Dean tortured me to see how far you could push before I cried."

"If I remember, it didn't take long."

"And if I remember," Kate said, "it didn't take long before you were both whining like babies."

"Karma," Kelly admitted. "And just when we were at our worst, Mom came in and placed a warm sugar cookie in each of our hands."

Kate nodded, remembering how the scent of vanilla lingered long after her mother had left the room. "Yeah."

The car rambled past Balloons and Blooms, the florist shop Darla Davenport had set up in her century-old barn.

"Dad ordered white roses for her casket." Kelly's voice wobbled. "He was concerned they wouldn't be trucked in on time and, of course, the price. I told him not to worry—that we kids would take care of the cost. I told him to order any damn thing he wanted."

Kate leaned forward and peered through her sister's sunglasses. "Are you okay?"

"Are you?" Kelly asked.

Instead of answering, Kate twisted off the cap of her Starbuck's Frappuccino and slugged down the remains. The drink gave her time to compose herself, if that were even possible. She thought of her dad. Simple. Hard-working. He'd taught her how to tie the fly that had helped her land the derby-winning trout the year she turned eleven. He couldn't have been more different from her mother if he'd tried. And he hadn't deserved to be abandoned by his youngest child.

"How's Dad doing?" Kate asked, as the iced drink settled in her stomach next to the wad of guilt.

"He's devastated." Kelly flipped on the fan. Her abrupt action seemed less about recirculating the air and more about releasing a little distress. "How would you be if the love of your life died in your arms while you were tying on her apron?"

"I can't answer that," Kate said, trying not to think about the panic that must have torn through him.

"Yeah." Kelly sighed. "Me either."

Kate tried to swallow but her throat muscles wouldn't work. She turned in her seat and looked at her sister. "What's he going to do now, Kel? Who will take care of him? He's never been alone. Ever," she said, her voice an octave higher than normal. "Who's going to help him at the Shack? Cook for him? Who's he going to talk to at night?"

"I don't know. But we definitely have to do something." Kelly nodded as though a lightbulb in her head suddenly hit a thousand watts. "Maybe Dean will have some ideas."

"Dean?" Kate leaned back in her seat. "Our brother? The king of non-relationship relationships?"

"Not that either of us has any room to talk."

"Seriously." Kate looked out the window, twisting the rings on her fingers. The urge to cry for her father welled in her throat. Her parents had been a great example of true love. They cared for each other, had each other's backs, thought of each other first. Even with her problematic relationship with her mother, Kate couldn't deny that the woman had been an extraordinary wife to the man who worshipped her. The chances of finding a love like the one her parents had shared were one in a million. Kate figured that left her odds stretching out to about one in a hundred gazillion.

"What's wrong with us, Kel?" she asked. "We were raised

by parents the entire town puts on a pedestal, yet we all left them behind for something *bigger and better*. Not a single one of us has gotten married or even come close. As far as I know, Dean has no permanent designs on his current bimbo of the moment. You spend all your nights with a stack of law books. I spend too much time flying coast-to-coast to even meet up with someone for a dinner that doesn't scream fast food."

"Oh, poor you. New York to L.A. First Class. Champagne. And all those gorgeous movie stars and rock stars you're surrounded by. You're breaking my heart."

Kate snorted. "Yeah, I live such a glamorous life."

A perfectly arched brow lifted on Kelly's perfect face. "You don't?"

While Kate enjoyed what she did for a living, every day her career hung by a sequin while the next up-and-coming celebrity stylist waited impatiently in the wings for her to fall from Hollywood's fickle graces. She'd chosen a career that tossed her in the spotlight, but she had no one to share it with. And often that spotlight felt icy cold. "Yeah, sure. I just get too busy sometimes, you know?"

"Unfortunately, I do." Kelly gripped the wheel tighter. "You know . . . you could have stuck around and married Matt Ryan."

"Geez." Kate's heart did a tilt-a-whirl spin. "I haven't heard that name in forever."

"When you left, you broke his heart."

"How do you know?"

"Mom said."

"Hey, I gave him my virginity. I call that a fair trade."

"Seriously?" Kelly's brows lifted in surprise. "I had no idea."

"It wasn't something I felt like advertising at the time."

"He was pretty cute from what I remember."

"Don't go there, Kel. There's an ocean under that bridge. So mind your own business."

Matt Ryan. Wow. Talk about yanking up old memories. Not unpleasant ones either. From what Kate remembered, Matt had been very good at a lot of things. Mostly ones that involved hands and lips. But Matt had been that boy from the proverbial wrong side of the tracks and she'd had bigger plans for her life.

Her mother had only mentioned him once or twice after Kate had skipped town. Supposedly he'd eagerly moved on to all the other girls wrangling for his attention. Good for him. He'd probably gotten some poor girl pregnant and moved next door to his mother. No doubt he'd been saddled with screaming kids and a complaining wife. Kate imagined he'd still be working for his Uncle Bob fixing broken axles and leaky transmissions. Probably even had a beer gut by now. Maybe even balding. Poor guy.

Kelly guided their mother's boat around the last curve in the road that would lead them home. Quaking aspens glittered gold in the sunlight and tall pines dotted the landscape. Craftsman style log homes circled the area like ornaments on a Christmas wreath.

"Mom was proud of you, you know," Kelly blurted.

"What?" Kate's heart constricted. She didn't need for her sister to lie about their mother's mind-set. Kate knew the truth. She'd accepted it long ago. "No way. Mom did everything she could to pull the idea of being a celebrity stylist right out of my stubborn head."

"You're such a dork." Kelly shifted in her seat and gripped

the steering wheel with both hands. "Of course she was proud. She was forever showing off the magazine articles you were in. She even kept a scrapbook."

"She did not."

"She totally did."

"Go figure. The night before I boarded that bus for L.A., she swore I'd never make a living hemming skirts and teasing hair."

"No, what she said was, making a living hemming skirts and teasing hair wasn't for you," Kelly said.

"That's not the way I remember it."

"Of course not. You were so deeply immersed in parental rebellion she could have said the sky was blue and you'd have argued that it was aqua."

"We did argue a lot."

Kelly shook her head. "Yeah, kind of like you were both cut from the same scrap of denim. I think that's what ticked you off the most and you just didn't want to admit it."

No way. "That I was like Mom?"

"You could have been identical twins. Same red hair. Same hot temper."

"I never thought I was anything like her. I still don't."

"How's that river of denial working for you?"

"How's that rewriting history working for *you*?"

Kelly tightened her fingers on the steering wheel. "Someday you'll get it, little sister. And when you do, you're going to be shocked that you didn't see it earlier."

The remnants of the old argument curdled in Kate's stomach. "She didn't believe in me, Kel."

"Then she was wrong."

For some reason the acknowledgment from her big sister didn't make it any better.

"She was also wrong about you and your financial worth," Kelly added. "You make three times as much as I do."

"But not as much as Dean."

"God doesn't make as much as Dean," Kelly said.

Their big brother had always been destined for greatness. If you didn't believe it, all you had to do was ask him. Being an NFL star quarterback did have its perks. Modesty wasn't one of them.

"Almost there," Kelly announced.

The green highway sign revealed only two more miles to go. Kate gripped the door handle to steady the nervous tension tap-dancing on her sanity.

Ahead, she noticed the swirling lights atop a sheriff's SUV parked on the shoulder of the highway. The vehicle stopped in front of the cop had to be the biggest monster truck Kate had ever seen. In L.A., which oozed with hybrids and luxury cruisers, one could only view a farmboy-vehicle-hopped-up-on-steroids in box office bombs like the *Dukes of Hazzard*.

The swirling lights dredged up a not-so-fond memory of Sheriff Washburn, who most likely sat behind the wheel of that Chevy Tahoe writing up the fattest citation he could invent. A decade ago, the man and his Santa belly had come hunting for her. When she hadn't shown up at home at o'dark thirty like her mother had expected, the SOS call had gone out. Up on Lookout Point the sheriff had almost discovered her and Matt sans clothes, bathed in moonlight and lust.

As it was, Matt had been quick to act and she'd managed

to sneak back through her bedroom window before she ruined her shaky reputation for all time. Turned out it wouldn't have mattered. A few days later she boarded a bus leaving that boy and the town gossips behind to commiserate with her mother about what an ungrateful child she'd been.

As they approached the patrol vehicle, a deputy stepped out and, hand on gun, strolled toward the monster truck.

Mirrored shades. Midnight hair. Wide shoulders. Trim waist. Long, long legs. And . . . Oh. My. God. Not even the regulation pair of khaki uniform pants could hide his very fine behind. Nope. Definitely *not* Sheriff Washburn.

A double take was definitely in order.

"Wow," Kate said.

"They didn't make 'em like that when we lived here," Kelly noted.

"Seriously." Kate shifted back around in her seat. And frowned. What the hell was wrong with her? Her mother had been dead for two days and *she* was checking out guys?

"Well, ready or not, here we are."

At her sister's announcement Kate looked up at the overhead sign crossing the two-lane road.

Welcome to Deer Lick, Montana. Population 6,000.

For Kate it might as well have read *Welcome to Hell*.

Late the following afternoon, Kate stood amid the mourners gathered at the gravesite for Leticia Jane Silverthorne's burial. Most were dressed in a variety of appropriate blacks and dark blues. The exception being Ms. Virginia Peat, who'd decided the bright hues of the local Red Hat Society were more appropriate for a deceased woman with a green thumb and a knack for planting mischief wherever she went.

No doubt her mother had a talent for inserting just the right amount of monkey business into things to keep the town blabbing for days, even weeks, if the gossips were hungry enough. Better for business, she'd say. The buzz would catch on and the biddies of Deer Lick would flock to the Sugar Shack for tea and a sweet treat just to grab another tasty morsel of the brewing scandal.

Today, the Sugar Shack was closed. Her mother's cakes and pies remained unbaked. And the lively gossip had turned to sorrowful memories.

Beneath a withering maple, Kate escaped outside the circle of friends and neighbors who continued to hug and offer condolences to her father and siblings. Their almost overwhelming compassion notched up her guilt meter and served as a reminder of the small-town life she'd left behind. Which was not to say those in Hollywood were cold and unfeeling, she'd just never had any of them bring her hot chicken soup.

Plans had been made for a potluck gathering at the local Grange—a building that sported Jack Wagoner's award-winning moose antlers and held all the community events—including wedding receptions and the Oktober Beer and Brat Fest. The cinder block structure had never been much to look at but obviously it remained the epicenter of the important events in beautiful downtown Deer Lick.

A variety of funeral casseroles and home-baked treats would be lined up on the same long tables used for arm wrestling competitions and the floral arranging contest held during the county fair. As far as Kate could see, not much had changed since she'd left. And she could pretty much guarantee that before the end of the night, some elder of the community would break out the bottle of huckleberry wine and make a toast to the finest pastry chef this side of the Rockies.

Then the stories would start to fly and her mother's name would be mentioned over and over along with the down and dirty details of some of her more outrageous escapades. Tears and laughter would mingle. Hankies would come out of back pockets to dab weeping eyes.

The truth hit Kate in the chest, tore at her lungs. The good people of Deer Lick had stood by her mother all these years while Kate had stood off in the distance.

She brushed a speck of graveside dust from the pencil skirt she'd picked up in Calvin Klein's warehouse last month. A breeze had cooled the late afternoon air and the thin material she wore could not compete. She pushed her sunglasses into place, did her best not to shiver, and tried to blend in with the surroundings. But the cost alone of her Louboutin peep toes separated her from the simple folk who dwelled in this town.

Maybe she should have toned it down some. She could imagine her mother shaking her head and asking who Kate thought she'd impress.

"Well, well, lookie who showed up after all."

Kate glanced over her shoulder and into the faded hazel eyes of Edna Price, an ancient woman who'd always reeked of moth balls and Listerine. The woman who'd been on the Founder's Day Parade committee alongside her mother for as long as Kate could remember.

"Didn't think you'd have the gumption," Edna said.

Gumption? Who used that word anymore?

Edna poked at Kate's ankles with a moose-head walking stick. "Didn't think you'd have the nerve," Edna enunciated as though Kate were either deaf or mentally challenged.

"Why would I need *nerve* to show up at my own mother's funeral?" *Oh, dumb question, Kate. Sure as spit the old biddy would tell her ten ways to Sunday why.*

The old woman leaned closer. Yep, still smelled like moth balls and Listerine.

"You left your dear sweet mama high and dry, what, twenty years ago?"

Ten.

"It's your fault she's where she is."

"*My* fault?" The accusation snagged a corner of Kate's heart and pulled hard. "What do you mean?"

"Like you don't know."

She had no clue. But that didn't stop her mother's oldest friend from piling up the charges.

"Broke her heart is what you did. You couldn't get up the nerve to come back when she was breathin'. Oh, no. You had to wait until—"

Kate's patience snapped. "Mrs. Price . . . you can blame or chastise me all you want. But not today. Today, I am allowed to grieve like anyone else who's lost a parent. Got it?"

"Oh, I got it." Her pruney lips curled into a snarl. "But I also got opinions and I aim to speak them."

"Not today you won't." Kate lifted her sunglasses to the top of her head and gave Mrs. Price her best glare. "Today you will respect my father, my brother, and my sister. Or I will haul you out of this cemetery by your fake pearl necklace. Do I make myself clear?"

The old woman snorted then swiveled on her orthopedic shoes and hobbled away. Kate didn't mind taking a little heat. She was, at least, guilty of running and never looking back. But today belonged to her family and she'd be goddamned if she'd let anybody drag her past into the present and make things worse.

Great. And now she'd cursed on sacred ground.

Maybe just thinking the word didn't count. She already had enough strikes against her.

It's your fault. . .

Exactly what had Edna meant? How could her mother's death be any fault of hers when she'd been hundreds of miles away?

Kate glanced across the carpet of grass toward the flower-strewn mound of dirt. Beneath the choking scent of carnations and roses, beneath the rich dark soil, lay her mother.

Too late for good-byes.

Too late for apologies.

Things just couldn't get worse.

Unable to bear the sight of her mother's grave, Kate turned her head. She startled at the sudden appearance of the man in the khaki-colored deputy uniform who stood before her. She looked up—way up—beyond the midnight hair and into the ice blue eyes of Matt Ryan.

The boy she'd left behind.

CHAPTER THREE

S he was back.

Ten years of anticipation tumbled through Matt's chest and left him breathless. When her mother passed, Matt knew she'd be back for the funeral. He'd been prepared. Still, seeing her across the casket and beside her father had been a shock. The sweat in his palms left no question.

Seeing her again brought him back to the day she'd left.

Without a note.

Without a good-bye.

Without so much as a kiss-my-ass.

It had been ten years since they'd parked at Lookout Point in his barely operable Chevy half ton and explored each others bodies long into the night. Ten years since they'd snuggled up in the bed of that old truck beneath a tattered plaid blanket where he'd planned to ask her the most important question of his life. Ten years since she'd snuck out of town and disappeared, taking his and her parents' hearts with her.

She wasn't a girl anymore.

Katie Silverthorne had developed into . . . well, she'd definitely developed. At fourteen she'd had freckles and a small chip in her front tooth from walking into an open school locker. At twenty she'd been a long-legged girl with fewer curves than a stretch of desert road. Now, the freckles and chip in her tooth were gone and she had curves in all the right places. The woman who stood in front of him with her ginger hair streaked blond, tawny gold skin, smoky green eyes, and lips so suggestive a man would be foolish not to kiss them, was anything but juvenile.

Too bad she was so cold-hearted.

If the situation were different, if they weren't standing just feet away from where her mother had been laid in the hard, frozen ground, Matt wouldn't hesitate to tell her what he thought. She didn't deserve pity. Why the hell would she even put up the pretense of grieving when he and everyone knew she didn't give a shit about either of her parents?

She didn't deserve the time of day.

But he respected her mother. Her father. And that changed everything.

After Katie skipped town, her mother had lent a warm embrace to his wounded soul and become his friend—a surrogate mother for his own who refused to lift her life out of a bottle. In turn, he developed a love and appreciation for both her parents and the incredible role models they'd become for him. For that reason alone Matt felt it necessary to offer his condolences to the *girl* who'd not only run out on him but her own parents.

"Your mother was a wonderful woman," he said, dropping his aviators into place. "We'll miss her very much."

Katie looked up at him. Uncertainty sparked in her eyes. "Thank you."

Matt forced himself not to stare at her glossy lips as she spoke, so he scanned the cemetery, the flower-carpeted grave, the departing mourners.

He found himself entirely too distracted by the woman in front of him who wore a clinging black jacket and a skirt too short for somewhere as off the beaten path as Deer Lick. Or her mother's funeral. She shifted her weight from one enticing hip to the other and the movement caught his eye.

"It's good to see you again, Matt," she said barely above a husky whisper.

Ten years melted away as he looked down at her, remembering the last time he'd held her. She'd been naked and warm in his arms and sweet as his Uncle Bob's huckleberry wine. But those days were gone for good and she'd broken too many hearts along the way.

"Wish I could say the same."

Stunned right down to her pink toenails, Kate watched Matt walk away. All six feet plus of lean, hard muscle sheathed in a khaki uniform.

She wanted to kick him.

Okay. So maybe he had a right to have an attitude with her. Maybe she might deserve his animosity just a teeny tiny bit. And maybe he hadn't gone the wrong-side-of-the-tracks path as she'd imagined. No beer gut. No balding head.

It was just too bad that he wasn't nearly as pleasant as that gorgeous face.

"Katie?" Her father waved her toward him. "Come here, honey. Time to go."

As she made her way over to join her father and siblings, taking care not to muddy the red soles of her shoes in the soggy grass, Kate glanced back where Matt remained near her mother's final resting place. A pretty, petite blond walked up to him and took his hand. He smiled down at her.

Wife?

Girlfriend?

Definitely attached.

And Kate definitely didn't care.

Whatever he did with his life or whomever he did it with didn't matter to her.

Her father tucked her beneath his protective arm and as a family—or what was left of them—they all headed toward the Grange a few blocks away. As they walked down the sidewalk, Kate gave a last glance at her mother's grave. And one more glance at the man who'd been an important part of her young life.

He, however, didn't look back.

Several hours later, the interior of the Grange remained packed wall to cinder-block wall. The empty casserole dishes and lunchmeat platters that cluttered the banquet table confirmed that Letty Silverthorne had been a popular woman. In the corner the jukebox played Nat King Cole's *Unforgettable*. Somewhere in the distance Junior Walker snorted a laugh as he recalled the time Letty had chased a skunk out of her garden, only to be sprayed in the keester before the animal trotted away. "Only good skunk is a dead skunk," he recalled her saying. Everyone laughed.

Kate remembered how every October her father would dress in camo, sling a rifle over his shoulder, kiss her mother on the forehead and head out to the forest to slay Bambi or Bullwinkle or whatever four-legged critter happened to end up in his crosshairs. A few days later he'd come home like Rambo with the carcass slung over his shoulder. Her mother would praise him with such enthusiasm you'd think he'd been nominated president of the NRA. Yet the woman would nicely shoo a stinky old skunk from her much-loved garden.

Letty Silverthorne, savior of skunks, would never dream of picking up a firearm. But it was okay if someone else did.

Kate sat on a metal folding chair, an untouched piece of pineapple upside-down cake on a plate in her lap, listening to the *remember when* stories fly about the room. She had no appetite for anything other than escape. No room for anything except guilt because *she* didn't have any recent Letty stories.

And she sincerely didn't know how many more she could take.

"You look like you could use a big brother right about now."

Kate looked up into Dean's handsome face—a face that graced wall posters, prime-time sports clips, and probably more than one woman's fantasies. She wanted to hug him for coming to her rescue.

He sat next to her, sprawled his long legs out in front of him and draped his throwing arm over the back of her chair.

"I saw you over there talking to that pretty redhead," Kate said.

Dean tweaked her nose like he used to when she was a kid. "Yeah, but you're my favorite redhead."

"Great. That means my roots are showing and I need to make an appointment with José as soon as I get home."

He gave her the smile that had landed him in the number one spot for *People* magazine's Sexiest Man Alive. "So when do you head back to Weirdoland anyway?"

"Day after tomorrow. I have three clients to dress for the music video awards next week and none of them can make up their minds between the designers I've chosen. They're all waiting for the fashion spies to let the cat out of the bag as to who's wearing what so they can choose a more chic designer." She took a breath. "Does that make sense? Even I can't decode it sometimes."

"You ever get tired of that game?" he asked.

"Do you ever get tired of football?"

He shrugged. "I'll never get tired of the game on the field. But sometimes the celebrity game gets kind of ridiculous. Like when you come out of your house and there are paparazzi everywhere just waiting to see what kind of jeans you're wearing. Personally, I don't think I'm all that special. I just know how to throw a ball."

"Stop dating supermodels and they just might forget about you," Kate said.

"Yeah." He flashed her a grin. "I don't get *that* tired of it."

She laughed and bumped his shoulder with hers. "When do you leave?"

"Same as you," he said. "Season's just started. And since I'm now at the ripe old age of thirty-four, I'm not about to move aside and let the new kid take over for long."

"Why? Are you worried about being replaced?" Kate asked. "For crying out loud, you made the Super Bowl last year."

"But we didn't *win* the Super Bowl."

"Ah."

"Yeah. The kid's like a wolf, always stalking me . . . waiting."

"Waiting?"

"He knows one more wrong hit to the shoulder and I'll have to call it a career."

"Would that be so bad?"

His chin dimple winked at her. "Does the end of the world sound too over-the-top?"

"*You're* too over-the-top. The last time I sat in Arizona's stadium and watched you kick the Cardinal's asses, I couldn't believe you were my freaking brother."

"Oh yeah? Well I'm still the guy who cut the hair off your Barbie and used it for my G.I. Joe camouflage tents. Besides, you aren't hurting in the superstar department either. I Googled your name the other day and came up with umpteen hundred thousand hits."

"You Googled me?" She pressed a hand to her chest. "I'm flattered."

"Don't be. I'm just being an overprotective brother. I check up on you and Kel all the time to see how accessible you are to the freaks among us."

"You mean stalkers?"

"Yeah."

It was nice to have a big brother. Even if she saw him more on Monday Night Football than in real life. At least she and her siblings made it a point to chat on the phone once a week. She credited that for keeping them close. "Don't worry. The only stalker I have is a calico cat that hangs around my condo."

"No boyfriends?"

"No time."

"That sucks." He folded his highly insured hands together

and dropped them between his knees. His green eyes darkened. "On the serious side . . . you, Kel, and I all need to sit down tomorrow and talk about stuff."

"What kind of *stuff*?"

"Dad stuff."

They both glanced over to where their father stood near the kitchen door.

"He's going to be all alone now," Dean said. "How will he run the bakery by himself? Who's going to take care of him?"

"That's exactly what I've been wondering."

"I'm worried about him."

Kate took a breath to clear the clog from her chest. "Me too."

"Then together we all need to come up with some solutions. Tomorrow. Okay?" Dean patted her knee and stole her piece of cake before he walked away.

Eager to sneak out, Kate stood. Since they'd ridden to the funeral together in their mother's car, Kate glanced around for her sister. She spotted her in a corner talking with the town veterinarian, an elderly man who, judging by his long hair and wooly sideburns, was simpatico with his furry clients. Kate motioned to the door. The almost imperceptible shake of Kelly's head translated to: *I'm stuck. Go ahead without me.*

Across the room, Junior Walker roared into another Letty story that involved an oversized loaf of wheat bread and a raccoon.

God, she had to get out of here.

Kate spotted her father still chatting near the kitchen and made her way toward him. The overhead light flashed across his balding head when he nodded at something the man across from him said. When she approached, the men opened up their circle to include her.

"My little Katie." Her father gathered her in and gave her a hug. "I'm so glad you're here, honey."

"Me too, Dad." Kate squeezed her eyes shut and hugged him back, glad to be in her father's arms again. But there was so much inside of her bubbling beneath the surface she could barely breathe. "I'm a little . . . tired. Would you mind much if I went home?"

"Of course not," he said. His eyes were rimmed with red. Kate knew he'd been in a state of tears all day. Some from laughter at old memories of the woman he'd loved for more than thirty-six years, some from the unbelievable sense of loss.

"Are you okay?" she asked, cupping his weathered cheek in her palm.

He nodded. "You go ahead. I'll be home soon."

"You sure?"

He kissed her forehead and gave her a smile.

As she walked away she glanced back over her shoulder. "Bring Kel home with you, okay?"

He waved his response then turned to rejoin his friends.

Friends.

They were what he needed now. Not comfort from a daughter he barely knew anymore.

Eager for fresh air, Kate pushed open one of the big steel doors and ducked her head against the breeze that had kicked up. Searching through her handbag for the car keys, she stepped beneath the overhang and bumped into something large and immovable. Her heels wobbled in the gravel. A big hand steadied her.

"Excuse . . ." Her head shot up. *Shit*. ". . . me."

Everything in Kate stopped cold. The blood drained from her head. Her ears buzzed. Her chest tightened the same as it had when she'd seen him earlier.

Matt's mirrored shades were gone and she looked right into the ice blue eyes she'd once gone crazy for. The thick fringe of dark lashes surrounding those eyes only enhanced the mesmerizing hue—like arctic icebergs surrounded by a stormy sky. His cheekbones were sculpted, his jawline chiseled in a masculine way that said the boy she knew was gone forever. In his place stood a man. A real man—who smelled like autumn leaves and wood smoke and a lethal amount of sexy.

Earlier today she hadn't been prepared for him, hadn't been armed for his harsh words and his cold demeanor. But she was ready now. *Bring. It. On.*

She forced herself to look up at his strong chin and the etched curve of those lips she'd kissed so many times. Way back then they had been remarkably soft and tender. Now they were pressed into a hard, implacable line. Through their school years, he'd been a great-looking boy but now . . . now he just looked dangerous. The shiny star pinned to his broad chest didn't help.

He gazed down at her through those pale eyes as if he could squash her like the ants crawling across the ground at their feet.

Okay, so she *thought* she'd been prepared for him.

Not the first time in her life she'd been horribly wrong.

Around them the night air swirled with the lingering aroma of pine and dewy blades of grass. The stars above twinkled brightly in the clear sky. And Kate wished she could just disappear in the dark.

"You lose your date?" she asked.

His lips tightened even more. "You lose your way home?"

"I'm here aren't I?" She clutched the cold keys in her hand until they dug into her skin.

"Nice of you to show up. I'm sure your mother would be very happy."

His words sucked the air from her lungs. "Okay, I get it," she said. "You don't like me. Can we at least be civil while I'm here?"

He shrugged one broad uniformed shoulder. "Sure."

Behind them the steel door swung open with a screech. Out barged Edna Price. With her came the melody of Frank Sinatra singing *My Way*.

Edna looked up and smiled at Matt. "Gotta get home and put the dog out. Can't leave her out for long though." She turned a frown toward Kate. "All she's good for is wandering."

The old woman's barb hit its mark. But, of course, Edna wasn't done.

"Emma Hart's in there looking for you, Matthew, honey. You don't want to keep a good woman like that waiting."

"I'll make note of that." Matt gave her a wave and a friendly smile as she hobbled away on her moose-head cane. "Good night, Mrs. Price."

He turned back to Kate. "So how long *are* you staying?"

"Two days." To guard against the icy daggers shooting at her she folded her arms across her breasts. "Think you can handle that?"

"Doesn't really matter to me."

"Well, at least you're honest," she said.

"At least one of us is."

One hand slid to her hip. The other white-knuckled her purse strap. "I never lied to you. Exactly."

"You never exactly told me the truth either. Would have been nice to know you'd been making plans to run away."

"You knew I was waiting for that scholarship. I didn't *run* away."

He laughed. "Honey, your tennis shoes left burn marks in the road."

She glanced across the parking lot for an escape. Her mother's boat was four cars down. If she walked fast, she could be there in a few seconds.

"Have you been sitting around for ten years thinking up nasty things to say to me?" she asked, irritated with herself for standing there and letting him grind in the guilt.

"Hardly. I've got more important things to do."

Before she could bite her tongue, she asked, "Like what?"

A smile curved his sensuous mouth. "Sorry, sweetheart, you lost the right to question me a long time ago." His gaze cruised up her body, taking its time at all the appropriate places.

She knew that look. The one that said no matter how long ago it had been he remembered that the last time he'd seen her she'd been naked in his arms and moaning his name.

She remembered too. It would have been nice if she could have packed away the memory of that night along with her clothes when she left town. But she hadn't. And for a long time after, she'd lie alone in her bed remembering his touch, his kiss, his attention to detail.

A shiver tingled down her spine and shot straight to her core. "Ancient history." She refused to let those memories haunt her anymore. Tonight she'd conjure up someone else to fantasize over. And he wouldn't have midnight hair or ice blue eyes or wear a deputy uniform or be too handsome for his own good.

She looked away from him again. Up this time. Anywhere other than at those pale eyes that watched her with such intensity.

"Wow. The North Star," she said, knowing it sounded lame the minute it left her lips. "I haven't seen that in awhile."

"That's too bad. Now if you'll excuse me, I need to be inside with the other mourners." He touched two fingers to the brim of his Stetson and he disappeared into the Grange.

Kate stared at the hard steel doors that divided them. He thought she didn't care about her mother, but it had never been about that. He should know it had never been about that. Matt Ryan had changed. Somewhere along the way he'd lost the warm-hearted boy he'd once been. As she headed toward the car the memory of a star-filled summer night hit her square in the chest.

"There's the North Star, Katie." He pointed his finger toward the half moon above them. "Make a wish."

"My mother says wishing on stars is a waste of time."

"Your mother doesn't know what she's talking about. A wish from the heart is a serious matter," he told her. When she hesitated he kissed her nose, her eyes, and her lips then said, "Do it for me. Please."

She looked up at the star and recited the poem. Star light. Star bright. And made her silent wish.

Then Matt pulled her close, kissed her deeply, and made love to her. Her first time. It was everything she'd ever imagined and more—sweet and gentle, hot and sexy. And oh so memorable. In

the aftermath when they were snuggled together beneath that plaid
wool blanket, holding each other like they'd never let go, he said, "I
made a wish too." Then he whispered it in her ear.

He should never have told her.

Wishes never came true when you said them out loud.

The door slammed shut behind him as Matt walked into the
Grange. She'd been in town less than forty-eight hours and
already she had him tied up in knots. How the hell had that
happened?

He'd known she'd come home someday. It was inevitable.
He'd known and he'd prepared himself. Or so he'd thought.

For months after she'd left he'd tried to erase the memory
of tangling his fingers in her hair, kissing her mouth, and slipping inside her where she was silky, hot, and eager. He'd tried
to erase the memories of all the times they'd laughed together
and held each other through times when it seemed no one
around them understood. She'd been his best friend. His first
love. And he foolishly thought she'd be his future.

Over the years he'd finally managed a comfortable sense of
numb whenever he heard her name or was forced to look at some
fashion magazine article her mother proudly showed him.

But seeing her today at her mother's funeral, at the funeral
of someone who meant the world to him, his defenses had been
down and he'd been blindsided. And all his good intentions
had been blown to hell.

"Matt?" Emma Hart appeared at his side. "Are you all
right? Why don't you come over here and sit down. Have a slice
of Letty's last pie." Emma led him past a row of tables and into

a folding chair across from Katie's quarterback brother, who was busy playing football god to the Deer Lick Destroyers' offensive line. The teenagers all but drooled as Dean explained how to get a consistent snap.

"Mr. Silverthorne insisted we save a piece just for you." Emma slid the plate in front of him. "He said his Letty would want it that way because you were like a son to her."

The knot in Matt's stomach blocked his appetite, even for a slice of Letty's famous cinnamon apple pie.

He poked his fork into the center of the crust and thought back to all the times she'd pushed him down into one of her Naugahyde chairs, shoved a hot slice of pie beneath his nose and conned him into telling her all his troubles.

"Want it a la mode?" Emma slid onto the chair next to him while in the distance Elvis sang about being lonesome. "I'm sure I could scrounge up a scoop of vanilla somewhere."

Matt gave her a smile and shook his head. "Wouldn't want to dilute it, being as it's the last slice."

Emma laid her hand on his sleeve, curled her fingers around his forearm. "I can't imagine how difficult this must be for you. I know how close you were with her."

Unable to speak, he took a bite of pie and savored the sweet, hot cinnamon flavor rolling around on his tongue. Letty had been the type of mother he'd always wished for. He liked to think they'd helped each other through some tough times. In Matt's mind, the Silverthornes were an ideal husband and wife, father and mother. And for the life of him he couldn't understand why their youngest daughter had deliberately chosen to hurt them the way she had.

As for him, he had more important things to do than worry

about her sudden intrusion into his life. He'd made a promise to Letty and he had exactly five months to make it happen. Before the election in January, he had to convince the good people of Deer Lick that he deserved to be their next sheriff. In order to do that he needed to find himself a wife who would make him even more acceptable in the eyes of the community.

There had never been a bachelor sheriff in Deer Lick and he had no intentions of losing votes on that one technicality. But more than needing a wife to make him a better candidate, Matt knew he was ready to fall in love again. For years he'd pushed women—good women—away believing it was safer. If he didn't get involved, he wouldn't get hurt. Now he was ready to fill his life with a family and commitment. He just needed to find the right woman to make that happen.

He took another bite of pie and glanced at the attractive woman next to him. Emma's soft blond hair, cool blue eyes, and calm demeanor were like a balm to everything inside him that raced and raged at Indy speed.

While he ate, she chatted about the community project her kindergarten students were involved in and how it would flow over into the entire school. Emma appeared to be a good teacher and an involved member of the community. She was sweet and respectable. Now was the perfect time to get to know her a little better.

The clock was ticking.

Kate hugged herself against the chill and made a dash for the car. She'd forgotten how cold this time of year could get back home and had left her warmer jacket stuffed in her closet at the

New York apartment she shared with a runway model. Male. Gay, of course. Not that there was anything wrong with that. Hollywood. New York. She was surrounded by gay. No wonder she couldn't find a man. At least one that might be interested in her. Of course, she hadn't been exactly looking either.

She unlocked the car door, although why she'd bothered to lock it in the first place she didn't know. No one in their right mind would steal this heap. And she was pretty sure around here automobile theft was low, if not nonexistent.

Sliding onto the seat, she turned the key and stomped on the gas pedal several times to rev the engine and get the heater going. As soon as she backed out of the parking space, curiosity sent her toward Main Street. With all the preparations for her mother's funeral the previous day, she hadn't had time to notice the changes and upgrades made to the town since she'd been gone. Mostly she just needed to drive and shake off the gloom that swirled over her head.

As she turned the corner, the *Sex and the City* theme played from within her handbag. She pulled out her cell phone and glanced at the name in the display before she answered.

"Josh, what's up?"

"It's a damned catastrophe, Kate. When are you coming back?"

"What's a catastrophe?"

"OMG, didn't you see *ET*?"

"Umm, no. My mother's funeral. Remember?"

"Oh. Sorry, sweetie." *He didn't sound sorry.* "Anyway, the so-called *Fashion Guru* slammed the outfit Inara wore to the premiere of *Last Breakfast in Eden*. I don't even want to tell you what she did to Stella's blue linen dress after I left her house."

A lump lodged in Kate's throat. "Don't tell me she sliced and diced an original McCartney."

"Worse. She bought a frickin' BeDazzler and added . . . are you sitting down?"

"Yes."

"Yellow rhinestones! And no, I'm not shitting you. We've only got four days before she attends the awards pre-show luncheon. I'm freaking out here, Kate. Somebody needs to get this trashy bitch under control!"

Kate gripped her forehead. Great. Strike three. Hello, *Variety* classifieds.

She took a deep breath.

Okay. No problem. She could handle this. She'd run interference with the entertainment media fashion hags before. She'd just do it again. She was a pro—who really didn't feel like dealing with such a trivial issue on the day they'd laid her mother to rest. But as soon as she hung up from talking with Josh, she'd order a bribe package to be delivered to the *Guru* and get her butt back to L.A. Pronto if not sooner.

Only one little problem remained. She'd promised her brother they'd sit down tomorrow and discuss how to help their father. Crap. She couldn't just bail on her dad the day after he'd buried his wife.

"Calm down, Josh. I'll call Inara. The soonest I can be there is late tomorrow night. And that's *if* I can wrap it all up here and get a flight out. In the meantime, I'm putting you in charge of not letting our pop princess out of your sight."

Kate ended the call, pulled to the curb, ordered her bribe package, and changed her airline reservations to an earlier flight. Once business was done, she pulled back onto the road and maneuvered the car around the corner at the Gas and Grub Roundup where her friends Maggie Densworth and Oliver Barnett had once stolen Olde English from the ice locker.

Oliver and Maggie consumed all six cans that night. Two months later Maggie announced she was pregnant. When Kate lamented her situation, Maggie told her it was no big deal. Shit like that happened all the time in a small town, she'd said. Maggie's dreams of becoming a TV news anchor had been squashed. And Kate was convinced that for *her*, a one-way ticket out of Deer Lick was the right and only decision.

Though Matt had taken precautions the night they'd made love, Kate had worried the following month. She didn't want to end up like Maggie—trapped in a dead-end town with a dead-end job and a kid and husband who'd forever regret the day he'd married her.

In a town the size of Deer Lick, everybody knew everybody's business. And while there were many couples who'd married young like her parents and stayed happily together, there were many more that hadn't. When marriage went bad, it got ugly and hateful and everybody got a black eye. Especially the kids who came from those busted and broken homes.

Matt Ryan had been one of those kids.

She may not have known much in those days, but she did know she cared about Matt too much to trap him into a repeat of the life in which he'd been forced to live as a kid.

She'd wanted more.

He deserved more.

The Buick sputtered past Purdy's Pawn Shop, which had expanded into the old Laundromat next door, and the Once in a Blue Moon Café where they served a heavenly Monte Cristo sandwich with homemade huckleberry jam. When she came to the red brick building in the center of the block, tucked between Buck's Gun Shop and the Once Again Bookstore, she pulled over and parked in front. Half whiskey barrels brimming with autumn mums framed the door and eyelet lace hung like a Victorian petticoat behind the plate glass window. The building looked dated and worn out. But she knew it was as reliable as the sweets served inside.

The Sugar Shack.

Kate had spent the early days of her life in that bakery kitchen, licking chocolate cake batter from the big wooden spoon her mother used. According to Letty, metal turned the chocolate bitter. Whether the story was true or not, Kate never found out. And when she'd had sweet chocolate smeared all over her face, she hadn't cared. The chocolate myth was just one of her mother's quirks that everyone accepted as gospel. Her mother had a million bakery mysteries that ranged from the possible to the absolutely ridiculous.

Sitting in the driver's seat of her mother's car, Kate stared at the darkened window of the brick building and fought back the emotion welled in her throat. The engine idled to keep the heater running. She turned on the radio—oldies, of course. Practically the only station in town. Unless you happened to favor country—not—or the talk radio station out of Bozeman—to which she'd rather gouge herself in the eye with a wand of cheap mascara.

Tom Jones serenaded her with *It's Not Unusual*. Her mother had adored the Welsh singer. Kate had always thought he had fish eyes and would get totally grossed out when her mother would giggle and swoon when old Tom swiveled his hips. Even after Kate had met the singer at a Grammy's after party, she still couldn't see understand her mother's fascination.

Over the years she and her mother had argued who was better: Elvis or Tom, Gilligan or the Professor, Bo or Luke. Kate never won a single dispute. Hard to do when you were arguing against the 1965 Deer Lick Debate Champ.

Kate slumped further down into the seat to stay warm. She leaned back against the headrest, closed her eyes, and listened to Mr. Jones croon away.

It's your fault...

She tried to push Edna's accusation and all the chaotic thoughts in her head to rest. But as she sat there, the air thickened with the cloying scent of vanilla. Despite the heater blasting, the interior of the car grew colder. Kate rubbed her arms. Maybe she'd done enough reminiscing for one day. Maybe she just needed to go home, crawl into the same small bed she'd slept in most of her life, and pray for complete oblivion.

Inside the car the temperature took another dip. She shivered and reached for the gearshift. As her cold fingers curled over the plastic knob, the air inside the car vibrated.

Suddenly Kate knew she wasn't alone.

Goose bumps rushed across her arms and up her spine. With one hand on the door handle, Kate snuck a peek over her shoulder, fully expecting to see some guy in a hockey mask waving a bloodied axe.

What she saw trapped a scream in her throat.

Surrounded by cookbooks, quilting fabric, giant knitting needles, and an odd hazy glow, sat her mother.

Looking anything but dead.

"Long time, no see, daughter."

Chapter Four

"So how'd I look at the funeral?" her mother's voice asked. "Okay? Or did Trudy White put too much blush on me like she does everybody?"

Kate twisted back around in the seat and faced the windshield. Her brain clicked through several cycles before she managed to come up with a relatively normal rationalization.

She was hallucinating.

No other explanation came to mind. It had been months since she'd had a decent night's sleep. She'd been overwhelmed by the approach of awards season. And then her mother's unexpected death . . . clearly she was exhausted.

As her heart tried to pound out of her chest, she reached up, adjusted the rearview mirror and scanned the reflection.

Just to be sure.

The radiance remained, floating above the clutter in the backseat. Nothing else seemed out of sorts. The glow could be just the moonlight bouncing off the oversized knitting needles. And the voice? Well, she'd always gotten good grades in her creative writing class. Looked like she was putting that imagination to good use. She shook her head to clear it and decided she definitely needed to get some sleep. Again, she reached for the gearshift.

"Katherine Spencer Silverthorne, are you going to answer me? Or just sit there and ignore me like you did your entire senior year?"

And now the voice in her head was pissed off?

Kate whipped around in her seat. Sure enough, there was her mother, wearing her famous red plaid flannel over a white T-shirt and denim overalls. A cranky expression crinkled the skin between her green eyes.

Had someone made a mistake?

The woman in the coffin had looked like her mother but maybe something else had happened. Maybe it was like the *Invasion of the Body Snatchers* and the woman in the backseat was really an alien. And to come up with such a ridiculous idea, maybe Kate had been living in Hollywood too long.

But how could the idea of a movie plot be any more bizarre than her dead mother sitting in the backseat?

Kate blinked. "M-mother?"

"Of course it's me. Who else would it be?"

"But you're . . ."

"Yeah." Her mother leaned forward. "I know."

Kate scooted toward the door.

"Too bad too." Her mother rubbed her chin. "I had a new recipe for better-than-sex chocolate cake I intended to try out for Nancy Yost's thirtieth birthday. You remember Nancy, don't you? She was the cutest, chubbiest little thing. Never did change much."

"Mother?"

"Katherine?" Her mother's head cocked in a perplexed puppy way. "Are you going to tell me how I looked or what? Did my Bobby pick out a beautiful casket?"

"You looked . . ." *Dead.* ". . . um, great."

"Not too much blush?"

"No."

"And the casket?"

"Oak with polished brass and ivory satin."

"Flowers?"

"A white rose spray and dozens of autumn arrangements." *Okay, this was just crazy.* "Jesus, Mom, what the hell are you doing here?"

"Katherine! Do not use the Lord's name and a curse word in the same breath."

"Sorry. I'm just a little . . . freaked out, you know?"

"Imagine how I feel. One minute I was getting ready to ice a batch of cinnamon rolls, the next I was looking down at myself wondering why I'd never dyed the gray out of my hair." Her mother glanced out the window, fidgeted with the wavy hair pulled up on top of her head. "I didn't mean to frighten you."

"Frighten me? You're scaring the crap out of me!" Then a thought screamed through her brain. "Wait. Does this mean I'm—"

"No, Katherine, you are very much alive."

Kate exhaled. Thank God. If she died now, she would have some very ticked off clients back in L.A. "Then what—"

"I had some unfinished business. And well, let's just say when that light appeared, I kind of ignored it."

"A light?" Kate asked. "There really is a light?"

Her mother's brows drew together. "You think so many people would lie about that?"

"I never really thought about it before." Kate faced forward and undid the seatbelt so she could shift easier in the seat. "I can't believe this." She looked up into the mirror. Again her mother had disappeared.

"Mom?" She heard a sigh.

"Don't bother lookin' in the mirror. I don't think I have a reflection anymore."

Kate looked into the backseat again and, sure enough, there she was. "Why?"

"I don't know." Her mother shrugged. "I think when you go through the light, you get all the answers, like in some kind of dead person's handbook or something. I'm kind of flying by the seat of my overalls."

"No. I mean why are you still here?"

"Don't you know?" Her mother's voice rang with disappointment. A tone Kate had heard millions of times before.

"Me?" She pointed to herself. "Uh-uh."

"Well, you don't just wake up one day and say, gee, I'm going to leave all this unfinished business behind. Life's a gift, Katherine." Her mother folded her ghostly arms across the red flannel. "You don't just toss it in a drawer like an old shirt figuring you can pull out a new one when the old one is worn out."

"I, um . . . have no idea what you're talking about," Kate said.

"Of course you don't." Her mother smiled the way she used to when she had something to hold over Kate's head. "But you will. Now answer your phone and tell that young man to stop bothering you."

"What?" As if on cue Kate's cell rang. She looked up. Her mother was gone. For real this time. Kate even leaned over the backseat but no sign remained of the woman who'd given her life. On the second chorus of the *Sex and the City* theme, Kate hit the talk button. "Josh? You are not going to believe—"

"Kate!" Josh's voice was in full bitch mode. "We have crisis number two. Michael Black refuses to wear the Hugo Boss tux. He swears he's going to wear something called *Wrangler* unless we find him a designer out of Nashville or at the very least, Texas. I know this is a bad time, but you seriously need to get your butt back here."

"I'll . . ." Kate's gaze wandered again to the empty backseat. ". . . be home tomorrow night."

And making an appointment with a head shrinker.

In the morning Kate awoke tucked into the twin bed in which she'd spent the better part of her life. Sleep had evaded her until exhaustion finally grabbed hold and she'd passed out. For hours she'd lain awake, thinking of her close encounters of the mother kind. She wondered if she'd imagined it. She wondered if maybe she'd really just been pushing herself too hard and needed to dig her toes in some sandy beach and enjoy some umbrella drinks served by a sexy cabana boy.

Maybe she just needed a sexy cabana boy.

She sat up and threw back the daisy sheets she'd picked out from a catalog in her junior year. Back when her mother had offered to let her and Kelly decorate their room however they wanted. Big mistake. Kelly's preference of a stern black and white pin-striped pattern had clashed with Kate's frivolous floral prints.

Their choices spoke volumes about their very different tastes. To prevent a constant bitch session, their mother had divided the room with a curtain rod and white sheet. On Kate's side there were still teen mag photos of Leonardo DiCaprio and Brad Pitt carefully stapled to the sheet. Apparently back then she'd been in a blond-haired pretty-boy phase of her life. Since then, she'd met both gentlemen and realized while great to look at, both were just regular guys. No reason, really, to initiate all that teenage lust. She was into more *manly* men now. Not actors. Or rock stars. Or any man who wore pants tighter than hers. Or spent more time in a day spa than Paris Hilton.

Kate crept from her bed, tossed a pillow at her snoring sister, and raced from the room to grab a cup of the coffee she smelled brewing in the kitchen. She walked down the hall in bare feet on carpet that needed to be replaced. As many times as she or Dean or Kelly had offered to buy their parents new flooring or furniture or even a brand new house, they'd refused. Their house was the nest they'd built with love, they'd said. They were just fine with what they'd had. As Kate stopped to look at the gallery of family photos on the walls, she understood what they meant. Love warmed every nook and cranny in this house. And it was that love that warmed her heart as well.

She found her father leaning against the faux marble counter where she'd first learned to properly ice a birthday cake. She'd done a disastrous job but he'd praised her as if her work had been good enough for royalty. On the counter beside him sat the morning paper and a steaming mug. He was dressed in the white pants, shirt, and apron he wore to the bakery every day.

"Dad?"

He turned and accepted the kiss she bussed on his clean shaven cheek. "Morning, sweetheart." His balding head gleamed as sunlight filtered through the window over the sink. The dark circles beneath his eyes made Kate wonder if he'd even slept a wink all night.

Her chest tightened and her concern for him increased. "You're not dressed for work, are you?" she asked.

"Of course." He sipped carefully from the mug. "Have to open up shop today."

"But . . . Dad. Don't you think it's a little soon? Don't you think you should—"

"I should what? Sit around and feel sorry for myself? Your mother wouldn't like that at all." He shook his head. "She'd look down at me, wag her finger, and tell me to get it together."

Or she'd be looking at him from the backseat of her battered Buick if he chose to drive it to work.

Before her siblings brought chaos to the table, Kate needed to find a way to break it to him that she had to leave in less than eight hours. She hoped the news wouldn't shatter his heart even more. She intended to come back as soon as possible, but that probably wouldn't help the hurt much. And there was again, that repetitive little problem of her misdirected good intentions.

"Dad? I thought since Dean, Kel, and I all have to leave soon we all might—"

"Come down to the shop with me?" Her father's face lit up. "Excellent idea, Katie."

She'd rather eat paste. Memories of long hours after school and the two years following high school, helping her mother decorate birthday cakes and cupcakes regurgitated in her brain every time she smelled sugar. Her legs still ached from all those hours of standing. She'd been pretty good at decorating though, and had even gotten into the creative flow *when* she'd been allowed to do her own thing. Even as a child she'd never been a paint-by-numbers/stay-within-the-lines kind of girl. Which was only one reason her parents' family business had never interested her. Her mother loved to dictate. Kate loved the freedom of choice. Their culinary tastes clashed like marzipan and vinegar.

Now that she was thirty years old and had a sugar-free career in California, there wasn't a chance in the world the bakery bug would bite her. Not. A. Chance.

"What's all the racket?" Dean shuffled into the kitchen, his stylish short hair as rumpled as the grey T-shirt and cargo shorts he wore. A five o'clock shadow dusted his dimpled chin. And he still looked like a superstar.

"Katie said you kids are coming to the Shack with me today." Their father took down two mugs from the cupboard and filled them full of coffee.

"No way." Dean scrubbed his multi-million dollar throwing hand across his face.

"Way," Kate grumbled.

"Remind me to kill you later," Dean grumbled back.

"Your mother would have been thrilled to see you all together in her bakery again."

"Together where?" Kelly wandered in, unlawyer-like in her

pink cat pajamas and disheveled ponytail. She smacked Kate in the head with the pillow Kate had thrown earlier.

"The bakery," Kate and Dean said in unison.

Kelly's response was silent but readable by the wide eyes and gaping fly trap.

Their father dragged down another mug and filled it for Kelly. Then he gathered them all in a group hug. Tears welled in his already red-rimmed eyes. "I'm so lucky to have all of you."

Lucky?

An icy fist slammed Kate in the gut. She looked at her siblings. They'd all three been gone from home for so long. How could her father possibly be happy they were only back for a couple of days?

And how could she possibly tell him she had to leave tonight?

The scuff marks Harvey Tittlebaum's shoes left on the dusty sheriff station floor were only one piece of evidence that Harvey had seen his way through yet another bottle of rum. Harvey liked his rum straight, he liked it in mass quantities, and he liked it early in the day. His wife, Lulu, however, had had quite enough of Harvey's all-consuming habit. An hour ago she'd called the station and told Matt to come pick up the S.O.B. or she'd fry him with her liver and onions.

"Did I tell you my wife stinks I'm drunk?" Harvey's words collided like trains on the same track.

Matt chuckled as he eased the elderly man onto the tufted mattress in a holding cell. "I believe she told me that herself.

Now, why don't you catch a little cat nap? I'm sure you'll feel better in no time."

"Hell, I feel perfeck right now." Harvey popped up from the mattress like a jack-in-the-box. "Bring on the party. Where's the dancin' girls?"

"Mr. Tittlebaum," Matt nudged Harvey back onto the mattress with little more than the weight of two fingers, "I think the only dancing girls you're going to see are in your dreams."

"Pfft! That's what Lulu says, 'In your dreams, Harvey!'"

The next sound Harvey made after he plopped down to the mattress was a loud snore. Matt shook his head and closed the cell door but didn't bother to lock it. Harvey wouldn't wake until later tonight. Hopefully by then his veins wouldn't be quite so pickled and he could go home to round two with Lulu.

The constant battle between the Tittlebaum's wasn't unusual in a town the size of Deer Lick. The entertainment in their community was what one could call lacking and old Harvey was a prime example of small-town boredom. Next in line were the kids who, if they weren't locked in their homes glued to some video game, were out scoring alcohol or pot. The outcome was never pretty.

Sheriff Washburn was too focused on retirement to recognize the problem or to want to find a solution. After forty years of service, he rightfully had his eye on the back nine at the Shadow Peak Golf Course and a place in the shade with a cold beer at the end of the day. When Matt became sheriff, he intended to tackle the situation full force before any more kids fell further down the rabbit hole. He'd made a list of methods to gain funding for the growing situation. Made a list of procedures to eliminate the problem. Now all he had to do was make sure the community put a check in front of his name on the ballot for sheriff.

Matt's boot heels echoed across the concrete floor as he walked toward his office. He hadn't gone far before Buddy Hutchins appeared. Matt had hoped his high school nemesis wouldn't make an appearance today. He should have known better.

"How can I help you, Buddy?" Matt's greeting was met with the same glare he'd faced when the two of them had played high school football together. Buddy had been a huge defensive back with a bad attitude. Things hadn't changed much over the years.

"You get a kick out of arresting my uncle on a drunk and disorderly?" Buddy growled. "He's an old man. Can't you go pick on someone else?"

Matt folded his arms. "Mr. Tittlebaum is not under arrest. He's currently sleeping it off." The stink of stale beer surrounded Buddy like flies on shit. "I'd suggest you do the same."

Buddy pushed at Matt's chest with both hands. "You threatening me, Ryan?"

The shove was enough to cause Matt to move back a step. But he didn't back down. "*Suggesting*, Buddy. It's a beautiful day. I'm sure you'd rather enjoy it from this side of the bars."

Buddy pulled back his fist and aimed it at Matt. "That's a threat! You son-of-a—"

The punch never landed. Matt caught it in his hand and used a familiar maneuver to restrain Buddy without much effort. "Assaulting an officer of the law is a federal offense, Son," Matt said as he guided Buddy back toward the holding cells. "Maybe you need to sleep it off alongside your uncle."

"*Son!* You're a piss-ant, Ryan."

"Yeah, I know." He pushed Buddy into his uncle's cell and turned the key in the lock. A rant of swear words followed Matt all the way back to his office. If not the brightest, Buddy was at least creative.

Matt dropped to his chair, ignored the creaks and groans of the age-old springs beneath the leather seat and tossed the arrest log on the desk he shared with James Harley and Stan Bradshaw. Across the scratched surface sat a picture of Stan's wife and twin boys. The only sign eternal playboy James took up residence was a half-empty mug of cold coffee.

With a few quiet minutes before he headed out to run the lake-to-Lookout Point patrol, Matt pulled his wallet from his pants and withdrew a wrinkled piece of paper. He unfolded it and stared at the names written in his heavy, barely legible scrawl.

"What the hell is this?" James suddenly appeared and whipped the paper from his hands.

Matt grabbed for it but James waved it above his head and grinned like the antagonist pain-in-the-ass he was.

"You makin' *another* list, Deputy Ryan? Seems you got a list for everything."

The chair creaked as Matt leaned back. He refused to give James any more ammo than he already held in his hand.

"Let's see . . ." James's dark brown eyes scanned the list. He forked his fingers through sandy colored hair that looked like he'd just done time in the sack with one of his many female admirers. "Emma Hart, Sarah Collins, Lacy Shaw, Diane Fielding . . ." He looked up, shaking his head. "You plan to keep all the single ladies in town to yourself?"

"It doesn't concern you."

"Uh-huh." James' grin widened. "You're not thinkin' about marrying one of these gals, are you?"

Matt fought the irritation that stung his cheeks. "Like I said, none of your business."

"Of course it is." James clasped a hand to the front of his shirt. "I'd be lax in my best friend duties if I didn't butt right on in. You want my advice—"

"I don't."

"I'd go with that Lacy Shaw. She's pretty hot. Nothing sexier than a woman in a nurse's uniform."

"I'm not looking for hot, James. I'm looking for respectable." Maybe to some, making a list of potential wives seemed a mechanical method. Too thought out. No emotions involved. But Matt was ready—now—to find someone he was compatible with. Someone who would make a good wife and mother. Someone who would keep his bed warm and be happy to see him each night when he walked through the door. The trick, however, would be dating more than one of these ladies in a town the size of a postage stamp without hurting someone's feelings.

He'd never considered himself a player. He'd always considered himself a one woman man, even when he'd never returned to a woman's bed more than once. But lately he hadn't had time for many outside pleasures. Dating had been dead last on his mind. He'd mapped out a life and he only had a few months to make it happen. If all went according to plan, by this time next year he'd be Sheriff of Deer Lick, have a wife, and maybe even have started a family.

Matt wanted a family.

He *needed* a family—one that would erase the years of dysfunction that had bred like cockroaches in his childhood home. Whatever welfare trailer-of-the-month that had happened to be.

Letty Silverthorne had told him he'd written himself a pretty tall order. But Matt knew what he wanted. Knew what he'd worked hard for these past eight years. And he had every intention of making all his dreams a reality.

All of them, except one.

He'd dreamed that Kate would realize she loved him and come back. But she hadn't. Time to move on.

"Well, if you want respectable," James said, "you'd best cross off Diane. I hear she's got a mean penchant for whips and leather."

Matt's head shot up to find the customary smirk tilting his partner's mouth. He and James had become friends over the six years they'd worked together. Before that, James had been untouchable, unreachable, and downright scary. Since he'd come over to the right side of the law, he'd become trustworthy and dependable. Seems James had hunted down his demons and won. Now he maintained a decent, if not a little wild, existence in his time off. But that didn't make Matt want to wring his neck any less. "May I have that back?"

James handed him the paper. "You've got to quit making so many lists, my man, and start living."

"That's what I intend to do."

"Right." James leaned a hip against the desk while Harvey's snores and Buddy's curses rattled through the station house. "So does that mean you're going to ask out that hot little red-head I saw you talking to in the Grange parking lot last night?"

Matt's pulse kicked up a notch. "That hot little redhead happens to be the youngest Silverthorne."

"No shit?"

"No shit," Matt answered. "And no, I won't be asking her out."

"Huh." James scratched his chin. "Mind if I do?"

Something zinged around Matt's heart and forced its way into his throat like a fifty pound bag of cement. Something that made him remember the way Katie had whispered his name when he'd held her in his arms. Something that brought back the same fresh, raw ache in his soul he'd felt the day he learned she'd left without even a good-bye.

Did he mind?

The sudden image of Katie in James's arms made Matt's blood boil. Fucking right he minded. "She's only in town for two days and her mother just died."

James shrugged. "Maybe she needs some consoling."

Matt's stomach churned as he shoved the folded paper into his jacket pocket and hoped to God he wouldn't have to kill his best friend.

Kate glanced around the bakery. Everything about the Sugar Shack screamed 1970s. The floor tiles, once a dusty pink, were now so yellowed with age they'd turned a putrid shade of orange. Dark paneling covered the walls and baskets of faded silk flowers decorated the top shelves. Everything was the same, even the intense smell of sugar.

Hands dusted with flour, Kate popped a tray of cooled cupcakes onto the work counter. Beside her, Kelly cut a tube of chilled dough to make their mother's famous honey wheat dinner rolls. On Kate's other side, Dean grumbled while he used a spatula to lift a batch of fresh-baked oatmeal raisin cookies from a metal pan.

"I'll bet *Sports Illustrated* would love to get a load of you wearing that apron," Kate teased. "Some big football stud, you are."

"Just because I can bake a mean pastry doesn't mean I'm not a killer on the field."

Kate laughed and patted him on the back, leaving a floured handprint on his baby blue shirt. "You keep convincing yourself of that, Bucko."

Kelly looked up. The frown wrinkling her smooth forehead ended their fun. "Come on you guys, quit goofing off. We need to discuss dad's situation while he's busy."

Kate glanced across the bakery where their father leaned against the counter talking with Gretchen Wilkes, a woman far too old to wear a mini-skirt and cowboy boots. "Yeah. Now's a good time. Especially since I have to leave tonight."

"You what?" Kelly's eyes widened. Her knife thunked into the cutting board. "You can't leave tonight."

"Yes I can."

"Uh-uh," Dean interjected. "We agreed we'd talk about dad's situation."

Kate piped a dollop of butter cream icing on a cupcake. "So talk."

Dean, being the oldest, gave Kelly that stupid eye signal he'd used in their adolescence when the two of them had plotted against Kate, the youngest and obviously, most naive.

"There's no way we can all just jump on a plane out of here," Kelly said. "Dad has no one."

"I'm aware of that, Kel."

"How's he going to bake all this stuff? It's going to take time to hire a good employee." Dean slid the cookies onto parchment-covered trays. "And how's he going to run the business alone? Forget about trying to run the household too. Mom took care of everything."

"Who's he going to go home to at the end of the day?" Kelly asked.

Kate looked up from the cupcake she was decorating with barely recognizable iced violets. "Why are you guys giving *me* the third degree?"

"We're not," Dean slammed his fist into a fresh glob of dough. "It's just something we need to discuss."

"So . . . let's discuss," Kate said.

"The football season is in high gear," Dean informed her as if she didn't already know. "I can't just walk away. I've got a contract."

"And I'm in the middle of a high-profile case," Kelly announced. "If I walk away, a child murderer might go free."

As their words sank in, Kate felt dizzy. The oven-warm smells of the bakery suddenly overwhelmed her. Her heart skipped and thudded. "This doesn't sound much like a discussion."

Dean plowed his fist into the dough again while Kelly slapped her dinner rolls onto baking sheets. Neither of them would look her in the eye.

"It just makes more sense that you would stay," Dean said.

Kate shook her head. "No. I have a job too. I have three celebrities to dress for awards shows next week. I can't just walk away either."

"Isn't there some way you can work without actually being there? You have a laptop. A cell phone." Kelly shoved her rolls into the deep wall oven. "Seriously, Kate. You can hardly compare making gorgeous people even more beautiful to putting a child murderer away for life."

"Or winning the Super Bowl," Dean added.

"Are you both crazy? You can't do this to me!"

Their father's attention broke away from his conversation with Gretchen Wilkes and he gave Kate a smile that reached all the way from his sad green eyes to her heart. Kate broke out in a cold sweat that had nothing to do with the heat of the ovens behind her. "Oh, my God. You guys already told dad I'd stay, didn't you?"

Kelly at least managed to look sheepish. Dean, not so much.

"Uh-uh." Kate thrust her index finger in the direction of the back door. "Outside. Now!"

Surprisingly the football hero and the fierce prosecutor ducked their heads and followed her orders. Once they reached the back alley, Kate shut the door, folded her arms and glared at her traitorous siblings.

"Kate—"

"You guys suck. You know that? I may not have a job that can save the world or that an entire team depends on, but my career is important to me too. You both said we'd *discuss* dad's situation. So that's what we're going to do right here, right now. *Discuss.* Not dog pile on Kate."

Dean and Kelly looked at each other.

"Stop that!" Kate yelled. "I know all about that weird nonverbal communication thing you do. It won't work this time."

Kelly rubbed her forehead. "I'm so sorry, Kate. There's no

way I can walk away from this case. You don't know what it's like looking into the eyes of this child's parents. I can't let them down. I've got to make sure their daughter's killer never hurts another child, ever again." Kelly's eyes darkened. "Or I'll never be able to live with myself."

Imagining the worst scenario, Kate's heart thumped hard. "He's a real bad guy, huh, Kel?"

"The worst." Kelly nodded slowly. "The best guesstimate I have for when the trial might be over is three to five months."

"The season will be over after the Super Bowl," Dean added. "I won't accept that it will end sooner for the team. They've worked their asses off this year."

Five months. Kate groaned silently.

Five looooong months.

How would she be able to keep her career alive after a five-month absence in a town that could forget a name in the span of an episode of *Entertainment Tonight*?

"We're so sorry, Kate. I'll come back as soon as I possibly can," Kelly promised.

"Me too," her brother echoed.

Kate exhaled. "I know."

Then, they all hugged. Because in the end, this wasn't about them. It was about their dad.

When all the baking had been done, Kelly and Dean went home and Kate returned to her cupcakes. Tension cramped the muscles in her neck and her grip on the pastry bag tightened. A big spurt of pale pink icing globbed onto the cupcake, ruining it for consumption other than the mouth of the trash can.

She did battle with a knot of fire in the pit of her stomach as she tried to dream up a way to help her father and attend, at least, her top three clients at the same time. Out of those three clients, two were her most difficult. It was too much for her to expect Josh to be able to handle all of them in her absence. But she was a pro. And it did make more sense that she be the one to stay and help. Her job wasn't expendable but it certainly was easier to maneuver than having to be in a courtroom every day. Or flying across the country from game to game. It wasn't as if she couldn't juggle things. Heck, she was the queen at multitasking. Last year hadn't she handled a movie star's fantasy wedding, a red carpet arrival, and a charity fashion show all in one day? Easy cheesy.

Right. And Valentino gowns grew on trees.

Amid her misery the bell over the bakery door chimed. She glanced up as the door opened. A gust of air blew in, bringing with it the scent of rain on the sidewalk, autumn leaves, and Matt Ryan. Her nerves unraveled with an unexpected tingle.

In a wide stance, he paused before her mother's lace-draped window and swept his gaze across the shop. When that gaze landed on her, his broad shoulders stiffened beneath the khaki uniform. The star pinned to his chest pocket lifted on a sharp intake of air. Slowly he removed his aviators from the bridge of his straight nose and that icy blue glare burned a hole right through her core.

Great.

Now all she needed was mean old Edna Price and her moose-head walking stick to show up.

Before the thought filtered from her head, the bell above the door jingled again. Kate cringed at the sight of the gray-headed woman as she hobbled through the door.

CHAPTER FIVE

Matt stepped from the autumn chill into the sweet, warm smells of the busy bakery. He gave a nod to Robert Silverthorne, who was placing flaky triangles of baklava into a pastry box for one of Deer Lick's most notorious man-eaters.

"Hey there, Matt," Robert said with a wave. "My helper'll be happy to take your order."

Helper?

Matt swept his gaze to the lunch counter and the redhead standing behind it.

The very last thing he expected when he stopped in for his customary tuna sandwich was to see her behind the counter frosting cupcakes. Like she belonged there.

She lifted her gaze and their eyes met. A flash of irritation seared him from behind those green depths. When the color returned to her pale cheeks, she tilted her head and her sleek auburn ponytail dusted the top of her shoulder. He could almost read her mind. Or at least the curse words bouncing around on her tongue.

Happy to take his order?

He didn't think so.

Last night he would have bet money she'd have been on the first plane out today. He didn't imagine the icy reception she'd received had been pleasant or comfortable for her. But she deserved nothing less.

Behind him the bell over the door jingled and Katie's lips pursed like she'd tasted something bitter.

"Afternoon, Matthew."

He turned toward the gravelly voice. "How are you today, Mrs. Price?"

"Oh, just fine and dandy. Course, my old bones aren't liking this cold weather none." She lifted her walking stick and gave it a wave. "You keeping your tradition of coming in for lunch?"

"Yes, ma'am." Matt held back a smile at the pinched expression surrounding her rheumy hazel eyes. He figured she suspected he'd come in for a different reason—a shapely reason that stood behind the counter in snug jeans and a figure-hugging sweater. "I'm hoping Letty's special recipes will still taste just as good as if she'd made them herself," he said, reassuring her he had no other motivation.

"Well, aren't you just the sweetest thing." Mrs. Price reached up and patted his cheek. "You'd best get that sandwich to go. Don't know what in blazes *that* one's doin' here . . ." She gave a head wag toward Katie. ". . . but you'd best check your order. See she don't cheat you."

Matt figured the target of their discussion could come up with a whole list of rotten things she'd probably like to do to his food. Cheating him on his order might be the least of them.

When Mrs. Price hobbled over to the display case, Matt stepped to the small lunch counter.

Katie looked up, gave him half a forced smile, and then slid a pencil between her fingers. Her hands were small and feminine, with short manicured nails painted a soft pink. If he closed his eyes, he could still imagine those warm hands on his skin, in his hair, cupping the fly of his jeans—

"Can I help you, Matt?" Her fascinating mouth formed the word that made up his name, but he barely heard it past the blood pulsing through his veins.

He let his gaze roam over her, stopping at the interesting places along the way. The little pearl buttons on her yellow sweater brought forth memories of a stormy spring night they'd once shared in the cab of his battered pickup truck. Memories of hard rain beating down on the metal roof and warm breath fogging the windows. Unbuttoning her cotton blouse and slipping his hands beneath the crisp fabric to touch her silky skin.

Every nerve in his body went on alert.

He remembered her warmth. Remembered her peaches-and-cream scent when he'd buried his face in the smooth curve of her neck. He remembered the taste of her on his tongue—all sweet and fresh and eager.

From behind the counter she watched him, and he couldn't help but remember the way she'd gazed up at him that night. Back when she'd been everything he'd ever wanted.

Back when he'd been nothing a damned fool.

"Hel-lo?" She wiped a smear of purple icing down the front of her white apron. That simple slide of her hand sent a responding upward tug inside his uniform pants.

"What are you doing here?" He crossed his arms and widened his stance, proclaiming this to be *his* territory. "I figured this would be the last place you'd want to be."

She shrugged. "Dad insisted on opening up shop today. We all told him it was too soon but—"

"Everyone grieves in their own way."

She glanced over her shoulder at the man in question. The hint of a sigh whispered through her lips. "I guess."

"Are you?"

Her gaze shot to his face. "Am I what?"

"Grieving."

While Kenny Chesney sang about the good stuff from the radio perched on a shelf above the mixer, the smooth skin between her perfect brows drew together. Then she flattened her hands on the counter and leaned forward.

"Is there something I can help you with, *Deputy*? A donut perhaps? Or did you specifically come in here to attack my moral fiber?"

Silence stretched between them as he debated whether or not to inform her he didn't believe she had any moral fiber.

But then she folded her arms beneath her breasts and shifted her weight to one enticing denim-clad hip and the thought flew from his head.

"Well?"

"Two tuna subs," he said. "No tomato. Two iced teas."

"For you and your evil twin?" she asked with a snarl. She jotted down his order then rang it up on the cash register. "That will be nine fifty-six."

"Don't need a twin," he said. The sleeve of his uniform rasped against his utility belt as he reached into his pocket, withdrew a ten spot and handed it to her. "I can get into trouble all by myself."

A simple curl to the corners of her mouth showed a bit of

the sassy side he remembered so well. She handed him back his change and her fingertips swept across the center of his palm. Electricity snapped between them.

She looked up, obviously aware. Maybe even surprised. "Is that something you do frequently?"

"Shock people?"

She shook her head and that sleek ponytail swung gently against her back. "Get into trouble."

He smiled.

She waited for his response, her eyes shifting from light to dark green. When she realized all she was going to get was a smile, she slapped his receipt down on the counter and pushed it toward him. "I'll have your order ready shortly."

He picked up the receipt, careful not to make contact with her again. One shock a day was enough for him. He'd already had two.

Since Edna Price had put some pretty awful thoughts into his head, he stepped back to watch Katie prepare his and James's lunch, making sure nothing but tuna salad went on his sandwich. She sliced through the crusty picnic rolls with such ferocity he expected to see blood drawn.

Reaching for the lettuce, she bent over the workspace and gave him an excellent view of how nicely her jeans fit. Then she flung lettuce leaves on each side of the bread, smashed down scoops of tuna salad, and slapped on wedges of Letty's home-made kosher dills. Her movements were swift and jerky, sloppy and careless. And he enjoyed watching every single movement, even though he had no business doing so.

Without so much as a glance in his direction, she rolled the sandwiches up in crisp white paper and stuffed them and the bags of chips into a sack. From a pitcher she poured two cups of home-brewed iced tea, then slid the bag and drinks across the counter.

"Have a nice day, Deputy Ryan. Come again soon."

Her polite business tone would have made her mother proud.

"Hopefully next time I won't be here," she added.

Okay, maybe not.

He didn't know why it gave him so much pleasure to have the ability to rile her up. Just a little. Paybacks were childish. And he was far from that. He was a man on a mission. He had an agenda. He needed to stick with that.

"Why Miss Silverthorne," he said, "if I didn't know better, I'd think you were trying to get rid of me."

"That's *Ms. Silver* to you. And . . ." Her bowed lips curled upward. ". . . you're a lot more perceptive than I gave you credit for."

He laughed—at her audaciousness and at his own reaction. He didn't know why that sassy smile made his stomach flip. He had no interest at all in what she called herself, what she did, where she did it, or who she did it with.

As long as his poor demented brain managed to remember that, he'd be good. Unfortunately, there wasn't a single inch of the rest of his body that *wasn't* interested.

While her sister finished packing her luggage for an early morning flight, Kate tore down the sheet divider in their room.

"What are you doing?" Kelly asked.

"If you think I'm going to be stuck in this miserable town

and stuck on one side of this miserable bedroom too, you're crazy."

Kelly neatly rolled the black silk blouse she'd worn to their mother's funeral and pushed it into her Liz Claiborne bag. "You're still mad."

"I'm not mad." Kate glared at her sister's reflection in the mirror above the vanity. "Just . . . I don't know. Tomorrow, while you and Dean go back to your normal lives, your normal jobs and your normal worlds, *normal* will no longer be a word in *my* vocabulary. In one short day my entire dialogue has flipped from St. Laurent, Hilfiger, and Armani to a dozen red velvet cupcakes, a double layer chocolate cake, and two tuna subs, no tomatoes—to go."

"I'm sorry, Kate. I really am."

Kelly looked duly apologetic and Kate tamped down her temper tantrum long enough to say "I know, Kel. I understand you have a child murderer to put behind bars. I know Dean has a multi-million dollar contract he can't walk out on. It's just—"

Her cell phone rang. She grabbed it up off her bed and answered without looking at the number. "Hello?"

"Please do not tell me you were serious about staying in Deer Poop or wherever the hell you are."

"I wouldn't lie about that, Josh. I can't come back until I get things here settled."

"Well, what am I supposed to do? Inara just showed up at Coco de Ville in a pair of mom jeans that would make Jessica Simpson cringe."

Kate closed her eyes. *God help her.* She had no doubt this whole staying in Deer Lick thing would shred her career. "Josh, I told you to watch her."

"Honey, you could shackle Robocop to her wrist and she'd still manage to create some kind of fashion catastrophe. The girl is a walking nightmare."

There was no use arguing with him. He was right. But she needed him to be her eyes and ears while she figured out how to juggle things between Glitter Town and Hick Town. Cajoling her assistant was the only weapon she currently held.

"Come on, Josh. I know you're up for this. Right now you have the perfect opportunity to step up your game. Weren't you the one who convinced Paris the yellow chiffon was a disaster for that Vegas nightclub opening? Weren't you the one who took Beyoncé aside and suggested her outfit would rock if she'd only remove her distracting bangles?"

"Well . . ."

"Come on, Josh. You are solid at stuff like that." God, she could almost hear him preen through the phone.

"I guess you're right."

Her stomach uncoiled half a knot. "I'm totally right. Sooo, can I count on you?"

"I guess so."

"Great. Then I have one more teensy-weensy favor to ask."

"You wouldn't be you if you didn't."

"I need some clothes. Would you pack me up a few week's worth, mostly jeans and sweaters, my Chucks, and . . ."

"I am *not* invading your underwear drawer. I don't do chicks' panties."

He didn't do chicks. Period. "You want me to go commando?"

An exaggerated sigh squeezed through the phone. "Fine."

"Ship them overnight," Kate said, "so I don't have to dig

into the high school wardrobe my mother never threw out."
She ended the conversation with a promise to conference call
him and Inara tomorrow afternoon regarding the singer's red
carpet choices.

"Problems?" Kelly asked. The smooth skin between her
brows crinkled.

Kate grabbed her old leather bomber jacket and cowboy
boots from the back of the closet and shoved her feet into them.
Her luck they still fit. She hugged her sister. "Go put that child-
murdering bastard in prison, Kel. I'll be fine."

Kelly hugged her back and Kate felt her sister's warm tears
press against her cheek. "Where are you going?" Kelly asked.

"I just need to get out of here for a little while."

"Want company?"

"Not this time." Kate gave her sister one more squeeze.
"See you in the morning."

Kate didn't need company.

She needed a drink.

The Naughty Irish was a local bar that made no bones about
living up to its name. Music might be the only exception, because good old American boys Mötley Crüe blasted from the
jukebox as Kate walked through the door.

A nontraditional blend of dark wainscoting, green walls,
and deer antlers decorated the place. And if you felt lucky, you
could spend ten dollars on a raffle ticket to support the local
4-H for a chance to be the proud owner of a Browning X-Bolt
rifle. Or so said the hand-printed cardboard sign.

Neon beer signs provided much of the interior lighting

and had been strategically placed to provide dark corners for those who got a little horny when under the influence. The P in the Pepsi stained-glass light above the pool table had been knocked out and the bulb beneath shot a streak of white across the room.

Kate allowed her eyes to adjust to the dim light. She stuck her hands in the pockets of her jacket and wove her way through the haze of smoke toward the long oak bar at the back. She studied the crowd as she scooted up onto one of two empty stools and wasn't surprised to find the place packed with camo jackets and ball caps labeled Mossy Oak. After all, it was prime-time hunting season. Of course, that didn't matter much to the people of Deer Lick who seemed to believe that camo went with every season and every outfit—including wedding attire.

The bartender slid a cocktail napkin in front of her and asked what she wanted to drink. The man looked like a military tank with a beer gut the size of a prize-winning pumpkin at the Harvest Hoedown.

"I'll have a lemon drop martini, please."

Tank looked at her like she'd lost every marble in her head. She wasn't in Kansas anymore.

"Oh, right. Uummm, a glass of Zinfandel?"

"We got house wine. White or red," he grunted.

Which would assure her of a headache in the morning. No thanks. "What's on draft?"

"Guinness and Moose Drool."

Eeew. "Guinness, please."

While she waited for her ale, Kate tapped her fingernails on her napkin and through the long mirror behind the bar watched a group of men in various stages of beard growth playing pool. They were watching her too. Like she was fresh meat.

In her thinking, men were all the same no matter where they came from. Beverly Hills, Manhattan, or downtown Deer Lick. Their pickup lines were altered only by accents or capacity of bullshit. And she'd become far too cynical to buy into any of it.

Tank slid a Guinness in front of her. Thirsty for a little mind-numbing reprieve, she reached for the mug.

"Kate!"

Kate looked up to see her old friend Maggie Densworth calling from all the way across the room. She dropped her serving tray to a nearby table and charged toward Kate with open arms. When she reached the bar, she grabbed Kate in a bear hug.

"It's great to see you!"

Maggie had changed. She was rounder, which made her appear shorter. Her long wavy brown hair had been replaced by a super-short bob. Her slender face had filled out and her cheeks now resembled ripe apples. Still, Kate returned the hug, remembering all the hours the two of them had spent dreaming, wishing for boys who were unattainable, and conjuring up ways to keep from being bored. Most of which granted them thirty days of restriction.

"I was so sorry to hear about your mom," Maggie said, hopping up on the bar stool beside Kate. "I wish we could have made it to the funeral but Adam had football practice and Brian had a dentist appointment."

"Adam and Brian?"

"Oh, God, it has been a long time since we've talked, hasn't it. Adam is my oldest, the one I was pregnant with when you left. Brian is my middle troublemaker. And Jeff is my baby. He's just starting kindergarten this year."

"Wow. You have three kids?"

Maggie laughed. "Yes, and that's it. We kept trying for a girl but no luck. And honey, I am done. There's not an inch of skin on this body without stretch marks."

At that moment Kate realized that an entire lifetime, and obviously a few stretch marks, had evolved without her. People had gone on with their lives. Made homes. Raised families. Supported and comforted each other in this small community she'd once shared. A knot formed in her chest. To clear it she sipped her ale, but the liquid didn't make the peculiar ache go away.

"So you and Oliver are still together?"

"Married ten years. He didn't say hi when you came in?"

"Oliver's here?"

"He poured your Guinness, honey."

Kate looked up at Tank, seeing no resemblance to the handsome young man she'd known way back when.

"Yeah, we've both put on a few pounds," Maggie laughed. "Ever since we bought the bar, our schedules have been crazy. Macaroni and cheese and Hamburger Helper aren't too good for the waistline. Ollie!" she shouted over the din of *Old Time Rock and Roll*. "I'm having a drink with our old friend Kate. Pour me a Moose."

Oliver waved and grabbed a mug from below the bar, tilted it beneath the spout and filled it without foam. He brought it down to Maggie and smiled. "Sorry Kate, didn't recognize you."

Kate smiled. She could say the same for him. "It's good to see you again."

"Consider me off the clock, sweetie." Maggie leaned across the bar and kissed his bald head. "Kate and I have years of catching up to do."

Oliver nodded and went to fill another order.

Maggie leaned back and gave Kate the once-over. "You look fabulous."

"Thanks." She could thank power bars and triple shot skinny lattes for keeping her fit. Or the typical Hollywood diet—starving. "It's so great to see you. So, you've been married for ten years? Wow. I remember when you wanted to get out of here and be a news anchor."

Maggie laughed. "Ah, foolish dreams."

"Why so foolish?"

"If I'd have gone off to be a news anchor, I'd never have the life I do."

"So you're . . . happy?"

"Happy? Deliriously." Maggie's smile filled her entire face. "When I've got my arms around my kids or when Ollie has his arms around me, I wouldn't want to be any place else."

"You don't regret—"

"Getting pregnant?" Maggie lifted her mug. "Not even for a second. Here's to old friends."

Kate tapped her Guinness against Maggie's Moose Drool and stared while her friend downed a good portion of the drink in one swift gulp. Kate was accustomed to watching celebs sip Cristal or absently stir their frou-frou umbrella drinks. She'd forgotten that Deer Lick had a reputation for being a little less refined. Not that there was anything wrong with that.

Kate sipped her ale and listened attentively while Maggie spun into stories about her kids or town gossip that had happened since Kate had left. It was the first time in a long time she hadn't been asked to talk about her *fabulous* Hollywood lifestyle. And she realized it wasn't Maggie being rude, it was simply Maggie wanting to share the happiness in her life. Before she knew it, Kate found herself engrossed in a conversation that had nothing to do with glamour and everything to do with baby spit and poopy diapers. And unlike the celebrity affairs where Kate became trapped while divas argued over who had the best plastic surgeon in Beverly Hills, she didn't feel like gnawing off her leg to escape.

"So I'm guessing you've run into Matt?" Maggie asked suddenly.

Just the mention of his name sent a warm tickle down Kate's spine that spiraled around to the pit of her stomach. She managed to shrug nonchalantly. "A couple of times."

Maggie leaned an elbow onto the bar and grinned. "And?"

"And what?"

"Honey." Maggie waved their empty glasses in the air until Ollie gave them refills. "You may have been gone a long time, but I can't imagine you've grown dense over the years. Or maybe seeing all those movie stars and rock stars has ruined your taste for gorgeous *normal* men. Especially one you had wrapped around your little finger before you left."

Kate had no intention of discussing Deputy Rude with Maggie or anyone else. So they had a history together. So what? A decade had passed. Yes, Matt could be classified as a total hunk. But she wasn't interested. What happened back then didn't matter anymore. It couldn't matter. Not even if there was a tiny little something that sparked inside her whenever she saw him.

She needed a break in conversation that wouldn't seem abrupt but would steer them to a different, less dangerous, subject. Only one justification would work. "Would you excuse me? I need to use the little girl's room."

Kate stood and weaved her way through the crowd toward the back. In the dingy and less than sanitary restroom, Kate did her business, washed her hands twice with soap and water, and glared at herself in the mirror. She looked wasted and blamed it on the cheap mirror and bad overhead light instead of the Guinness she'd consumed.

When she was done, she tugged her sleeve over her hand and opened the door. She stepped out into the dark hallway that led from the bar to the restrooms and, from the sound of banging pots and pans, Kate guessed the kitchen. Why bars and restaurants always stuck the bathrooms by the kitchen was anyone's guess and pretty disgusting.

She looked down, smoothed her hands over the front of her sweater and ran into a huge wall. Her head jerked up and she found a pair of icy blue eyes glaring down at her.

"That's twice in one week you've barreled into me, *Ms. Silver.*"

His voice was low and deep. Yet even over the jukebox, she still managed to hear the bite of sarcasm in his tone.

"If I didn't know better, I'd think I had a target on me," he added.

"Sorry, I leave the shooting practice to my dad." Her gaze dropped from his eyes to the star pinned on his wide chest to the semiautomatic strapped next to the handcuffs on his utility belt. He stood close and the scent of him filled her head with autumn leaves and warm male. "What are you doing here?" she asked.

He rocked back on his heels and peered down at her more closely. The red glow from a Fat Tire Ale sign slashed across the left side of his face. "Got a complaint about some rowdy clientele. Would that mean you?"

"I never get out of line. Unless the occasion calls for it."

His eyes skimmed her from head to toe. And that gave her a boost of alcohol-induced confidence. She smiled and folded her arms beneath her breasts. His gaze followed and fixed onto the front of her sweater. Yep, he was definitely checking her out.

"You wouldn't happen to be flirting with me, would you, Deputy?" she asked. She did not receive a smile for her comedic efforts. Instead, his dark brows came together over those blue eyes and he leaned down. So close his cheek brushed her hair. Then he breathed deep.

"How much have you been drinking?" His eyes may have wandered a moment ago, but now his tone was all business.

"Not nearly enough," she said, taking a step backward.

"You driving?" he asked.

"Nope. I'm just standing here talking to you."

"Still a smartass."

"Can't arrest me for that." She walked away.

"Don't drive," he warned in a big bad wolf growl. "Or I'll make use of these handcuffs."

She looked over her shoulder at him where he still stood in the dark hallway looking one hundred percent badass cop. "Is that a threat, Deputy Ryan? Or a promise?"

CHAPTER SIX

A definite chill frosted the air when Kate stepped out of the bar several hours later exhausted from Maggie's breakneck speed of catching up on each other's lives. It had been great to see her old friend and Kate had been happy to find the rhythm in their friendship hadn't missed a beat. Within just a few minutes, they'd been laughing and gossiping as if the ten-year absence had never happened.

The knowledge filled her with unexpected pleasure. She didn't have friends like that in Hollywood. What she did have were acquaintances. The closest that came to any description of *friend* were her assistant, her hairdresser, and the girl who sold her a cinnamon bagel every Saturday morning. A pretty pathetic list Kate realized.

As she walked toward her mother's beast of a car, she breathed in the pungent scent of wood smoke. A fresh breeze caught the ends of her hair and whipped it across her face. The only winds she was familiar with anymore were the suffocating hot Santa Ana's. Winds that seemed to harbor a taste for fanning flames that transformed expensive Malibu mansions into matchsticks.

Realization crept up on her and caused her heart to do a funny little flip. She'd missed the scents of home—the miles of open pastures, pine needles dampened by a warm rain, the aroma of home-baked meatloaf or pot roast wafting through open kitchen windows. And the bouquet of fresh bread or cookies baked in the ovens in her family's bakery.

She dug her keys from her jacket pocket and noticed the quiet. Instead of the high-level traffic sounds she'd grown used to in L.A., there were only the muted sounds from the bar and the tap-tap of her boot heels against concrete.

She stuck the key in the car door, wondering again, why she bothered to lock the old heap. She slid onto the front seat and reached to turn the key in the ignition. But when she looked up through the windshield and couldn't decide whether The Smoke Shop sign had one pipe or two, she knew she couldn't drive. She'd have to call her sister or walk. At least the nip in the air would sober her up.

From the radio Tom Jones began to croon. A strong sense of déjà vu fell over her and she hoped the prior events were a one-time hallucination.

It's not unusual. . .

"You are not driving this car, young lady."

Shit.

Knowing it was useless to look in the mirror, Kate turned in her seat. And there she was—red plaid shirt, denim overalls, messy gray bun on top of her head, hazy glow floating all over the backseat. "Mother."

"Katherine."

No need to acknowledge the scowl marring her mother's face either. It reached all the way into her words. Kate turned around in her seat, dropped her head back to the headrest and stared out the bug-splattered windshield. She wondered briefly when the men with the nice white jacket would arrive.

"Young lady, you are in no condition to drive."

"I'm not driving. I'm sitting. Besides I only had two beers."

"Three. And they were Guinness. Much more potent than a Coors Light."

"You were in the bar?" Kate asked. Great. Now she was being spied on? By a ghost? In the space of a pause, the air in the car grew heavy. The pressure pushed on her chest, squeezed the breath from her lungs.

"Not exactly."

Kate closed her eyes and rubbed her fingers against her temples. "Then if you weren't *exactly* in the bar, how do you know how many beers I had?"

"A mother just knows these things."

"So . . . ghosts have ESP too?"

"So . . . daughters never stop being smartasses?"

Kate flinched. That was the second time tonight she'd been labeled. Maybe it held some merit.

"This is so unlike you, Katherine."

The tone in her mother's voice sounded exactly the same as the time Kate had taken on a dare and gone cow tipping with a group of friends after they'd bowled at Strike-Out Lanes. The cow had tipped over all right. On her. In a field overflowing with cow pies. Her friends had had to wake up the farmer to get her rescued from her bovine imprisonment. It had taken three showers to get the stink off. Her restriction had lasted an entire month.

"Not really," she said. "You just don't know me very well anymore."

"A mother always knows her child. Always knows what's best for her."

Right. If she'd left her life up to her mother, she'd either be putting buns in the oven or have one in *her* oven.

"Why do you think I'm here?" her mother asked. "For my health?"

Kate's eyebrows shot up her forehead and she couldn't help but glance in the mirror. "Am I supposed to laugh at that?"

Her mother hooted. "No, but you've got to admit that was pretty good."

"Hysterical."

"And still you have no sense of humor," her mother said. "Well, that's why I'm here."

"To make me laugh?" Kate asked, getting more confused by the minute. For Pete's sake, if she was going to lose her mind by seeing dead people, they could at least have the decency to make sense.

"Not to make you laugh. Although that might be a nice side effect."

"Then why *are* you here?"

Her mother paused as if searching for the right words. "Well, since I blew my chance to make amends while I was living, I'm here . . . ummm . . . to . . . help you. Yes, that's right. To help you find the meaning of your life."

"You sure about that?"

"It's difficult to explain."

Just what Kate didn't need, a confusing *and* meddling ghost. "Look, Dr. Phil," she said, "how about you just tell me how to help Dad. He's lost without you. The meaning of *his* life is gone. We're worried about him. And I'm just not sure how to handle all this."

"My Bobby will be just fine, Katherine. Don't you worry about him."

"I think you overestimate him, Mom." She breathed in a gulp of thick air and it clogged her throat when she thought of her heartbroken dad. "He wanders around the house like he's looking for something. He won't sleep in your bed. And he's already thrown himself back into work."

"What would you expect him to do? Sit around and rot? That's my job. Ha! Get it?"

Kate cringed at the thought. "Not funny, Mom."

"See. There you go again. No sense of humor." Her mother paused again as though pondering some miraculous discovery. For a woman who seldom was at a loss for words, she sure seemed to be searching for them in her afterlife.

"What you need, Katherine, is to put a little spark in your life. But right now you've got your head so far in the clouds that he could fall right into your lap and you wouldn't even recognize him."

"He? Him?" Kate's brows lifted. "I'm not looking for a boyfriend."

Her mother released a heavy sigh.

Was that even possible?

"Boyfriend! I'm talking about soul mates, Katherine. That's what my Bobby and I are. That's why he's going to be just fine.

He knows I'm waiting for him—not that I want him to hurry up. But he knows our love reaches far beyond earthly boundaries. And that's what you need to find."

Kate shook her head and the vinyl seat squeaked. What she needed was another Guinness. She and her mother had barely spoken for ten years and the woman was worried about Kate finding a man? What about the argument they'd had before she left home? Sheesh. Still, if her mother wanted to discuss men, she'd try to comply. Arguing had never gotten them anywhere except estrangement.

"Mom. I barely have time for a dinner date let alone a *soul mate*. What I need to find is a way to help dad get his life organized so I get out of this hick—"

A sharp rap on the window startled her and sent her heart racing.

Kate looked up.

Through her side window, the white neon light from Bill's Barber Shop reflected off a shiny pair of handcuffs that swung like a pendulum from a very large, very masculine hand.

Matt had just about finished his shift and decided to make another round past the bars to make sure everything was in order.

Okay, that was a lie.

He'd made another round past the *Naughty Irish* to see if Katie had gone home or if she was still perched on that bar stool with her group of pool-playing, camo-wearing admirers still gawking at her like she was a ten-point buck on opening day of hunting season.

Some things never changed. Especially in Deer Lick. New blood meant new challenges for the bored twenty-something-year-olds, the newly divorced, and those who didn't quite take the sanctity of marriage as seriously as they should. When that new blood was in the form of a shapely firecracker like Katie, it was hard to tell what would happen. Usually someone ended up in cuffs.

Looked like tonight was the firecracker's turn.

When Katie rolled down the window, Matt flipped the cuffs into his palm and took perverse pleasure in the frown that pulled at the corners of her luscious lips.

"You scared me," she said with a squeak that told him she was about fifty percent pissed off and fifty percent amused. Police training hadn't been necessary to figure out that one. Just personal knowledge.

Gravel crunched beneath his boot heels as he took a step back, peered down into her mama's car, and tried not to laugh as he gave her his regulation cop glare. "May I see your license and registration, ma'am?"

She craned her neck to look up at him. Her smoky green eyes narrowed. "I'm not driving."

He scanned the car from the front bumper to the back.

"The car is not running. The car is in *park*," she informed him in what he now called her big-city tone.

"You're behind the wheel. And I have every reason to believe you were about to drive home."

"And that's illegal?"

"How much have you had to drink tonight, *Ms. Silver?*" he said, using the name she'd tossed at him yesterday. Did she think she was too good to use her real name? Or had she shortened it because people in Hollywood had only learned to spell two syllable words?

"One beer."

"How many?"

"Ummmm . . . two?"

He leaned a little closer, slapped the handcuffs against his palm. "I didn't quite hear you."

Her eyes widened and she sighed. "Maybe three."

"Uh-huh."

"I swear." She lifted her hands and clasped the steering wheel. "That's all I had. And I wasn't going to drive."

"You always sit in the car and argue with yourself after only three beers?"

"I wasn't arguing with my—"

"Would you mind stepping out of the car, please?"

"Seriously, Matt, I—"

"Step out of the car." His request had little to do with police maneuvers. He just wanted to see her again—the tight jeans hugging her slender thighs, the way the oversized leather jacket fell across her small shoulders, the way the emerald sweater beneath dipped low and hugged her breasts.

Yeah, he was a glutton for punishment. No doubt about it.

She glared up at him from the driver's seat. Seemed to weigh her choices. Then with an exaggerated exhale of breath she yanked the keys from the ignition.

"Fine." She pulled back the handle and pushed the door open.

Had he not stepped back, the metal would have crashed into a certain part of his anatomy he'd like to keep intact, healthy and ready for action.

She stumbled her way out of the car and glared up at him. "I am *not* drunk."

"Uh-huh."

"I'm not." She weaved just a little and leaned toward him. "So you . . ." Her long slender finger poked at his chest. ". . . just put those handcuffs away."

He took a step closer, crowding her. To intimidate her? Or just for his own damned pleasure? "Or what?"

She probably wasn't as drunk as he'd first thought, but she was definitely in no condition to drive. Standing this close her scent drifted up and caught him off guard. Surprisingly she didn't smell like a brewery or heavy bar smoke like most people he pulled over under suspicious circumstances. Instead she smelled like wintergreen gum, aged leather, and warm woman. An enticing combination that had him fighting the urge to tangle his hands in her silky hair and haul her against him.

"Or . . ." She looked up and gave him a lopsided grin with that soft luscious mouth. ". . . hey, do you flirt with all the people you pull over, Deputy Ryan?"

"I don't flirt when I'm wearing a firearm."

"Seriously?"

She moved closer. So close her breasts were nearly pressed against his chest. Her heat radiated through the fabric of his uniform. She lifted her hand and traced the shape of his badge with a manicured nail. His heart rate kicked into overdrive and he fought back urges he hadn't had to suppress in years.

"Because I've seen that look before," she continued. "And unless you—heeey!"

The click of the cuffs securing her wrists echoed in the clear fall night.

"What are you doing?" she asked, her mouth gaping like a fish.

"You seemed to be intrigued by my handcuffs." He circled his palms around the metal, making sure they weren't too tight. But all he really felt was her soft skin against his calloused fingers. He thought the move clever, a distraction. He couldn't have been more wrong. Touching her was like touching fire. Unfortunately he'd always been a man who didn't mind getting a little singed now and then. "Thought I'd show you how they're used."

"Am I . . . under arrest?" Her body tensed. "You didn't even read me my . . . whatchamacallems. It doesn't work like this on *Law & Order*."

"And this isn't a reality show either, sweetheart." He slid his hand beneath her elbow, led her to his patrol SUV, and helped her up onto the front seat. He reached across her to fasten her seatbelt and made another too-stupid-to-live error that pressed her warm breasts against him. Oh sure, he could remove the cuffs, make her more comfortable, but right or wrong this was a whole lot more fun than putting the cuffs on most of the drunks he came up against.

"I don't think you're supposed to call me sweetheart. Isn't that sexual harassment? Aren't you supposed to shove me in the backseat?" she asked acidly, her green eyes narrowing. "Isn't that where hardened criminals like me go?"

"God, you are drunk." He wasn't about to spoil the fun by telling her the only place he planned to take her was home. He closed the door and then went around to slide into the driver's seat. The dashboard clock verified his shift was officially over so he made a quick radio call to log out. The code numbers he used forced her brows together.

"What's that mean?" Katie asked. "Are you telling them to get the drunk tank ready for me? Which, by the way, I am not."

"Harvey Tittlebaum and his nephew Buddy are already occupying the drunk tank tonight. Course, they might like a little female company."

"You cannot be serious."

Matt started the engine and drove off down Main Street. "Naw, that would be cruel and unusual punishment for the two of them. So I guess we'll have to find someplace else to stick you." He glanced across the cab and managed to keep a straight face. "We usually cuff our additional drunks to the commode. Unfortunately the tile floors do have a tendency to get cold this time of year."

"Great." She slumped in the seat and dropped her head back against the headrest. "Just what my father needs, to have to bail his drunk daughter out of the slammer restroom."

Matt looked over at her, the storefront lights flashed across the misery darkening her beautiful face. To her credit, she didn't start blubbering like most of the drunks he picked up. Suddenly he didn't have the heart to tease her anymore. And he wasn't exactly ready to take her home either. "I'm not taking you to jail."

"You're not?" She sat up. "Then where are you taking me?"

"Somewhere to sober up. Your dad has enough on his plate. You want him to see you like this?"

"Oh! No. You're right. I can't go home." Her tone spiraled into panic. "Not smashed like this."

"Thought you said you weren't drunk."

"Maybe a little."

"Maybe a lot," he said.

"No. A *lot* was that party-till-you-puke Friday night after the Deer Lick Destroyers won the state title. After *you* scored the winning touchdown." She chuckled. "God, I spent the entire next day hugging my knees and worshiping the porcelain king. *And* trying to convince my mom that I had the flu."

"Did she believe you?"

"No." Her nose wrinkled. "I had to scrub the mixing pots for a week. Do you remember that night?" she asked.

He did. But his version was quite different. While he vaguely remembered scoring that touchdown, he did remember Katie dancing by the bonfire near the back of Old Man Carver's plowed alfalfa field. He remembered how she'd come to sit on his lap, her body warm from the fire. He remembered her breath sweet from the wine when she kissed him. And he remembered wanting her so bad he'd ached.

Kate had been an affectionate drunk back then. He glanced at her across the SUV and wondered if she'd be just as amorous now.

The patrol vehicle rolled to a stop in a dark alley. Kate knew she'd had a bit too much to drink, but she wasn't disoriented and that was definitely the back entrance to the bakery. "What are we doing here?"

"You said you wanted to sober up." Matt turned off the engine. "I hear this place makes the best coffee in town."

She looked across the interior of the SUV. The red, green,

and yellow dashboard lights bounced off the star pinned to his shirt. "Maybe so, but I don't have a key."

He got out of the SUV and came around to open her door. "I do," he said as his big warm hand reached beneath her elbow and he helped her down from the seat while tingles slid from her heart and into her stomach.

With her hands cuffed and the Guinness weaving through her bloodstream, she lost her balance and bumped against his wide chest. The alley was dark, the night sky darker, so when she looked up she missed the expression on his face. What she didn't miss was the tension in his arms, his hands, or the solidness of his strong body. "Sorry," she said.

They might have stood like that—chest to breast, thigh to thigh—for a minute or five hours. Kate wasn't sure. She was only sure her heart fluttered like hummingbird wings against her ribs and his matched hers beat for beat. Of course, she could be misreading all those cardiac rhythms.

As though he recognized they were in a dangerous position, he quickly uncuffed her. Though the metal bracelets hadn't been tight at all, she rubbed her wrists. She just needed a distraction from the devastatingly handsome man standing in the dark alley with her, who, despite his outward antagonism, was obviously interested in her. Or at least parts of him were.

He said nothing as he stuck the cuffs into his utility belt and then turned toward the back entrance to unlock the door. She watched him flip on the lights and then stroll over to the coffee pot like he'd done it a million times.

"Exactly *why* is it you have the keys to my parents' bakery?" She tossed her jacket on the chair by the door and followed him to the prep counter where the coffeemaker sat next to the stack of baking sheets she'd washed before leaving earlier. The scent of sugar floated around them as he reached for the box of filters and dumped in a few scoops of coffee.

"They gave it to me when I worked for them."

"You worked for my parents?" She came up beside him and planted her hands on her hips. "When?"

"After you left."

That settled over her like a tsunami. "So, you like, what? Decorated cupcakes?"

He grinned. "Your mother always said I made a mean raspberry torte."

She tried to picture big bad Matt Ryan wearing a white apron and dusting confetti candy bits on a birthday cake. The image didn't fit any better than her being back in Deer Lick.

"I don't get it. If you needed a job, why didn't you just keep working for your uncle?"

"Because after you bailed, your folks needed me."

Ouch. Okay, so her parents needed someone to help them out. She had left them short-handed. At the time she hadn't exactly considered what kind of situation her departure would put them in. She'd been selfish. And now, the thought of how'd she'd left them high and dry stung.

But Matt hadn't said they needed *somebody*, he'd said they needed *him*. That was different. And that didn't sit well with her at all. She nudged him out of the way and tugged the glass carafe from his hand. "I can do that."

He pulled up a stool and sat down. "I miss her."

Kate looked up in time to catch a wistful look darken his eyes. "My mom?"

"Yeah. She was a good friend." He stretched his long legs

out in front of him and chuckled deep in his chest. "Of course, I did everything I could to keep on her good side. You did not want to piss off Letty Silverthorne."

"Seriously. She was never the kind to easily forgive and forget."

"You're a lot like her in that sense."

She fought the urge to punch him. Unfortunately he was telling the truth. "That's what Kelly tells me. She thinks Mom and I are cut from the same fabric."

"I can see that. Your mom was a good woman."

She pushed the electrical plug into the outlet. "Does that mean you think I'm a good woman too?" Fishing was so pathetic. But these days Kate would take whatever compliments she could wring from someone.

He gave her that smile that made her heart flip like an IHOP flapjack.

"Make a full pot of that and I'll help you drink it."

"Nice deflection, Deputy." She looked up. "You sure? Seems to me you'd want to call it a night."

He watched her, seemed to study her actually, before he answered. "I'm in no hurry."

His scrutiny made her uneasy and only managed to scramble a million questions through her mind. Some she could sift out. Others were best left tucked in her brain for safe-keeping.

Apparently she'd missed a lot of Matt Ryan's life. And though she'd thought of him once in awhile, her reflections on what he'd done with his life had never consumed her. She'd been much too busy building a career. She bit her lip as she waited for the carafe to fill with water. He sat there on that stool like he owned the place. His dark hair a bit messy like he'd run his fingers through it. The expression on his handsome face unreadable.

Curiosity nipped at her with sharp little teeth. A sure sign she should just let things go. A sign she chose to ignore. She'd never discovered the identity of the blond by his side at her mother's funeral. Now seemed as good a time as any to ask the big question. "No *little woman* to go home to?"

He looked up from the newspaper he'd found on the counter. "Not yet."

"Huh. I figured you'd be married by now." She ended her comment with a chuckle.

"Something funny about that?"

"Actually . . ." She chuckled again and pushed the coffeemaker ON button. ". . . I also figured by now you'd be bald, pudgy, and a grease monkey still working for your uncle.

His blue gaze intensified as stared at her without blinking. "Guess you figured wrong."

Boy did she. She turned toward him, leaned against the counter and folded her arms. "I never imagined you, of all people, would go into law enforcement. I mean, you do have a pretty wild background."

"People grow up, Katie. And people forgive."

"It's Kate. Nobody calls me Katie anymore except my dad."

"Is there anything about you that's still part of the girl before she left?"

She shrugged. "Not much. Hard to remain a small-town girl in a city that eats them up and spits them out."

He shook his head. "Can't figure out why anyone would ever want that kind of life."

Sometimes neither could she. But she'd eat worms before

she'd let him know. "Because it's exciting. It's fast-paced. It's glamorous. Do you know I have an entire loft stuffed with couture and a collection of designer jewelry most other stylists would kill for?"

He stared at her as though she were speaking Martian.

"But it's not just about the clothes. It's about the red carpets, the star-studded galas, champagne, caviar . . ." Those moments made it easy to forget all the hours she spent on her knees. In cat hair. Sewing crystals on the pants of an unappreciative pop princess. ". . . never a dull moment, you know?"

He leaned back and folded his arms. His biceps expanded. Kate knew those muscles were from hard work and not a workout machine. Which made them way more sexy.

"Guess I'm okay with dull." He shrugged. "But then, that must have been one of the things you hated about me back then."

Looking for an escape from the intensity in his eyes and the sting in her chest she said, "I never hated you. I just wanted something more than this town could give me."

He stood and came toward her. "You mean something more than I could give you."

Her heart tripped. *Yes.* "Honestly, Matt. I'd been waiting for that scholarship for two years. When it came, I left. I never added you into the picture. We were young and what happened between us was . . ." *Incredible. Unforgettable. Unbelievable.* ". . . a mistake."

Unexpected and old feelings rushed back as he stood next to her. She reached for the carafe. Carelessly poured the coffee into the cup. And missed.

Hot drops of liquid splashed over her hand and she jerked

it away just in time before the entire contents burned her. The cup crashed to the floor. "Ow, damn it."

"Are you okay?" He took her arm and held her hand up to examine it.

"I'm fine." Except for the warmth of his palm surrounding her wrist. Except for the heat radiating from his body. Except for the hard jolt of desire that reared its horny head.

He looked down into her eyes, looked at her mouth and lowered his head. Mesmerized she watched it happen, in slow motion, until his amazing lips brushed her hand with a kiss and every fiber in her body went into a meltdown of need.

Then he gave her *the look*—that sexy half-lidded look that once had her ripping off her shirt and shucking her panties.

"I never saw it that way," he said.

"What?" Her hand, still cradled in his palm, tingled and she had no idea what he was talking about.

"A mistake." A slow smile curved his lips. "Us."

Now what in the hell was she supposed to say to that? Especially since her heart seemed to be trying to beat its way out of her chest.

"I had dreams," she said, easing her hand from his. "Didn't you? Didn't you ever wish you could get out of Deer Lick? Didn't you ever wonder what the rest of the world might be like?"

"Me? Nope." He shrugged, leaned down, and picked up the shards of glass. "I'm like a tree. I've got roots that go way down deep. And I don't plan on digging them up."

"Never?"

"Never." He took a step closer to toss the broken cup in the trash can behind her."

"God, this place would drive me crazy." She shook her

head, to shatter her overpowering imagination. "It doesn't even have a movie theater. How can anybody live in a town without a movie theater?"

"We never missed it as kids." He leaned a hip against the counter. "Most people use those mail-in DVD places. That way you don't have to worry about someone's cell phone going off and interrupting the movie. You can watch it from the comfort of your sofa or even your own bed. I guess that's where I differ."

"Why's that?"

He gave her *that* look again. "The last thing I want to do in bed is watch a movie."

She laughed. "I'm not even going to ask. But I'm sure you don't spend much time there alone."

"Jealous?"

"You wish." Kate reached for another cup and glanced over her shoulder. Arms folded across his chest he stood there, watching her.

"Don't pretend like you know anything about me anymore, Kate. You don't."

"I never said I did. I just assumed."

"Don't." His eyes narrowed. "How would you like it if I assumed you slept your way to the top of your career? Don't they have something called a casting couch?"

"I don't sleep around." She folded her arms. "Besides, I'm a stylist, not an actress."

"Says who?"

Kate watched her parents' quaint log cabin come into view as the patrol car rolled to a stop at the curb. Her mother had decorated the small front porch with pots of golden mums. An autumn wreath with an orange satin bow hung on the front door. Her mother had a knack for all those homey touches. Which had been only one of the issues that had driven her and her mother apart. Kate had never been into gingham and cute. She'd always been more a fan of silk and fabulous. Still, she had to admit, the homey touches gave an air of welcome you just couldn't achieve with rhinestones and feathers. Her chest tightened as she glanced across the darkened cab to Matt. He'd been silent since they'd left the bakery.

She'd never gotten that cup of coffee. Matt had suddenly been in a hurry to get back to the station. So she rode the entire way home with the window down, hoping the cold air would drive the leftover Guinness from her system. Yet even now, as Matt put the SUV in park, opened his door and got out, her head spun like she was on a merry-go-round at full speed.

And she wasn't exactly sure it was from the ale.

Always the gentleman, Matt came around to her side, opened her door and helped her down from her seat. Her cowboy boots landed on the dewy strip of grass bordering the sidewalk. The warmth of his palm encircled her arm until she took a step backward and his hand dropped to his side.

"Thanks for the ride," she said. "And for not arresting me."

He nodded that beautiful dark head. "Next time you might not be so lucky. I'm usually only good for one get-out-of-jail-free ticket."

She smiled. "Well, I appreciate it." More than ready to be away from his overwhelmingly male presence she stepped toward the sidewalk then turned with a wave. "Thanks again."

With one foot on the street and one on the curb he stopped,

looked back at her, then came toward her with his hands in his jacket pockets. "Let me ask you something."

Uh-oh. "Sure."

"You're successful, right?"

She gave a half-hearted shrug. "I'd consider myself that, yes."

"And you go to all these star-studded parties and hang out with celebrities and rock stars?"

"Absolutely." *Where was he going with this?*

"Yet you tell everyone you're too busy for a relationship."

"Says who?"

"Your sister. Your brother. Your . . ."

Traitors. "Okay, okay, I get it."

"Are you?"

She folded her arms. "What do you mean?"

"I mean, you're so damn eager to tell everyone about your fabulous lifestyle . . . how's that really working for you?" He paused, the glint in his icy blue eyes visible even in the dark of night. "What keeps you warm at night?"

"A silk comforter."

He grinned down at her.

"Are you insinuating that I don't have a life?" She propped her hands on her hips. "Because I do. I have a life. I can promise you that." *Liar, liar, pants on fire.*

He smiled in a non-convinced way that made her want to use those smirking lips for something else. "I do," she insisted. "*And* I have an original Valentino hanging in my closet that I plan to wear to the People's Choice Awards next year. How many women can say that?"

He chuckled as he walked away. While he slid into the

driver's seat, he asked through the open window, "Tell me something, Kate. Exactly how many orgasms is that worth?"

She was so not going to let him get the best of her. "I guess that all depends on how you wear the gown. With or without panties."

He grinned and put the SUV into gear. Before he drove off he said, "Now there's something worth thinking about."

Kate gritted her teeth as the taillights grew smaller in the distance. She'd love to be able to shout out "Liar!" but the accusation wouldn't fly. He was right. She was too busy to even buy herself a vibrating *gift*. Sure, she'd had sex in the past ten years, but she'd also had lovers who were more into their own satisfaction than hers.

Matt Ryan did not fit into that category.

Not even when he'd been barely above drinking age.

Resigned to the sinking reality that orgasms were a small part of her past and there seemed little hope for them in the near future, she walked to the front porch and quietly unlocked the door. Since it was late, she didn't want to wake anyone. Or, at least, she didn't want anyone to wake and see what a hot mess she'd become.

When she eased the door open to the living room, she found her father fast asleep in his recliner, a framed photo of her mother clutched to his chest.

Kate stood there, looking at him. Looking at the restless expression on his face. And she could not stop the tears that welled in her eyes.

Poor daddy. Her soul ached for him.

She didn't know what to do to help this man she loved with all her heart. She wasn't wise enough to know how to help him find peace. So she did the only thing she could think of at the moment. She gathered up the crocheted afghan her mother had made for one of his birthdays and covered him, tucking the soft knotted yarn beneath his chin. Then she kissed him on top of his balding head.

"Night, Daddy," she whispered. "I love you."

He exhaled softly as she tiptoed away. When she reached the bedroom door, he murmured, "Sweetheart, I knew you'd come."

Kate gripped the doorknob. There was a smile in his voice. In that instant, Kate knew she wasn't the only one her mother visited. A warm tingle spread through her heart. Maybe there was something to be said about this soul mate thing her mother claimed existed.

She slipped inside the bedroom, careful not to wake her sleeping sister, and let the leather jacket slide down her arms. She sat on the edge of her bed, toed off her cowboy boots, and wondered.

Could there actually be someone out there just for *her?*

And if so, would she ever find him?

CHAPTER SEVEN

W hile the sun dipped below the peaks of the Rockies, Kate sat behind the desk in the small bakery office and interviewed yet another unqualified applicant eager to fill her mother's baking shoes. A week had passed since her siblings had gone back to their normal lives. Dean's football team had won their Sunday night game. Kelly had called and implied she was pantyhose deep in good fact-finding on the killer and promised she'd get back as soon as possible. In the meantime Kate was still stuck in Deer Lick.

It had also been a week since Matt had so kindly reminded her of her nonexistent sex life.

That she wasn't so happy about.

While Chelsea Winkle, current student body president of the senior class of Deer Lick High and head cheerleader for the Deer Lick Destroyers, explained her method of decorating Halloween spider cupcakes, Kate's mind wandered. The meeting she'd had that morning via Skype with Josh and Inara had almost imploded.

The pop singer needed to wear something spectacularly

casual to the red carpet premiere of Hugh Jackman's latest action flick. Again, her client complained about Kate's modest choices. After an hour long power struggle, they set up Josh's computer so Kate could look through her wardrobe storage for something alluring but not too sexy that might please the difficult diva. They'd finally agreed on a Dior animal print halter dress Kate had been saving for herself. Oh well, anything to keep the styling machine moving in her favor.

Chelsea abruptly ended her monologue. Kate stopped doodling on Chelsea's application, looked up, and smiled at the teen who fit the perfect example of an all-American girl—blond hair pulled up in a ponytail, blue eyes, naturally straight teeth, and a dusting of freckles across her nose. The teen grinned and nodded at Kate as though she'd just divulged the secrets of the universe.

"So . . . Chelsea . . . have you ever taken a professional cake-decorating class?"

"Oh. No. I just get all my terrific ideas from my mom's *Better Homes and Garden* magazines. You should see the one I found last Christmas for peppermint pie."

"Wow. Sounds . . . interesting. Have you ever worked in a bakery before?"

Chelsea's blue eyes widened. "Gosh, no, Miss Silver. But I help my mom bake chocolate chip cookies for my dad all the time."

From a package, no doubt. Kate stood. "Thanks for coming in, Chelsea. I have a few more interviews before we can make our final decision."

Chelsea stood too. "Oh. Okay. Well, I hope I get the job. I really, really, really need the money for the *cutest* prom dress I saw over in Bozeman. I can't afford it without a job."

Kate remembered the days of proms and Valentine's dances. And she remembered the importance of just the right dress to a young girl who wanted to look like Cinderella. Even if only for a night. "Are there a lot of girls like you?"

Chelsea cocked her head. "What do you mean?"

"Girls who can't afford to buy a prom dress."

"Yeah. A lot of us try to hit the thrift shops but this area isn't really known for its ball gown occasions. So the selection is pretty sad."

An idea burst into Kate's bored little brain that rocked her from head to toe. An idea that had a little to do with the small shop for rent over on Fourth Street and a whole lot to do with her Hollywood connections. "To be honest, Chelsea, I'm not going to be able to offer you the job here at the bakery."

The teen's smile slipped. "Oh."

"But I'm pretty sure I can offer you a job of another kind. One you just might be perfect for."

"Really?" The smile returned.

With a hand on the back of Chelsea's fuzzy blue sweater, Kate led her to the front of the shop. "Why don't you give me a call in a couple of days and I'll fill you in."

"That would be great, Miss Silver. Thank you so much."

"Call me Kate and we've got a deal." She extended her hand.

The girl eagerly reciprocated. "Thank you . . . Kate."

Once the door closed behind the teen, Kate's father looked over at her with questioning eyes. Kate shook her head. Her father nodded, then went back to making the dough for tomorrow's selection of pies. Kate pulled her cell phone from her apron pocket and punched in number one on her speed dial.

"Josh? Listen, I've got an idea and I need your help . . ."

An hour later Kate had put her plan into action. A satisfied smile curled her mouth. The clock edged toward six o'clock and she and her dad could finally lock the door, clean up, and go home.

Her feet were killing her and her hands were raw. She looked down at her chipped nails. She needed a manicure, a massage, and a martini. Unfortunately all she was going to get was a shower, leftovers, and a lumpy bed.

Kate flipped on the turn signal at Main and Whitetail Rd. She had just enough time to grab a six-pack of Pepsi from the Gas and Grub before she went home to warm a bowl of the beef stew her father had made the night before. She'd never been much of a leftover kind of girl. Not even after she moved to Hollywood and her leftovers often consisted of delicacies her caterer pals snuck into her empty fridge. But her dad's homemade stew and warm biscuits brought forth wonderful memories from when she'd been a kid. Maybe she needed to admit that parts of her childhood hadn't been completely hideous.

She pulled into the G & G's vacant parking lot where the only sign of life came from the window and a life-size cardboard cutout of a busty blond in a Hawaiian bikini. For those who weren't happy enough with her overflowing triple D's, her hip-shaking movement had been motorized.

Kate pulled open the glass door and waved to the cashier—a kid barely old enough to sell alcohol, let alone the porn magazines they kept stored behind the counter. She grabbed her Pepsi from the cooler and then cruised the aisles, managing to talk herself into a package of Flamin' Hot Cheetos. She usually preferred a Butterfinger with her soda, but the overpowering sweet smell of the bakery killed her sugar craving. On the way to the register, she plucked a package of teriyaki beef jerky from the shelf and a tube of ChapStick and then tossed everything on the counter.

As the kid rang up her purchases, the glass door opened and a breeze shot through the front of the store. Kate turned to see who else was stocking up on snacks, only to find Edna Price staring at her as though she'd sucked lemons.

Great.

"You still here?" the old woman asked.

"If by *here* you mean in Deer Lick, I guess you're forgetting you saw me just this morning when I bagged your brownies."

"I always did think you were a smartass."

"Join the crowd," Kate muttered.

"That'll be $13.45," the kid said.

Kate pulled a twenty from her wallet and handed it over.

"Didn't your mama teach you to respect your elders?" Edna asked, cupping both wrinkled hands over the moose's head.

Kate accepted the bag from the kid and headed toward the door. She'd had a long day and she was still excited about her new venture. The last thing she needed was a wrestling match with the town crone. "Look, Mrs. Price, I'm sorry if my presence here offends you. I'm only trying to help out my father."

"Help him?" The old woman's gray brows lowered. "Where were you when he and your mama needed you before? You were selfish then. Appears not much has changed."

It wasn't the first time Mrs. Price had reminded her of her choice to leave without telling anyone. It wasn't the first time the memory of the night she and her mother had argued struck her square in the chest with an iron fist. Nor was it the first time she'd been filled with deep regret.

"You know, I . . ." She looked into Edna's disapproving gaze and realized nothing she could say would change the woman's opinion of her. ". . . nevermind." Kate pushed open the door and fled out into the cool night air. She didn't need to explain to a judgmental old woman why she had left. She just wanted to go home, eat her father's stew and her Cheetos, and go to sleep. Maybe tonight she'd be too exhausted to be haunted by the reoccurring nightmare of her mother's last words that fateful night. The night her mother had called her a worthless dreamer who would never amount to anything.

But she doubted it.

Fatigue crept into her bones as she slid into the Buick and turned the car toward refuge. A near full moon shone down on the quaking aspens lining the road, turning the autumn foliage to glittering gold. An elderly couple strolled hand-in-hand past homes filled with warm light. They paused briefly to kiss. The sweetness of the act made Kate sigh. When she'd been a teen, she'd somehow overlooked the charm of her hometown. She'd looked past the Norman Rockwell appeal of kids playing in their yards without fear of gang wars erupting around them. That one could still go out at night without the worry of being robbed. Kate glanced across the seat at her purse, which held an arsenal of protection devices and laughed. No one needed Mace in Deer Lick.

From the radio Tom Jones began to sing *It's Not Unusual*.

"Edna means well."

The abrupt sound of her mother's voice shoved her heart into her throat and nearly caused her to crash into the Weber's

Mobile Window Repair van parked on the side of the road.

"Geez! Mom! A little warning you're here next time? Please?"

"Sorry."

"And what's with Tom Jones singing every time you decide to pop in?"

"It's my theme song."

"Your—"

"Hey, I figure if it's good enough for the WWE wrestlers, it's good enough for me."

"I'm pretty sure *The Rock* never exploded into the area with Tom Jones blaring."

"Well, I'm not much into that heavy rap stuff."

"Yeah, I just don't see you as the Eminem type."

"What does candy have to do with music?"

"No. Mom. Eminem is . . . nevermind." Far be it for her to have to explain the intricacies of the rap world. It wasn't like her mother was going to go out and buy a CD or a concert ticket.

"Well, I'm still sorry about Edna back there. She just doesn't know how to hold back on what she's thinking."

"There's the understatement of the year." Kate glanced in the rearview mirror even though she knew it was useless. "I know you two were good friends. Maybe you could pay her a visit and ask her to back off."

"Yeah. Can't really do that."

Kate glanced over her shoulder. Her mother sat in the middle of the bench seat tapping her chin with her forefinger. "Why not?"

"That's not my mission."

"Your mission? Oh. That's right." Kate shook her head. "The one to find me a love that reaches beyond earthly bounds."

"It's more complicated than that."

"Really? Well, while you're at it, could you make sure he has a penthouse in Manhattan, a mansion in Malibu, and a fabulous live-in chef?"

"Is that what you think life is all about, Katherine?" The twinge of sadness in her mother's tone was barely audible, but it was there all the same.

"It doesn't hurt."

Her mother actually tsked. "You have so much to learn."

"You know, Mom, I'm really not doing so bad with my life. I have a successful business. I wear beautiful clothes. I have friends." At least a few. Though none with benefits.

"I never said you were doing bad, Katherine. I said you needed someone special in your life."

"I can always buy a dog."

"You just don't get it, do you? You can't keep running."

Kate could almost hear her mother shaking her head. Though curiosity prodded her to turn to see if she was right, she kept her eyes on the road, dodging a squirrel with a death wish. "What do you mean? I'm not running from anything."

"Honey, you ran ten years ago and you haven't stopped since."

The old anger and desolation she felt that night slammed into her heart. "I didn't run. You drove me away." Her jaw tightened. "Do you even remember what you said to me?"

"Of course I remember. I also remember that you took it the wrong way."

"I don't think so. Look," Kate said, gripping the wheel tighter, "I don't want to talk about this."

"Don't you think it's about time we did?"

"We'll only argue. We always do."

"Arguing isn't always a bad thing, Katherine."

"Says who?"

Beneath her fingers the steering wheel wobbled. Then a tire blew with a loud pop.

"Damn it!" Kate guided the crippled car to the side of the road. "I don't even know how to change a tire."

"Then it's time to learn."

"Are you going to give me a lesson?" Kate turned, only to find the backseat empty. "Mom?"

When there was no response, Kate got out of the car and kicked the flat tire on the way to the trunk. She managed to pull out the spare and the jack. Her hands were filthy before she even got started. With her hands on her hips, she stood back looking at the car for some indication of how she was supposed to do this. But all she saw were parking lot dings and rust. She rummaged through the glove box for the owner's manual but only came up with a few yellowed napkins, the car registration, and proof of insurance.

Dropping to her knees she tried to look under the Buick for a hook or some hint of where the jack was supposed to go but nothing jumped out and waved a flag at her. She guessed she'd have to crawl under to see what she could find there.

The gravel bit into her back and she was halfway beneath the beast when headlights streaked across the asphalt. A car came to a stop behind her. Her heart squeezed in her chest.

Please God, don't let it be that Mike guy with the hockey mask and an axe.

A door opened and closed and heavy footsteps walked toward her.

"Trouble?"

From beneath the car Kate glanced at the huge black boots straddling her legs. She closed her eyes. Yes, *he* was definitely trouble.

She skootched out from beneath the Buick and brushed the grime from her hands. "Deputy Ryan. What a pleasant surprise."

Matt leveled a look at her, mostly to keep from smiling at the streak of dirt she'd smeared across her forehead and the obstinate tone in her voice. "What are you doing under there?"

"Looking where to put the jack. As you can see, I have a flat."

"Don't you know it's dangerous to crawl under a car that isn't secure?" He extended his hand to help her up. She eyed him warily before she placed her cool palm in his. When he gave a gentle tug, she came up and into his arms. For several heartbeats she stood there looking up at him through those smoky green eyes while he looked down at her, resisting the urge to lower his head and kiss those full, seductive lips.

The idea was not only bad, it bordered on insane. He broke the hypnotic hold she held over him, picked up the tire iron, and set it by the flat. "I take it you've never changed a tire before."

She stepped back. "No. I have roadside service on my insurance."

"Of course you do," he said, reaching inside the car to set the emergency brake.

"What's that supposed to mean?"

When he walked toward the back of the car, she stood in his way, arms folded. He could have stepped around her but what would be the fun in that? So he cupped his hands on her elbows, lifted her, and set her aside.

"That means that you're going to learn how to change one. Just in case your roadside service is too busy playing Texas Hold 'em or something."

"Oh." She looked at him like she didn't believe that was what he meant. And she was right.

He kneeled on the asphalt. "Come on. Get down here."

She knelt beside him with the knees of her jeans digging into the pebbled surface. "Aren't you afraid you're going to get your uniform dirty?"

He laughed. Shook his head. He'd love to get dirty. But not the way she was thinking. "Take this . . ." He handed her the tire iron. ". . . and loosen the lug nuts."

She gave one a good attempt then looked at him with despair in her smoky eyes. "It's too tight."

"Let me help," he said.

She held out the tire iron.

"Uh-uh, Hollywood, you've got to learn to do it yourself."

He scooted behind her, wrapped his arms around her until his hands were on top of hers, and realized he'd made a big, big mistake. Not only were his arms framing the sides of her luscious breasts, but his crotch was pressed against her warm backside. And chances were in about two seconds she'd know she didn't exactly turn him off.

She swiveled her head and said with a smirk, "Is this the way you help *everyone* learn to change a flat?"

"Nope. Just the pretty girls. The boys are on their own."
Holding her between his arms was torture. Heavenly torture.
His only distraction came in the form of helping her loosen the
lugs one at a time.

Once that was accomplished, he handed her the jack and
showed her where to place it under the car. She grunted a little but
managed to get it in the right spot. Then he handed her the tire
iron again. "Put this in that slot and use it to pump up the jack."

"Ooh, I love it when you talk dirty."

He shook his head. She had no idea. Or at least she didn't
remember.

She gave the jack a go with about as much success as the lug
nuts. After several unsuccessful attempts, she looked over her
shoulder at him, batted her eyelashes, and said in a very Mae
West voice, "A little help would be soooo much appreciated."

Before he knew it, his arms were wrapped around her again.

The jack wasn't the only thing she raised.

Trying to keep his erection under control was a ridiculous
feat. Especially when she smelled like sugar and vanilla and all
he wanted to do was lick her all over.

When the spare was in place and he'd survived the torment
of having her in his arms, he tossed the flat and the jack in the
trunk. And while every ounce of common sense told him to
give her a wave, get in his car, and get the hell out of there, his
legs carried him forward. Toward her. The queen of his fantasies for too many years. Hell, even with tire grease on her forehead and road dirt smudged on her cheek she turned him on.

He opened her door and watched while she slid onto the
seat. He waited until she started the car before he started to
walk away.

"Matt?" she called from the open window.

He stopped. *Do not turnaround.* Man, were his feet *ever* going to listen to him? He retraced his steps and found himself, once again, beside her door like a big dumbass.

She looked up at him, smiled, and crooked her finger. With his testosterone churning and his common sense on temporary leave, he leaned down.

"I just wanted to thank you for your help," she said, then leaned forward and kissed his cheek.

Her lips were warm. Soft. And everything inside him shattered. She wasn't the girl he'd fallen in love with. She was the woman who'd walked away without even a good-bye. He had a life planned. And it didn't include her.

"I would have helped anyone," he said, breathing back the pain lingering in his chest. "Tonight it just happened to be you."

Kate watched Matt stride back to his patrol car. He held his head high, his shoulders straight, and his message couldn't have been any more clear.

Tonight it just happened to be you translated to *you're no different than anybody. You mean nothing to me.*

She turned the key and the engine kicked over with a groan. Once Matt was in his car, he started it right up and drove off. Kate watched as his taillights disappeared around the corner.

Seemed like all she ever did was watch his taillights disappear.

He didn't have to stop and help her. She would have figured it out eventually. But even as much as he appeared to dislike her, Matt Ryan had a chivalrous streak in him a crater wide.

He smiled at crabby old ladies. Helped pregnant women cross the street. He'd even stepped in to help her parents when she'd left. Everywhere she turned it seemed he was coming to the aid of someone even when he wasn't wearing a uniform. The town adored him.

Something light and fluttery danced through her heart. He was a freaking pain-in-the-ass knight-in-shining-armor she couldn't help admire. Still, if she could just chisel away at all that wonderfulness, she was sure she'd find something rotten. Even if it was that he only flossed once a week.

With a sigh she released the emergency brake and put the car in drive. Half a block later Tom Jones invaded the radio. *It's not unusual. . .*

Oh dear God.

"Well that went spiffy."

Kate braked and turned in her seat. Her mother frowned at her from the back. Her normal golden glow looked a bit more chartreuse. Kate wanted to laugh. She was starting to enjoy her mother's little intrusions. And wasn't that weird? "Are you eavesdropping on my life?"

"No, dear. Just your poor attempts at a love life."

"I'm not looking for love, Mother."

"Well, honey, there's your first mistake."

On Sunday afternoon, her only day off, Kate stood in the middle of the empty shop she'd rented. Her imagination whirled like pixie dust as she planned out how to decorate it on a shoestring budget. And where would she find the time? Seriously. Between interviewing applicants for the bakery job, working eight to ten hours alongside her father and trying to keep her Hollywood clients happy, she barely had time to sleep.

Five months. She was going to be here for five months and even as busy as she might be, she was still bored out of her mind. She needed to fill every hour of every day to keep the gremlins from sucking up the part of her life she'd worked so hard to put together all these years. To keep her from choking on the lingering guilt. To keep her from falling in step with the other six thousand residents of Deer Lick, Montana.

She breathed in the musty air and had to admit that even though she probably had a screw loose for taking on extra projects, she thrived on a good challenge. Even if it killed her. So while her back and leg muscles ached, she picked up her cell phone and dialed Chelsea Winkle.

Within half an hour, Chelsea and her cheerleading squad were standing in the middle of the vacant space while Kate explained what needed to be done and how much she would pay them for their work.

"Who's the artistic one in the bunch?" she asked.

Both Chelsea and a brunette named Madison raised their hands.

"Okay. I need both of you to create the sign that will go out front. Nothing too over-the-top. Something whimsical that will catch the eye of every teenage girl in Deer Lick. And it's got to withstand brutal weather."

"Can we use pink?" Chelsea asked. Her ponytail swung as she cocked her head. "I really, really love pink."

"Of course, but try to stay away from loud colors," Kate said, smiling. "We're not going for in-your-face. We're going for fantasy."

Chelsea and Madison looked at each other and grinned. "Definitely pastels."

"As for the rest of you, I need someone to make a trip to the hardware store for the wall paint, and I need the rest to hit the thrift shops for some tables, maybe a desk, even something that could be used as a front counter. Use your imagination. We'll paint everything white so don't worry about the color."

"This is going to be so much fun," Brandy, a too-thin girl with dark hair and braces squealed.

"Do what you can today, then meet me back here tomorrow after six. We'll have to work fast. My assistant will be sending the first shipment out in a few days."

Kate stood back as the girls went out the door giggling like the teens they were. She remembered that youthful exuberance. In fact, she felt a little tug of it now in the center of her heart.

Chelsea stuck her head back through the door.

"Forget something?" Kate asked.

"I forgot to say thank you."

Ah, small-town politeness. The teens in her adopted hometown of L.A. rarely put their cell phones away long enough to say thank you to anyone. "You're welcome, Chelsea."

"Kate?" She used the name timidly. "If you don't mind me asking, why are you going through all this trouble when you're only going to be here for a short time?"

Kate gave a little shrug. "I remember being your age." She glanced out the big bay window and watched a mother kneel and hug her small child as they stood outside the dentist office across the street. Unexpectedly, Kate's heart went a little squirrely. "I guess this is payback for all the good times I had." *And for all the hell she'd raised.*

Chelsea gave her a smile. "Well, I hope you'll change your mind and stay. I like you."

Kate smiled back. "I like you too."

And she did. Something about the girl reminded her of herself before Hollywood dug its claws in and jaded the youthful enthusiasm she'd had when she'd first arrived. Not that Hollywood was all bad. Just that Deer Lick was a complete one-eighty.

When the door banged shut behind Chelsea, Kate glanced around the empty space again, seeing, in her mind, how it would look by this time next week. A tingle of satisfaction rippled through her just before a hint of panic slapped it down. Her one day off was almost over and she wondered if she'd bitten off more than she could digest.

A wave of fatigue rolled over her head. She needed something to get through the coming week of insanity and sore muscles. Maybe she could go home and take a nap, or watch an old movie on TV with her dad. Or bake some cookies. Or . . . *cookies?* What was she thinking? She locked the shop door and crossed the sidewalk to jump into the Buick and head . . . somewhere. She started up the car, pulled away from the curb, and shook her head when Tom Jones started to sing.

"You look awfully satisfied with yourself," came the comment from her invisible backseat driver.

"I am," Kate said. She didn't want to tell anyone of her newest venture. She'd even made the girls swear to secrecy. She had no desire to look like a fool if she couldn't pull it off. But since her mother knew she'd downed three Guinness the night Matt had handcuffed her, she probably didn't have any secrets. Nothing like a nosy ghost. She smiled.

"What are you up to?"

"Don't you know?" Kate asked.

"No. I try to give you a little space now and again."

"When did that start?"

"Hey, I gave you a sheet across your room so you could have some privacy from your sister, didn't I?"

"Why, yes. Yes you did. I'm not sure I ever thanked you for that."

"You didn't."

"Well, I'm thanking you now. I really appreciated your understanding that we needed a little space to ourselves."

Her mother was silent.

"Mom? Are you okay?"

"Obviously not."

"I didn't mean *that*. I meant—"

"I know. You've just never been big on thanking me before."

Kate swallowed. "I'm sure I did when it was appropriate."

"No. What you did was argue every point until I wanted to stab my eyes out with a toothpick."

"I guess I didn't realize . . ."

"There's a lot you never realized, Katherine. That's one of the reasons I'm still here."

"I know. I know. The eternal love thing."

"That too. But more importantly . . . the day you ran away I made a promise to myself that before I died I'd make sure you understood all those things I said to you back then."

Kate's neck muscles knotted. "I understood."

"No, honey, you didn't. And when I found myself looking up at that beckoning light, I knew I couldn't cross over until I kept that promise."

Kate swallowed again past the lump lodged in her throat. Memories of screaming at her mother and her mother screaming back made it hard to breathe. "Mom, I don't want to be the reason you can't enjoy eternity. Everything is okay."

Her mother shook her head. "I can't tell you what it was like the day I held you in my arms for the first time. You were such a small, sweet little thing. And from the moment I looked into your eyes, I hoped you'd be the one."

"The one?"

"The one who'd want to stay close to me and your daddy. The one who'd inherit my love of this town, of doing things for the community, of realizing that nothing is greater in life than the love of the right man and raising a family of your own."

The lump in Kate's throat grew and slid down into her chest. "Mom, I—"

"Katherine, after you left, I realized that I suffocated you. It wasn't fair for me to put all my hopes and dreams on your shoulders. You had a right to your own." Her mother buried her face in her hands. "It's just that I . . . I loved you so much."

Kate blinked away the tears welled in her eyes. When the moisture cleared, her mother was gone.

"Mom? Mom? Come back!" she called out. "Please?" A reply never came. For the first time since Kate could remember, she did not want her mother to leave. The block wall between them had started to crumble. Kate wanted to knock it down entirely. Her mother had never said those things to her before. She had no idea her mother felt that way. No idea at all.

She sat with the car running for quite a while before she gave up and realized her mother wasn't coming back. Kate hoped her mother's disappearance was only a short-term thing and they could continue to work out the wrinkles in their relationship. She hoped that with all her heart.

Within minutes, Kate found herself driving toward the lake. When she'd changed the flat tire, she'd seen her old fishing pole in the trunk. The idea was absurd. She didn't even know if she remembered how to tie her hook or cast her line. But she did remember loving the tall pines that surrounded the lake, the cry of the osprey as they glided across the sky searching for fish. She remembered the fresh scented air and the exciting tug on her line as she hooked a nice fat rainbow trout.

Most of all, she remembered the sense of calm—the sense of belonging that blanketed her when she stood on the shore and looked out over the water.

And right now, oddly enough, she needed to belong.

CHAPTER EIGHT

As the sun sank lower in the sky and the clouds became tinted with a spray of pink and gold, Matt realized that Lacy Shaw and he were far from compatible.

Currently, she sat on the opposite end of the Adirondack style sofa he'd purchased on a recent trip to Billings. She swirled her iced tea in the tumbler he'd given her an hour ago when she'd arrived on his doorstep. Uninvited. The tray of pumpkin cookies she'd brought couldn't make up for the fact that she was boring him out of his mind. He felt bad about that.

"I just adore sunsets, don't you?" she asked, now twirling her finger through her shoulder-length red hair. "I mean, ever since I moved here from Nevada, I've been in love with sunsets. Did I ever tell you why?"

Oh no.

As she rambled on about working nights in the Desert Springs emergency room in Vegas, Matt tried to look interested. He smiled at the appropriate times. Nodded as though he was listening intently to the story she told about some heart attack victim not wanting to leave the casino until he'd finished his roll at the craps table. But all Matt was really doing was looking at her hair and thinking about a different redhead. One who, unfortunately, grabbed his interest so much he could barely get an ounce of sleep.

Lacy scooted closer to him and leaned her elbow on the back of the sofa, attempting an alluring pose with her slender figure. But Lacy didn't have the smoky green eyes that charged his batteries. She didn't have lips that were so luscious he just had to have a taste. And he wasn't being fair to her by leading her to believe there could be anything more between them than friendship.

The woman beside him was smart and sweet and any man would be lucky to have her as his wife. Unfortunately nothing about her gave him any kind of a buzz. There was zero, zip, nada chemistry between the two of them. And while he might be looking for a respectable wife, he didn't want to commit his life to someone who wouldn't want to be a little *disrespectable* behind closed bedroom doors.

Lacy was more the flannel granny gown type.

He wanted a woman who'd use *him* to keep her warm at night.

He pulled up the sleeve of his shirt and glanced at his watch. "Darn it," he said in his most disappointed voice. "I hate to break up our visit, Lacy, but I've got to run patrol tonight."

"Oh." She looked up at him as he rose from the sofa and held his hand out for her. "I had hoped we could get to know each other a little better."

He sighed appropriately. "Me too. Unfortunately there's no one else to take my shift tonight so . . ."

She smiled and nodded. "Walk me to my car?"

He did. And after he brushed her cheek with a kiss and waved as she pulled out onto the road, he looked down the sandy shoreline to the lone figure casting a line into the lake that sparkled in the evening light.

He'd noticed her the moment he'd stepped out the door. There was no mistaking the way those jeans hugged her rear end or the lightweight sweater smoothed silkily over her breasts. Or the highlights and contrast in her hair as the waning light caught it and made it look like spun fire. His spine tingled as if the feathery tips of that luscious hair were dancing across his naked skin.

Matt stood there in a wide stance, arms folded, watching her ignore him. He'd caught her glancing at him from the corner of her eye when he said good-bye to Lacy, and several more times while he stood there watching her. No doubt she was ornery. But surrounded by ancient pines and golden leafed aspens, she sure was something to look at.

A smile spread across his mouth. He'd be willing to bet Kate Silver was a woman who wore nothing to bed but sweet-scented lotion.

Suddenly her pole bent and she squealed. Her hands worked fast on the reel. She kept her tip up and pulled in the fish just the way she had when she'd been a kid—like she was hauling in Moby Dick. When the rainbow flopped on shore, Matt walked toward her.

It would be ungentlemanly of him not to help.

It would also be stupid of him to step any closer. He already knew he couldn't get his mind off her. Knew she made his pulse race and his body harden. Knew she was one hundred percent wrong for him. Unfortunately he was getting into a really bad habit of not listening to his own good advice.

"That's a nice one," he said, stopping next to her as she bent down to pick up the trout.

"I know." She looked up and grinned like a kid who'd been handed an all-day sucker. "Isn't it awesome?" Proudly she held up the wiggling fish for him to see.

"It's a beaut. It'll taste great cooked on the grill."

"You want it?" she asked, holding it toward him.

He shook his head. "Too much for me. I'll share it though."

"Sure." She thrust the fish toward him. "I hope your friend will enjoy it."

Run. Now was his chance to thank her and escape before he dug the hole any deeper. "That's not who I meant I'd share it with." *Damn his uncontrollable mouth.*

She glanced at their surroundings as though looking for someone else. When she realized there was no one else, she looked back at him and cocked her head. "Oh. You mean . . . you want to share it with me?"

He shrugged.

"Won't your girlfriend mind?"

"She's not my girlfriend." *And why did she need to know that?*

"Right. Friend with benefits then?"

Did that bother her? "Guess you've been away too long to remember that's not really possible in a town this size," he said. "People talk."

"Then you might as well give them something good to talk about."

Oh, he had. A time or two or three or a thousand. But things were different now. His reputation couldn't take a hit of any kind. It wasn't likely he'd give Kate any ammunition against him. She'd already ruined him once before. "This isn't California and people aren't prone to behave the way you do in Tinsel Town."

She studied him and her nose wrinkled just slightly. "I'm not so sure I want to share my fish with you, Deputy Ryan. You have a nasty habit of saying all the wrongs things to me."

"Or maybe it's the truth and you just don't want to hear it."

"See." She flung her hand upward. It came down with a smack on her thigh. "There you go again."

He drew an X over his chest. "Cross my heart I'll do my best to refrain."

Her smooth forehead furrowed. "Why do you want to share dinner? You don't even like me." She stood there, holding her trout by the line, mistrusting him one hundred percent.

So now the shoe was on the other foot.

He chuckled and took her by the elbow. "Come on, Hollywood. Let's get that lunker on the BBQ before it shrivels up. I'll even let you clean it."

"Gee thanks."

They walked side by side down the shore toward his cabin. The entire concept was bizarre. If anyone would have ever asked him if he'd be inviting Katie Silverthorne to dinner a decade after she dumped his ass, he'd have given them the number to Montana's best psychologist.

Or maybe he should look up that number for himself.

"No tackle box?" he asked. "What'd you catch that thing on?"

"If you can't catch 'em on worms, you can't catch 'em."

Matt laughed at the image of her digging up a slimy creature from the earth. But that image was short-lived and quickly replaced with what he'd really like her hands to be doing.

"I swear I had no idea you lived here," Kate said, cupping a wine glass in her hand while she leaned against the deck rail. "But I must say you've done a really nice job fixing up the place." In addition to earning the trust of the community, the man had built himself a home. Was there anything he couldn't do?

He stood beside her, the tails of his blue flannel shirt lifted with the breeze as he flipped the fish in the grilling basket. The flames sizzled and popped as the juices dripped down into the fire. Night had fallen crisp and cool. Barely a ripple marred the surface of the lake. The crickets were doing their thing, their melody accompanied by a frog quartet spaced around the perimeter of the yard. Kate took a sip of the chilled zinfandel and wished she'd brought a jacket.

"I bought the place after Old Man Anderson passed away." He looked up and Kate caught his blue gaze in the candlelight flickering from the punched-tin lamps perched on the deck posts. "It was in shambles. Took me five years to finish."

"Five years?" She sipped her wine again, mesmerized by the easy way he handled himself with the grill. By the way he moved—slow and sure. There was nothing sexier than a man who felt comfortable in his own skin. And looked damned good in it too.

"Yep. I pretty much gutted the whole thing," he said. "After I added the second story and the deck, I called it good. I started out with eight hundred square feet and ended up with over two thousand."

Kate glanced up to the second story veranda and the golden light illuminating from behind open French doors. Sheer curtains billowed with the breeze from what Kate guessed was the master bedroom. She wondered how he'd decorated it. Did he have a king-size bed topped with a cozy down comforter and fluffy pillows? Or was he the sleek modern type with a black and gray bedspread? She watched him push the halved potatoes around on the grill and imagined he'd be the former. There was a side of Matt that boasted warmth and deliciousness. While a whole different side warned her to be cautious. He was a complex man. The sturdy house he'd built reflected the fact that he could do just about anything he set his mind to. She just didn't know what his mind was set to anymore. She raised her glass and nodded. "You did good, Deputy Ryan."

He looked up at the house with pride and gave a short nod. "Thanks."

She sipped her wine and before she could bite her tongue the intoxicating effects had her asking, "Have you always lived here by yourself?"

With a stainless spatula he slid the grilled trout and roasted potatoes onto plates without looking at her. But he smiled. "That's a pretty personal question, Hollywood."

"Just making conversation." A task that wasn't coming easy for either of them.

Without giving her an answer, he set the plates on a planked cedar patio table and motioned for her to sit across from him. She watched the way his muscles moved beneath his flannel shirt, the way the candlelight gleamed off his dark hair, and she realized she could watch him all day. Of course, self-preservation demanded it would be a frigid day in Tahiti before she'd let him know that information.

"Have a seat," he said, and waited until she did before he joined her.

She set her wine glass next to her plate, stuck her fork in the meal, and closed her lips over a bite of steaming trout. The burst of lemon and butter flavor exploded across her tongue. "Mmmmmm." She closed her eyes. "Very good. The last time I had trout was with Drew and Cameron. They—"

When she looked up, he was watching her. Intently.

"Drew and Cameron?"

"Barrymore and Diaz."

"You always do that?" he asked.

"Do what?"

He popped a bite of potato into his mouth, chewed, and swallowed before he answered. "Name drop."

"I don't mean to. It's just—"

"Your life."

"Yes."

"And these people are important to you."

"Well, yes, they are my clients."

His gaze speared her. "And these are the clients that keep you warm at night?"

Something flashed between them that made her heart race and a shiver of awareness skate through her stomach and pool between her thighs. She could only imagine exactly how warm that big body of his could keep a woman. "The salaries they pay me provide a very comfortable lifestyle. So yes, in a sense, they keep me warm."

He leaned his forearms on the table and his dark brows drew together. "So your clients pay you to be their friend?"

"It's not like that," she said, trying her best not to sound defensive. "There are dozens of different kinds of friendships. There are those you call to commiserate with, those you meet up with just to chat, and those you meet to chat with and talk business."

"What about those who are there to hold your hand when you're scared? Or bring you soup when you're sick? Or call just to tell you they're glad to hear your voice?"

She lifted her glass. "Touché."

"Sorry," he said. "I'm really not trying to push you into a corner."

"Then what *are* you trying to do?"

"Your life is so different. I'm just trying to figure it all out."

"Wow. That surprises me."

One broad shoulder lifted in a shrug. "So how'd you make it all happen? Your career, I mean."

Kate sipped her wine and watched him over the glass rim. No sarcastic grin curved his mouth. He looked to be genuinely interested. "School of hard knocks. At first I thought all I had to do was finish my degree and I'd walk into this glamorous life where all the stars would be breaking down the door to hire me." She laughed. "Talk about a backwoods babe in the concrete jungle."

He drank from his Sam Adams, lowered the amber bottle then sucked a drop from the beautiful curve of his top lip. "But you made it work."

"Yeah, I did. After I learned the basics, I developed my own style. Which apparently had been struggling to get out of me for years."

He gave her a knowing smile. "I do remember you had a very different fashion sense than most of the girls at Deer Lick High."

"Ah, yes, my Daisy Dukes, crop top, and hoodie days."

"You wore them well."

"All that skin showing? I gave my mother nightmares."

"I didn't mind."

His deep chuckle gave her an odd sense of comfort. One she wasn't quite sure she should explore.

He leaned forward. "Tell me more."

"Really?"

"Yeah, how did you go from *backwoods babe* to a Hollywood success?"

"Mostly I chatted up anyone who may have had a contact in the industry and I got my name out there. After a few years I finally got a call from a stylist who needed an assistant." She sipped her wine. "The best day ever was when I threw away my apron and quit my waitressing job."

"Doesn't sound like it was easy."

"Maybe not, but I wanted it. It taught me a lot about myself. I learned that I couldn't just sit around and wait for things to happen; if I really wanted something, I had to make it happen. I learned that I'd never be happy stuck in a cubicle and pushing paper. And I learned that making things interesting or fun or beautiful is a big part of who I am. If I couldn't do that . . . well, I'd be a pretty unhappy camper." She glanced away from the intensity in his eyes. "That probably sounds shallow to someone like you who's all about serve and protect."

"Not shallow. Just different. I admire creativity. As a kid I could never even stay in the lines when I colored."

"Staying in the lines is overrated. So what about you?" she asked, eager to sway the conversation away from herself. She might like styling for people who craved the spotlight, but she never truly felt comfortable there herself. Especially when the source of intimidation sat only two feet away. "How's your mother?"

"Same story. Different day." He gave a barely visible shake of his head. "She met husband number six last year. I'm not even sure she's legally divorced from number five. She moved to Alabama. Still drinks. Never hear from her unless she needs money."

"I'm sorry." Kate reached across the table and placed her hand on his arm. Beneath her fingers his muscles tightened.

"Shit happens." He moved his arm from beneath her touch and picked up his fork.

The action should have been a clear sign that he wasn't a touchy-feely kind of guy. She remembered differently. She remembered plenty of times when he couldn't get enough of her hands all over him. But when times had been tough, when he'd had to deal with his mother's public drunkenness, or when his mother would punish him for the misery she'd made of her life, Kate had just held him in her arms. Obviously he was still trying to tuck away those painful years and move forward. Time to change the subject.

"Soooo, now that you have your house done, what's your next project?" she asked.

He took a bite of potato, chewed it thoughtfully. "Sheriff Washburn's retiring. I plan to take his place."

"Seriously?"

"It's been my goal for a long time."

"It's a lot of responsibility."

He nodded, sipped his beer and said, "I'm ready for it. A lot of changes need to be made around here. Deer Lick may be small, but it's not without its problems."

"Who are you running against?" she asked, a little impressed by his sudden enthusiasm.

"A guy from Wyoming. Small-town deputy."

"Like you?"

"Nothing like me." His brows came together. "His platform is to keep things operating the way they are. But drugs are creeping into the community and the situation can't be ignored."

She sipped her wine. "That's pretty admirable."

He glanced out across the lake. "I care about this town, the people in it. It's a good place to raise kids." His eyes came back to hers. "I'd like to keep it that way."

Their conversation came to a halt even as they watched each other. The differences between them were enormous. He was focused on taking care of his community, making a family, and raising kids. She was focused on staying on top of her game and grabbing handfuls of happiness here and there.

For now, the beauty of the night surrounded her as she shared a delicious meal with a gorgeous man while sipping very good wine. Who could ask for more? With her plate nearly empty, she pressed the napkin against her mouth. "Dinner was really great. Thank you."

"No problem. Thanks for catching it." He stood to remove their plates.

"Let me help you with that." She reached out her hand and accidentally brushed her fingers against his. The same spark that flew from their fingertips that day in the bakery ignited a warm tingle through her stomach.

Their eyes met and he shook his head, obviously dismissing the connection. "I've got it covered."

She watched him disappear into the dark house. A single light came on followed by the sound of dishes being dumped in a sink. She strolled to the edge of the deck and looked out over the lake. The moon glimmered on the still water and the scent of pine filled her head. She breathed in, knowing she needed to leave, yet not being able to tear herself away. If only she could trap the moment in a bottle and take it with her.

His slow and steady footsteps approached from behind and a warm jacket draped over her shoulders. She slipped her arms into the sleeves.

"Thought you might be cold," he said. "You shivered a couple of times during dinner."

The jacket smelled like him—warm, spicy, sensual male.

She turned, practically into his arms. "Thank you."

He lifted the collar of the jacket and tugged the lapels together with his big, strong hands. His gaze moved over her face, slowly, caressing her with his eyes. Her breath caught in her chest and her heart thumped with wild anticipation. All the warm feelings she'd once had for him, all the memories of lying in his arms, kissing him, tasting him, came rushing back.

He stood close—so close the angles of his handsome face sharpened and his eyes flashed a deeper, more penetrating blue. The breeze ruffled his hair and carried the clean scent of his skin. Around them the air grew thick. Her stomach knotted with a familiar desire.

They stood like that for what seemed like hours before he said, "Everything sane inside me says I shouldn't kiss you."

His blunt words doused the flames that licked at her core.

"Then don't." She started to pull away.

"I can't help myself," he said, his voice husky. Instead of letting her go, he tugged the jacket lapels toward him, lowered his head, and covered her mouth with his.

The touch of his lips, the taste of him was new, yet recognizable. And nothing had ever felt more right.

Burning with desire and aching with emptiness, she leaned into him, rose onto the balls of her feet, and wrapped her arms around his neck. His arms surrounded her in one smooth motion and they came together—heartbeat to heartbeat. Their tongues touched, swirled, and caressed while time melted away. She ran her hands through his hair, gripped the soft strands between her fingers while he made love to her mouth. Her head buzzed and she felt weightless in his arms. His hand slid down the curve of her back and cupped her bottom, bringing her against the thick, hot bulge that conveyed his own urgent need.

As she tried to get closer, the *Sex and the City* theme chimed from the cell phone in her back pocket. On the second chorus her hands were holding nothing but air.

"You'd better get that," Matt said, now standing an arm's length away. "Might be someone important."

Feeling a sudden emptiness in her gut, she debated on whether to throw the phone in the lake and finish what they started or . . . "Shit." Kate yanked the cell from her pocket and thrust it to her ear. "Hey . . . Josh."

Matt turned his back then moved farther down the deck to give her privacy.

"Tell me something good," she said into the phone.

"Oh, it's good all right," Josh snapped. "Inara was just arrested at Club Bardot for indecent exposure."

"What? How the hell did she manage that?"

"A combination of one too many Iron Butterflies and the bartender's paring knife."

"Don't tell me."

"She de-feathered the Marchesa mini in *very* conspicuous places."

A headache the size of the Hollywood Bowl exploded behind Kate's eyes. "I told you not to tell me."

"Sweetie," Josh said in an overly sympathetic tone, "Redneck playtime is over. You need to come back before that singing psycho destroys more than just your relationship with your designers."

"I'll . . . be back soon." Chewing her thumbnail, Kate thought of her father, the chasm left in the bakery by her mother's death, and the project she'd just started for her party gown–deprived teen girls. Not to mention the man who'd just kissed her socks off. She heard Josh's not so subtle warning. Hollywood or Deer Lick. Career or family.

No contest.

Kate hit *end call* and looked up to where Matt stood with his shoulders unyielding and his defenses locked tight.

When she walked up behind him, he asked, "Boyfriend?"

"No." She pressed her lips together where the taste of him still lingered and she laid her hand on the arm of his flannel shirt. "Can we get back to where we were?"

He turned and looked at her. Really looked at her. Like he could see deep beyond the surface and into the veins pushing the blood through her heart. "I don't think so, Hollywood."

"Why not?"

"Because I'm not here for your entertainment."

"Excuse me?"

"You." He pointed. "Me. Nothing in common."

Before she could blink, he was walking toward the house. "Wait a minute." Her hands slammed down on her hips. "*You* kissed me. You can't do that, then just walk away and act like I don't exist."

He gave her a wave. "Drive safely."

"Seriously?" she shouted. "If you're mad because I got a phone call from another guy while you were kissing me, don't be. Josh is gay. As in, has never been with a woman his entire freaking life gay!"

He stopped with his hand on the doorknob. "I'm not mad."

She followed him up to the door. "I thought we were having a nice time."

He turned toward her. A cold mask of indifference marred his gorgeous face. "This isn't a good idea."

"Why?"

"Because I don't want to talk to you. You irritate the hell out of me."

"Then why did you kiss me like *that*, if I irritate the hell out of you?"

His pale eyes darkened ever so slightly as he leaned his shoulder against the door frame and folded his heavily muscled arms across his chest. "Temporary insanity."

"Bull. You want to know what I think?"

"No."

She moved up onto the step, invading his personal bubble. He didn't back up. He didn't back down. And neither did she. "I think you're remembering old times and how great we were together," she said. "I think you liked me a lot then." She paused. No response. "I think you still like me."

"You should probably stop thinking so hard."

Between a wicked heartbeat and a breath, she curled her fingers into the soft flannel covering his wide chest and pulled him toward her. She pressed her mouth against his.

He probably didn't want to kiss her again, but hey, he was a guy. And when she slid her tongue across those chiseled lips, they softened and he kissed her back. In the quiver of an eyelash he had her melting in her Chucks. She leaned in, wanting more. Needing more. Not caring who was wrong or right or even what happened ten years ago. She wanted him. Bad. A slow moan rumbled in her chest.

His hands wrapped around her arms and he tugged her against him. Yes. Now they were getting somewhere.

Mid-kiss he set her away.

Before she could ask "What the frig?" she found herself staring up at him from the bottom step.

"Go home, Kate."

The hike back to her car wasn't long, but darkness fell around her like a thick blanket and made it difficult to see. The soles of her Chucks ground against the gravel road and the wind pushed at her back—almost as if steering her away from Matt. She shook her head. Even Mother Nature knew they were one hundred percent wrong for each other. She kicked at a stone in her path. "Impossible, stubborn shithead."

As she approached her mother's beast of burden, Kate heard a whine from a thicket of Silverberry. She stopped and her imagination flew into action. Wolves were always spotted in the area, but they rarely came close to town. Still, it would be her luck to end up on the ten o'clock news as a wolf snack.

The whine came again and Kate realized the sound had a pathetic ring to it, not an *I'm going to eat you* quality.

She squatted down and tried to look through the bushes, but it was too dark to see anything. Then the bushes moved and a dark shape came toward the edge of the road. It didn't appear to be very large—or threatening. Most likely a dog. So Kate made a kissy sound and patted the ground.

"Come here, baby," she said in a low, calm tone. "I won't hurt you. I promise." It took her several minutes of coaxing before the animal crept through the brush and Kate found herself looking into the frightened eyes of a golden retriever puppy she guessed to be about three months old.

"Oh, you poor little thing." She held out her arms and the pup slowly walked into her embrace. He quivered against her and she could feel his ribs as his tongue slipped out and licked her chin. Too thin. Scared. Obviously hungry. Kate's heart broke. There was only one thing she could do.

She picked up the pup, held him close, and pulled the front of Matt's jacket around him. She walked the rest of the way to the car with the dog tucked up under her chin. As she placed him on the front seat and slid in next to him, the pup crawled up onto her lap. She smoothed her hand over his head. "It's going to be all right. We'll find your parents and get you back home." The puppy's stomach growled and Kate's heart shattered just a little bit more. "But first we need to get you something to eat."

Kate struggled through the front door, her arms filled with the puppy and a bag full of puppy supplies from the Gas and Grub.

"What have you got there?" Her dad chuckled and rose from his recliner to give her a hand. He took the bag and set it on the kitchen counter.

"Well," Kate said, stroking the pup's head, "I'm not sure if I found him or he found me.

"So you're playing rescuer again? That didn't take long."

Kate put the pup in her dad's arms while she withdrew the puppy chow from the grocery bag. "What do you mean?"

A smile split across her dad's face as he held her new friend close. "Have you forgotten how many dogs and cats and baby raccoons you rescued when you were a kid? You were always bringing something home, begging us to let you keep it. Your mom and I thought for sure you'd end up being a veterinarian."

Kate cut open the top of the puppy chow and wrinkled her nose. "I might love animals but I can't stand to see them hurt. I would have made a terrible vet." She poured the food into a cute dog food bowl she'd also bought. The matching water bowl had a design of red with purple paw prints and yellow dog bones. She set the bowl down and her dad released the puppy. The pup went straight for the bowl.

While he wolfed down his food, she filled his water bowl and put on the red dog collar she'd bought as well. She'd resisted the one with pink rhinestones. No male dog in his right mind would be caught dead in rhinestones. Well, at least not a Montana dog.

"Looks like your new friend will be styling now," her dad said. "What are you going to name him?"

She pulled out the fleece dog bed she'd purchased and looked up. "Oh. I'm not keeping him. I'll find his parents."

"Looks to me like his owners might not have wanted him. He's awful thin."

"How could anybody not want him?" She kneeled down and baby-talked to the dog. "He's such a cute widdle boy." The pup responded by wagging his tail and slurping a lick up the side of her face.

Her dad laughed. "Well, it looks like he's going to claim you whether you want it or not. Nice jacket by the way."

Kate stood and looked down at the embroidered logo on the front of the jacket that read *County Sheriff*. Engrossed with her canine rescue she'd completely forgotten she'd had it on.

"I went fishing at the lake and . . . I ran into Matt Ryan. I didn't know he lived in Old Man Anderson's place."

"Yeah, he's done a nice job of fixing that up. Now all he needs is a nice wife and some kids to fill it. Did he tell you he was running for sheriff?"

Kate nodded and lifted the puppy to take him outside to do his business. "He mentioned something about that."

"So you two are on speaking terms now?" he dad asked.

Speaking terms? No. Tongue tangling terms? Maybe. "Ummm, not really."

Her dad leaned against the kitchen counter and crossed his arms. "So how'd you end up with his jacket?"

"Ummm . . . I was cold and I . . . guess he was just trying to get another vote."

"But you won't be around long enough to vote for him, will you?"

Her chest tightened. Would she?

K ate closed her bedroom door and set the puppy down. He'd been a good boy outside and she hoped he'd be housebroken enough so she wouldn't wake in the morning with dog doodles all over her floor. He sat on his haunches and looked up at her, cocking his head in that funny dog way that made her laugh.

"You are cute, I'll give you that." Kate stuck her hands in the pockets of Matt's jacket while she watched the puppy roll on his back, wiggle, and snort. In the right pocket a piece of paper poked her hand. She withdrew the note, unfolded it, and stared at the bold handwriting.

> *Emma Hart*
> *Sarah Collins*
> *Lacy Shaw*
> *Diane Fielding*

Kate turned the paper over but the back was blank. Obviously he'd made a list. But for what? She checked the pockets for anything else but came up empty. She laid the list on her bed and looked at it while she changed into the flannel *Princess Power* pajamas Kate Hudson had given her on her last birthday. She set the puppy's fleece bed beneath the opening of the antique vanity her mother had rescued from a home that had burned in Bozeman when she was a kid. A quick coat of white paint had restored it. Later, Kate had added the gold details when she'd gone through her Princess Jasmine phase.

She squatted down and patted the floor. The puppy, full from a good meal, waddled over and plunked down beside her. "This is your bed." She patted the warm fleece. "You can take it with you when we find your parents. But for now you can sleep in it here. Okay?"

The puppy looked up at her then placed his front paws on her leg and licked her chin. She laughed, kissed his moist nose, then set him in the doggie bed, and waited until he lay down and made himself comfortable.

"Night, night, little guy." She turned off the overhead light, grabbed Matt's list from her comforter and crawled beneath the sheets. She clicked on her bedside lamp and studied the names. Who were these women? What did Matt have to do with them? Were they suspects? Criminals? Terrorists? Prostitutes?

Prostitutes in Deer Lick? Okay, that was funny. The only street walkers she'd ever encountered were drunks leaving the bar or dumpster-diving raccoons. But these names had to mean something. She studied the list some more. Coming up with no answers, she refolded it, placed it on the nightstand and turned off the light.

A minute later the puppy whined. She figured he'd do that for a few minutes then, feeling safe, fall asleep. But he had other ideas and he jumped up on her bed.

"Hey." She rubbed his head. "What are you doing up here? You have your own place to snooze."

The puppy grunted, then lay down in the crook of her

knees, snuggling himself as close to her as he could get. Kate laughed and said, "Okay, but just for tonight."

The puppy sighed. Kate tucked her hands beneath her cheek and closed her eyes. Moments later they popped open again. There'd be no sleeping tonight.

Not until she figured out Matt's mystery list.

Chapter Nine

Dawn had yet to break as Kate sat in the storeroom of the bakery looking through her mother's recipes and trying to come up with something new to break the monotony of doughnuts and dinner rolls. The puppy snored at her feet in his fleece bed beneath the table where she sat. Somehow she'd let him talk her into bringing him to work, though she knew a bakery was the last place a dog should be hanging out.

After taking his picture she stapled it to a *FOUND* flyer she'd scribbled and taped to the front window. Hopefully someone would recognize him and could take him home to his parents. Not that she minded the feel of his furry body curled around her feet or the cute little groans he gave when he stretched. But she was just sure someone out there must miss him terribly.

She reached down, stroked his head, and then continued to flip through pages and pages of recipes without much success. She wanted something really different. Something that would rock Deer Lick on its boot heels.

Anticipation drove her to grab her laptop and scan the Internet. As she checked bakery websites from Vegas to Savannah time flew. Somehow she ended up on cable TVs *Cake Boss* site. From lopsided Mad Hatter types to extravagant black and gold tiered wedding ensembles, the cake creations were amazing. Breathtaking. A tingle went up her back and her creative fingers started to twitch. She continued to click through until Google sent her to a site that made her laugh out loud.

Her wheels started to spin.

If she wanted to rock and shock Deer Lick, she'd found a way to make it happen. What she had in mind would not only get the gossip going, it might very well put the Sugar Shack on the map.

By the time the bakery's back door opened and her father stepped into the storeroom, Kate had her *treat* dilemma figured out and had ordered the supplies online. In the meantime, she'd make some standard yet tasty varieties while she waited for her weapons of mass deliciousness to arrive.

"You're here early," her dad said, hanging up his coat on the hook near the door. "And I see you've brought a friend."

Kate pressed the key to shut down her computer and looked up. "I'm sorry, Dad. When I tried to leave this morning, he whimpered so bad I just couldn't leave him. I put up a flyer on the front window."

Her dad smiled, patted her on the shoulder, and said, "Its okay, sweetheart. Just keep him in the storeroom."

"I will. I promise."

She closed the cover of her laptop while her dad put on his apron.

"I see you have your mother's recipes out," he said, reaching behind to tie the apron strings.

"I thought I'd try something new." She looked up and caught the concern in his eyes. "You wouldn't mind, would you?"

"Heavens no. Your mother was always whipping up something. And it wasn't always gossip."

He paused and Kate knew he was picturing her mother in his head. She smiled, remembering how her mother loved a good scandal. So did Kate. Maybe she walked in her mother's shoes a little more than she realized.

"Did you find something in her files?"

"Actually, I'm kind of winging this one. I've got a couple of ideas. The trick will be to see if I can make them happen."

Her father smiled, crossed the storeroom and wrapped her in his arms. "You can do anything you want, Katie girl. I believe in you. I always have."

If only her mother had said those words ten years ago. Things could have been much different. Kate allowed her father's love to wash over her as she hugged him back. "Thank you, Daddy."

He gave her an added squeeze. And even when he stepped away she still felt the warmth of him in her heart.

"Well, I'd better get to those donuts. The morning crowd will be banging on the window soon." He smiled again and stood there looking at her the same way he had on the day she'd pulled in that derby winning trout.

"What?" she asked.

"I'm just so glad you're here, honey. I've missed you."

A lump lodged in her throat. "I've missed you too, Dad. I really have."

He gave her a wink, then disappeared through the door. She heard his footsteps on the concrete floor, then the familiar sounds of the bakery coming to life.

Today was going to be a great day. She could just feel it in her bones.

Today sucked.

Kate looked at the clock. It was only noon and already she felt like she'd been standing for ten hours.

Angie Dewhurst wanted a refund on the cinnamon rolls she'd bought yesterday because they didn't have enough icing on top. Of course, Angie didn't bother to return the defective pastries. Her children, supposedly, had devoured them regardless of their lack of sugared trimmings. From Kate's point of view, Angie Dewhurst needed to lay off the icing and find her way to a nice salad.

Jeremy Morrison ordered a full sheet cake for Arnold Aiken's bachelor party. Jeremy wanted the cake to be filled with three different flavors and he wanted a naked woman on top. Jeremy didn't know he'd just handed Kate the ticket to her new line of pastries. She'd never created pink icing boobs, but now was a great time to learn.

Their weekly delivery of supplies had been delayed due to an early season snowstorm coming out of Idaho. And so far, everyone who looked at the puppy flyer commented that he looked just like any other golden retriever and they had no idea who he might belong to.

Just when she thought the day couldn't get any worse, the bakery door opened and Edna Price hobbled in. Damn. Too late to hide. Kate forced a smile to her lips while Edna approached.

"You still here?" Edna asked, propping her moose-head cane against the counter.

"Yep," Kate ground out between clenched teeth.

Edna eyed her up and down. "You got on your mama's apron?"

"I don't think she'll mind."

"Hmmmph. Give me an egg salad on rye. No mustard. I'm allergic."

"I wouldn't dream of it, Mrs. Price." Kate turned toward the prep counter and glanced at the bottle of Gulden's sitting next to the mayo. She grabbed two slices of rye, a scoop of egg salad and resisted the temptation to squirt a tiny drop of mustard on top. Her intention had been to smash down the mix and make the messiest sandwich she'd ever created in her life. But for some reason, just as she thought she was getting used to being detested, hated, and despised, the need to please nudged her conscience and she gently ejected the egg mix onto the bread. Next she carefully placed perfect lettuce leaves on top and wrapped it with two pickle spears instead of the usual one. Any extra points she could gain from Countess Crotchety couldn't hurt.

She slid the wrapped sandwich into a bag and handed it to Edna who looked at it with mistrust.

"You put a pickle wedge in there?"

"Two pickles wedges."

Edna's rheumy eyes widened. "I'm not payin' extra."

"I wouldn't ask you to." Kate reached for the customary bag of Lays.

"No chips. They make my fingers swell up like bloated udders. But I'll take one of them instead."

"No chips. Got it." Kate reached inside the display case and folded a square of parchment over the brownie Edna had chosen.

"How much do I owe you?" Edna asked, digging into her worn red change purse.

Kate slipped the brownie inside the bag, refolded the edge and politely handed it back to Edna. "My treat today, Mrs. Price."

Grey brows slammed together. "I don't need no charity."

"Consider this a peace offering. If you'll excuse me, I have another customer," Kate said, referring to the gorgeous blond hunk in uniform standing behind the countess.

Edna turned and tapped the deputy on the thigh with the moose-head. "Well, well, James Harley. Fancy seeing you in here."

"Just picking up lunch, Mrs. Price. And might I say you're looking especially lovely today."

Kate watched the deputy's dark brown eyes twinkle as he flashed a billion dollar movie star smile at the old woman. Kate had met plenty of BSers in her day. James Harley just might be their king.

"Flatterer." Edna actually giggled and there was a little spring to her step as she hobbled to the door. Then she stopped and looked back at Kate and held up the lunch bag. "Mighty nice of you," she said, and then she was gone.

James Harley stepped to the counter and flashed Kate that same charming grin. Whatever he was selling, she wasn't buying.

"How can I help you, Deputy?"

He leaned against the counter and gazed into her eyes. "A

date Friday night sounds good. Just you and me and a bottle of cabernet beneath the stars."

"Shucks." Kate laughed. "I'm only here on a day-to-day basis. By Friday I could be in Morocco."

He straightened his broad shoulders and grinned even wider. "Well, that's the most interesting rejection I've ever received."

She leaned forward and patted his hand. "I'm sure you don't get many. Now, what would you like to order?"

Without looking at the menu he said, "Two tuna subs. No tomato. Two iced teas."

"Sooo, I take it you work with Matt Ryan?" she said as she went to the prep counter, grabbed the picnic rolls and sliced them open.

"How'd you know?"

"Oh, just a wild guess."

He grinned. "It's the uniform, right?"

She lifted the sliced roll. "The sandwich. Tuna sub, no tomato. His standard."

"Ah, yes. Well, our boy doesn't like to venture outside his comfort zone much."

How was that possible for a man who risked his life every time he put on his uniform? Kate finished the order and placed the bag of food on the counter. "Can you hang on just a minute?"

"You bet. Change your mind about Friday night?"

"Sorry." She went into the storeroom and returned with Matt's jacket. "Would you mind returning this to Deputy Ryan?"

James's brows lifted and a smile exploded across his calendar boy mouth. "Sure."

"And tell him I found his *hit* list in the pocket. So if anyone shows up dead, I'm onto him."

"His hit list?" James reached inside the pocket and withdrew the folded note. He scanned the paper then laughed. "Sorry, beautiful, this isn't what you think."

"Oh?" She accepted the twenty dollar bill he handed her and punched the amount into the cash register. For a moment she didn't think he'd tell her what the names on that list meant. Curiosity gnawed at her insides.

James refolded the note, slipped it back into the jacket pocket, and grabbed the bag and drinks from the counter. As he juggled everything in his hands he said, "Our boy just loves to make lists. And that one is probably his lamest."

"Why's that?"

"Because *that* is his potential wife list."

With the bakery closed and only the kitchen area lights on, Kate dropped the container of maple ice cream onto the counter and glanced at the blackness beyond the front window. She'd been at work since before dawn, now here she still was after dark. But while fatigue crept through her body, excitement pushed it aside. Tonight she'd try her hand at a new creation. She felt a little like a pastry Picasso, eager to get her creative juices flowing.

Something equally as intriguing slipped into her head as she pried open the ice cream container lid.

Matt's wife list.

Four names had been on that paper. Which one had been

the redhead she'd seen at his cabin? Was she his top choice? Last in line? Exactly what kind of woman was he looking for? Why would someone as gorgeous as Matt Ryan need a list? With all his good deeds and homegrown spirit he definitely made ideal husband material. And as for his talent in the bedroom—or in her case the back of a pickup truck—he'd had that aced at twenty-two years old.

Her cell phone rang and stole her mind from all things tingly and sweaty. She wiped her hands on her apron and lifted the phone from the counter. "Hey, Josh."

"Please tell me you've changed your mind about staying in Deer Spit."

Kate wedged the phone between her ear and shoulder. "No can do, Tonto. I'm up to my elbows in ice cream and brownies."

"Careful you don't get fat."

"Don't worry, I won't."

"You work in a *bakery*."

He made it sound like she worked in a sewage plant. Kate glanced at the display case where cream puffs snuggled temptingly beside a row of baklava. Okay, so she might have snarfed down a brownie or two. Or three. No big deal. Her jeans still fit. For now. Besides, brownies were a hell of a lot tastier than her usual Pepsi and Power Bar. "Working in a bakery is an honorable way to make a living."

"Yeah, if someone offers you a cable show and a wad of cash."

"It's homey," she insisted.

"It's lame," Josh said with a final dig. "News update. Faith Hill called. She wants you to create the wardrobe for her upcoming tour."

Grabbing a new package of baking cups from the shelf, Kate asked, "When does the tour start?"

"In March. She was a little anxious to find you were on extended LOA."

Kate sighed. "Give her my cell number. I promise I'll be back . . . way before then. I have several good possibilities to hire for the bakery and dad seems to be adjusting okay."

"Hallelujah. Do you still want me to send the gowns?"

Ah, her little side project. She couldn't possibly let those girls down. "Yes. ASAP." She had a lot to do in just a few weeks. But if she could survive fashion week in New York, she could endure anything. Who needed sleep? "In fact, send them overnight. The girls are almost done painting the place and the racks have been installed. So I have a place to hang them now."

"Oh goody."

"Look, Josh, I know you've been doing a great job with me gone. I want to thank you for saving my bacon."

"Just bring that bacon home fast, sweetie, cuz breakfast is being served short order."

"Right. Josh? One more thing, and I hate to ask, but what's up with Inara?"

"You don't want to know."

Great. Kate tossed the phone on a pile of towels, scooped the ice cream into a large bowl, and stirred it with the wooden spoon.

She'd lied to Josh.

She didn't have a single prospect to hire for the bakery. The girls had barely begun to paint the furniture they'd found for the dress shop and the racks were in boxes on the floor. Her dad still wasn't sleeping in bed at night. She had to find the puppy's parents. And her brother and sister were incommunicado.

How the hell could she walk away from all that?

An even bigger question had started to poke its dirty little head into her conscience . . . did she even *want* to walk away?

She'd just begun to feel like she had a handle on things. Well, mostly the relationship with her mom. They'd chipped off a piece of the barrier between them and Kate couldn't help but be optimistic that good things were in her future. It honestly felt like someone had pulled a dark shadow off her heart and replaced it with a sprinkle of some kind of happy dust. Like she was in the process of reinventing herself. Again.

It was one level of crazy to admit to mending the relationship with her mother from beyond the grave, but that she would even consider walking away from the career she'd worked so hard to build? Anyone who knew her would call her a certifiable wacko.

She'd be the first in line.

But the longer she stayed, the more she began to care. And the more she began to care, the more she could see herself staying put. Who knew?

Humming with the song on the radio she pulled the muffin pan closer, slathered peanut butter over the brownies in the half-filled baking cups then added the ice cream. After she smoothed the ice cream down, she sprinkled toffee bits, iced the tops with buttercream, drizzled them with caramel and sprinkled on slivers of dark chocolate. Then with a sense of creative satisfaction she stuck the entire pan into the freezer.

Finally done for the day, she went back to the prep table and began to gather up her tools. A loud creak came from the back door. Kate turned just in time to see the knob twist. Heart pounding in her throat she picked up a chopping knife and held it in front of her as the door swung open.

"Burning the midnight oil?"

Breath whooshed from her lungs when she saw Matt standing there in his deputy uniform and the jacket she'd handed off to James Harley earlier that day.

"What are you doing here?" she asked, taking a deep breath to bring her racing heart down to normal. "You scared the heck out of me."

"You plan to use that thing?" He took a few steps closer. Humor flashed in his eyes as he gave a nod to the sharp implement in her hand.

"Got a good reason why I shouldn't?" she asked.

"Probably." He gave her a rare smile that made him even more handsome than normal. And that was really saying something. "But I figure I could disarm you faster than it would take to make up a story."

"Oh yeah?" Her fingers tightened around the wooden handle.

The words had barely left her mouth before he pulled the knife from her hand, wrapped his arms around her, and held her hands behind her back.

"Yeah," he said.

"Wow." She looked up at him. "You work fast." With her breasts mashed against his big solid body, breathing became impossible. In this case, she didn't mind suffering. "What are you doing here? I thought I irritated the hell out of you."

"Among other things." He looked down at her. His cool gaze searched her face. Lingered on her mouth.

Trapped within his arms she felt the heavy pull of desire and a hot tingle spread across her chest. Only a slice of air separated their mouths. The scent of his aftershave filled her head with images she had no business thinking. Matt was a part of her past not a part of her future.

Too bad her body had other ideas. "Well, you irritate the hell out of me too."

"Bet I can change your mind."

His cockiness triggered her temper. "You know, Deputy Ryan, this is the second time you've shackled my wrists. Is this your subtle way of telling me you're into bondage?"

A slow sensual smile curved his lips. "Would that shock you?"

"I live in Hollywood. Nothing shocks me."

His quiet humor curled around her. "You sure about that?"

Her eyes widened.

Her lips parted.

And Matt lowered his head.

He hadn't intended to walk in the bakery and kiss her, but that's exactly what he'd done. He didn't even have the sense to be appalled at his behavior. He was too busy drowning in the savage lust beating through his veins, pounding in his chest and grinding through his groin. From the moment she'd curled her hands into his shirt and he'd surrendered to what he thought was one last taste of her, he'd thought of nothing else than tasting her again.

He savored the sugary scent of her skin while he fought the

urge to back her up against the counter, slide those jeans down her legs, and bury himself inside her slick, hot body.

Her mouth tasted sweet like rich chocolate, and by the way she had her body pressed up against him, she was as hungry for him as he was for her. He let go of her hands and she brought them around to cup his head. Then those exploring fingers glided across his shoulders and down his chest. The touch of her palms spread fire across his skin, lighting him up with pleasure and pain.

He cupped the back of her neck and her silken hair draped over his hand. He imagined how it would feel fanning across his bare chest and the kiss delved deeper. She moaned into his mouth while his opposite hand snuck beneath the hem of her sweater. Her skin was warm and soft as he slid his palm down the small of her back and tucked his fingertips between worn denim and soft skin. He pulled her tight against him. He ached for her. Needed her. While his tongue plunged into her mouth, her hands walked down his chest and she reached for the buttons on his shirt.

His mouth found the curve of her neck. In total submission, she dropped her head back to give him access.

Sanity roared back and popped him on the head. As much as he ached for her, he set her away from him. Their eyes met. With ragged, uneven breathing she stared back.

"Still think nothing can shock you?"

A slow smile curled her lips. "You're pretty good at that, Deputy."

"Thanks."

"But you'll have to do better than that to upset my banana cart." She reached for a muffin pan and began sticking frilly paper cups inside the molds.

"That sounds like a challenge." One he definitely wouldn't mind taking her up on. "What are you doing?"

"I'm creating." She poked a finger in the center of a cup and pressed it into place. "I figured as long as I'm here I had better keep myself entertained. So I'm coming up with some new items to add to the menu."

He planted a hip against the counter. "You always were the ambitious type."

She looked up at him and frowned. "Is that another dig?"

"No." He laughed. "I just remember you were always up to something. Like the time you hauled me to that old blow-me-down barn to salvage wood. Then you had me helping you build dog houses for the next three weeks so you could donate them to the animal shelter."

"You didn't seem to mind."

"That's because you were wearing short shorts and a tank top and bending over all day. I'm a guy. Of course I didn't mind."

"Well, my idea kept some poor homeless doggies warm."

And for weeks afterward, thoughts of her pounding nails had kept him warm too. But it had always been more than just sexuality with Kate. For a long time she'd been the only person he'd been able to count on when his world had been a total bag of shit. They'd spent hours and hours together talking, laughing, dreaming. She'd listened to him and never judged him for the life he'd been born into or the way he dealt with his mother.

She'd loved him. Or so he'd thought. And she'd given him the one thing no one else had been able to. She'd given him hope for a better life.

He watched as she went to the freezer, yanked open the steel door and pulled out a tray. Her movements were almost musical, like inside her head she was dancing and her arms and legs followed the rhythm. He remembered that about her too. She'd always been an inspiration to watch whether she'd been scooping up chili for the walking tacos they sold at the FFA booth at the fairgrounds or cleaning out the stalls for her summer job at the Clear River Lodge. She put her heart and soul into everything she did, even if it meant she ended up smelling like donkey dung.

"Here," she said, lifting a cupcake from the pan and handing it to him. "Try this and tell me what you think." She leaned back and folded her arms.

"You're not trying to poison me, are you?"

The overhead lights hit her eyes and he could swear they sparkled with mischief. "Would that shock you?"

"Not at all." He bit into the cake and flavor exploded across his tongue. The rich chocolate and caramel were the same he'd tasted when he'd kissed her. He closed his eyes, savored the smoothness, the passion of the dessert. He heard himself moan.

"You like it?" Excitement danced in her words.

He moaned again. "I think you're onto something here, Hollywood."

She clapped her hands and gave a little jump of pleasure that landed her right in his arms.

Without hesitation she stood on her tiptoes and kissed him on the cheek. It took everything he had to keep from wrapping his arms around her and holding her there, right against his heart. He'd been in love with Kate over ten years ago, when neither of them knew much about anything except they liked being together. And even now when he knew better, even now when he was a thirty-two-year-old man established in the community and well in control of his life, chances were he was still probably a little in love.

Now *that* would shock her.

Because it sure as hell shocked him.

CHAPTER TEN

The following morning, Matt stood at the kitchen window looking out over the lake. The cup of coffee in his hand had grown cold while he berated himself for giving in to the urge to stop at the Shack last night where he'd proceeded to kiss Kate. God. Why did he continue to torture himself? Hadn't he learned his lesson? When it came to Kate, obviously not.

To make matters worse, he'd enjoyed himself. Over coffee and her mouthwatering cupcakes they'd laughed about old times. They'd talked more about her career and he'd gained a better understanding of what she actually did to be paid such a high salary. He'd been impressed, even proud of her. But the conversation they'd had did nothing to disprove she was anything more than a temporary fixture in Deer Lick. She loved what she did. And once she finished up here, she would leave. She made it clear that this town couldn't hold her. What made him think *he* could? He hadn't been enough for her then. Why would he be enough for her now?

Little had changed. He was still the same man. A little more mature. A little rough around the edges. But he still had the same soul. He still had his pride. And as much as he wanted the woman who'd set his soul on fire years ago, he would never let her strip him of his pride. At least, never again.

He sipped the cold java and frowned. He'd best take his own advice and stay away from her. He'd set his life in motion. He wouldn't allow anything or anyone to stand in his way.

Prepared to take action on getting back on track, he strolled into the kitchen, dumped the coffee in the sink, and poured himself a fresh cup. Then he sat down with his To Do list and picked up the phone. He punched in the numbers to call Emma Hart and ask her out for a date. He'd take her someplace special. Someplace dark and romantic. Someplace where he wouldn't be tempted to think of Kate. Or her soft mouth. Or how much he wanted her. Body, heart, and soul.

Kate sighed with relief as she locked the back door to the bakery and headed toward her mother's car. Matt had not made an appearance for his tuna sub today. Apparently the gods had been listening last night when she'd prayed herself to sleep. She had no control when it came to that man. He was like an inviting tropical pool on a hot summer day. And she'd be smart to remember her lack of swimming skills.

She opened the car door and the pup jumped in. Or he attempted to. His back legs just weren't long enough or strong enough to complete the process. With a chuckle, she picked up his hindquarters and gave him a little help. As she started the engine, he sat beside her on the bench seat, his pink tongue lolling happily from between his tiny teeth.

"Day's not over, pup. We still need to put in some time at

the dress shop." His warm brown eyes sparkled up at her and her heart melted. She stroked his head. "I'm sorry your parents haven't come to claim you yet. I put an ad in the paper and dropped some flyers around town but . . ." She hugged him and ruffled his soft fur. "I guess I can't keep calling you pup, can I?"

Kate shifted the car into drive as he gave a little whine and wagged his tail. A chill engulfed the interior of the car and from the radio, Tom Jones began to sing.

"Why don't you call him Tom?"

"Mom!" Kate hit the brakes and swung around in her seat. "Where have you been?"

"Tom's a good name."

"He doesn't look like a Tom," Kate said, stroking the puppy's soft fur.

"Rover?"

"No."

"Fido?"

"Come on, Mom. You can be more creative than that."

"He's *your* dog."

Kate glanced down. "He's not *my* dog. He belongs to somebody."

"Yeah." Her mother chuckled. "You."

"I can't have a dog. I'm never home." A niggling misery squeezed her heart when she thought of all those times she *was* home. And alone. And lonely. "He's going to grow up and be huge. I couldn't take him to red carpet events like Paris does her dog-of-the-month. He'd never fit in a purse. He needs a place to run, chase squirrels and be who he really is. He wouldn't be happy in Hollywood."

"Are you?"

"Am I what?"

"Happy in Hollywood?"

"Well . . . of course I am."

Her mother let go a long sigh. "You sure about that?"

Kate pulled the car to the curb in front of the shop. "Are we back at this again? Why does everyone keep questioning my life?"

"Why do you keep feeling the need to defend it?"

Good question. Why did she? Her life in Hollywood was like a giant Scrabble board where she had too many missing pieces to complete the game. All the wham-bam-snap-and-sizzle was there, but too little of the warm and fuzzy. She stroked her hand across the pup's soft fur. She'd kind of grown fond of warm and fuzzy.

Kate put the car in park and turned in her seat. The shadows clouding her mother's eyes knocked the breath from her lungs. "Mom? What's wrong?"

"I'm sorry. I really don't mean to back you in a corner. Old habits die hard, I guess." Her mother swept her finger across the empty place where her wedding ring had sat for thirty-six years. "It's just that . . . I love you, Katherine. And I'm worried about you."

Kate closed her eyes, letting her mother's "I love you" settle into her soul. She let it curl around her heart. When she opened her eyes to respond, her mother had disappeared.

Kate snapped the last clothes rack into place and grumbled to the pup stretched out on his side, watching every move she made.

"Other than Hollywood, you name one other place I could have had all those opportunities." She crossed the room to fluff the creamy satin curtains that framed the front window. "I've been living the life I always dreamed of. I make tons of money. I have friends in high places and . . ."

The dog sat up and cocked his head.

"What?"

He whined.

She propped her hands on her hips. "You don't believe me?"

He sneezed.

"Fine. Jump on the bandwagon."

He gave a little bark as if clarifying he already had one paw onboard.

"Excuse me. Kate?"

Kate turned. In the doorway stood the pretty blond who'd been with Matt at her mother's funeral. Her straight hair had been pulled back into a ponytail. The gray overcoat she wore looked two sizes too big for her. "Can I help you?"

The blond smiled, extended her hand, and stepped forward. "I'm Emma Hart. I'm sure you don't remember me since we've never really met . . . properly. I was in the same grade as your sister. I just wanted to say I'm so sorry about your mother. She was such a wonderful woman."

"Thank you." Kate shook her hand and returned to her curtain fluffing, if only as a distraction from the pity in Emma's eyes.

"Cute puppy," Emma said, kneeling to the ground. Obviously she didn't care if her gray slacks became a dog hair disposal. "Is he yours?"

Kate shook her head, gave the curtains a final tug, and

turned. "I found him out by Ma—" Not knowing the extent of Matt and Emma's relationship, Kate quickly corrected herself. "By the lake. I've been trying to find his parents."

Emma scratched him beneath his chin and his hind leg twitched. "He's adorable."

"He likes you. Maybe you'd like to give him a home."

"I'm afraid he wouldn't get along with my cat, Oscar. He's old and cranky and a little possessive."

Kate moved behind the front counter and began to sort through the inventory photos she'd taken of each gown after they arrived that afternoon. "What can I do for you, Emma? I'm sure you didn't come in here just to talk about my stray dog."

"You're very perceptive." Emma bit her bottom lip, approached the front counter warily, and set her black vinyl purse on top. Her hands shook. "Actually I can't believe I even got up the nerve to come here in the first place."

The way Emma rushed her words, Kate realized she was making the woman uneasy. And that she was probably coming off as a bit bitchy. Even if it didn't matter to Kate who this woman was or her involvement with Matt, she had no right to be rude. Kate gave her a comforting smile. "Take your time. No need to be nervous. The dog doesn't bite and neither do I."

"I'm glad." Emma laughed, then her smile faded. "Okay. Here goes . . . I'm a schoolteacher and I'm totally fashion blind. The only sense of style I have is enough common sense not to wear the hideous teacher sweaters my colleagues give me for Christmas. You know, the patchwork kind with mice and rabbits and ABCs on them?" She shuddered. "I don't want to hurt their feelings, but those sweaters are dumpy and frumpy. For heaven's sake, I'm only thirty-two, not sixty-five and ready to retire."

Kate laughed.

"At work I do need to dress appropriately. And since my work is the biggest part of my life, well . . . in my off hours I'm afraid of venturing beyond jeans and sweatshirts."

"And that gets a little boring, right?" Kate said, wondering where this conversation was headed.

"Yes." Emma's eyes widened and she nodded. "And as much as I hate to ask for help, I'm desperate. I admire your work—your style, so much. Kate Winslet looked absolutely stunning at the Golden Globes this year."

The compliment flowed over Kate and made her smile. Too bad all she'd really done was to match a vintage Valentino with the right chandelier earrings to accomplish the look. The actress really didn't need any help when it came to adding the gorgeous factor. "Thank you."

"Which is why I need to ask for your help."

"My help?"

"Yes. For the first time in my life I need to look fabulous."

"Well, you've come to the right place. The name of this shop is Cindi Rella's Attic."

"Perfect."

"What's the occasion?"

"I've been asked out for a very romantic date. Actually, it's our first date and I'd love to look stunning. Maybe even a little bit . . . sexy." She gave a nervous chuckle. "Nothing like my usual self."

"Wow." Kate could feel Emma's anticipation all the way across the counter. "Sounds exciting. Who's the lucky guy?"

Emma smiled. "Matt Ryan."

Kate's heart took a little sidestep.

Of course it was Matt.

Who else in the world did Kate think would ask Emma out?

The *first* date thing had thrown her. And now, what would she say? She couldn't say no. Emma seemed like a really nice woman, someone she could picture as a friend.

But last night Matt had had his lips on *hers*.

So why did he keep kissing her if he wasn't interested?

Was it some kind of perverse payback?

And why the hell had she enjoyed it so much?

The following Friday night, to keep her mind from speculating how Emma and Matt's date was going, Kate threw herself into completing the final touches on the shop. Cindi's Attic would soon open to the darlings of Deer Lick. She hung the last gown on the rack and adjusted the hangers until they were all separated by the exact same width. A lump of pride clogged her heart as she stood back and took it all in. The pink-and-white striped curtains that hung from a PVC pipe frame her father made to create two dressing rooms. The chandelier's sparkling crystals that glittered across the ceiling. And the two wicker chairs and table that highlighted the front window.

Her girls had put some amazing details into the place that made it look more like a chic Manhattan boutique than a former craft supply shop.

Her young celebrities had really come through as well. Not only had they supplied her with a myriad of elegant creations, but the sparkly accessories to complete the look. Even a few tiaras.

Each dress had come with the name of the celebrity who donated the item as well as the background of where it had been worn. For these local girls to know that they were stepping into the same designs that had been displayed by the likes of Taylor Swift, Kristen Stewart, Selena Gomez, or a number of other popular celebs would only add to their overall experience.

Anxious to complete her To Do list, she stepped over the dozing pup to arrange the costume jewelry in the glass case. The bell above the glass door chimed and Kate looked up.

In the heart of Girly Central, looking as though he would fit in anywhere, stood Matt. Though Kate could tell the fabric wasn't designer quality, the charcoal suit he wore fit him as though it had been tailored specifically for his broad shoulders and trim waist. The royal blue tie accented his piercing eyes.

A silent sigh pushed from her lungs.

GQ really didn't know what they were missing. Deputy Matt Ryan was drop-dead spectacular. Aside from the scowl on his face, of course. Whatever he was pissed about this time, she really didn't want any of that action. He ran more hot and cold than the natural springs that fed into the creek behind Shoreline Lodge.

"Go away." She turned her back to him and resumed her work. The pup rushed for protection behind her legs and gave a little growl at their intruder.

"Not until I find out what the hell you're up to."

She waved a hand over the glass surface. "Clearly I'm arranging jewelry."

"That's not what I meant." His strong jawline clenched and Kate had to admit she'd never seen him quite so tweaked. Well, except for the moment he'd discovered she'd come back to Deer Lick. And when Josh had called and interrupted their kiss. And, oh, about a hundred other times she could think of.

She exhaled a hard breath. "Then why don't you tell me what you meant, *Deputy Ryan*."

He closed the door behind him, stepped closer, and towered over her. The spicy scent of his cologne and his blatant masculinity stroked every drop of estrogen humming through her body.

"What the hell did you do to Emma?" he demanded.

Great. Just what she needed, a small-town critic. She stared at him. "You didn't like what you saw?"

"I didn't like that you took a nice girl and turned her into one of your Sin City harlots."

"A harlot?" she sputtered. "Are you kidding me? Who even uses that word?" She studied him—the glare speared in her direction, the twitch in his jawline, the stiffness to his broad shoulders, the clenched fists hanging at his sides. What was all this animosity really about? Emma? Her? Or him?

"Emma was very excited you were taking her somewhere romantic. She wanted to impress you." She folded her arms. "Not that you deserve it."

"She didn't need to do anything to impress me," he said. "I like her just the way she is. Or was."

"So does that make her number one on your potential wife list?"

His eyes widened. "How do you know about that?"

"Evidence." She smiled at his obvious surprise. "I found the list in your jacket pocket. When I gave it to James to return to you, I mentioned I'd found your hit list. He enlightened me."

"And you think that's funny?"

"Not at all. But I do think it's shocking that a man like you thinks he needs to make a list for something like that. I never thought of you as so cold and calculated." Especially when his smokin' hot body had been pressed against hers. "Why don't you just fall in love the old-fashioned way?"

"Because I don't have time."

"Are you kidding? Nobody's got anything *but* time in this town. What's the rush?"

He shoved his hands in his pants pockets, looked down at the ground then back up to her. "I told you I'm running for sheriff."

Missing the connection she lifted her eyebrows, walked toward him, and said, "And?"

"There's never been a bachelor sheriff in the history of Deer Lick," he said as though he hated to spill the obviously important information.

"Ah. And you don't want to lessen your chances."

"There's too much at stake."

Kate's heart pinched when she pictured this gorgeous man walking down the aisle with a woman he didn't love. She pictured him waking every day to a bleak existence just because he thought he had to be married to be elected sheriff. He deserved that position. He cared more about their town than anyone she'd ever known. All anybody had to do was watch him. His commitment to the community was as obvious as the big red nose on Ronald McDonald's face.

She thought back to the boy he'd been. The way he'd held

her in his strong arms. The way he'd made her feel cherished and secure. The encouragement he'd given her when she told him of her desire to learn fashion. She knew him now as a man who'd do anything to protect what he loved. And he loved Deer Lick. Enough to marry a woman he might *not* love.

Personally, he drove her crazy—sent her sanity pinging right up the Dope-O-Meter. But she'd never wish for him to live a life of misery. He deserved more.

She reached out and touched the sleeve of his suit. "What about love, Matt? How are you going to live with someone if you're not in love with them? How can you build a family if there's no love?"

Anger rolled off in him waves. His eyes narrowed. His scowl turned stormy as a thunder cloud. But that didn't stop him from grabbing her with both hands and pulling her hard against his chest. It didn't stop him from lowering his head and pressing his tantalizing lips against hers. It didn't stop his slick tongue from entering her mouth and kissing her with an out-of-control cyclone of need and lust and hot, hot passion.

Equally, that dark look didn't stop her from wanting to glue herself to him, or stop her from pressing herself against him, or wanting to tear his clothes off so she could get her greedy mouth and hands on all that warm, sexy skin.

When he sucked her tongue lightly into his mouth, her nipples peaked against her soft cotton sweater. He tasted like peppermint and a long denied pleasure grabbed hold of her deep inside. It spread like a firestorm across a dry forest.

She wanted this man. Needed to wrap herself around him. Needed him to slide his erection into the liquid heat that pooled between her thighs. Her own unfulfilled need threatened to overpower her. And while the idea should scare the hell out of her, she just didn't give a damn. In his arms, she was lost. Completely, irrevocably lost.

His grasp on her tightened a fraction just before he stepped back and untangled her fingers from his hair. "Damn it." His arms dropped to his sides. "How long are you going to stay in town and keep messing with me, Kate?"

Kate licked her lips to keep from biting away the humiliation of once again falling under his spell. Of being rejected. Again. "Hey, I was in here minding my own business until you walked in."

His dark brows lowered. "Then do me a favor."

"What?"

"Stay the hell away from me." He yanked open the door. "Because it's obvious I can't stay away from you."

The taillights of Matt's SUV had barely disappeared before Kate locked the shop door and headed home. The pup lay on the seat by her side, his head propped on her thigh.

Her chest ached.

She could blame it on heartburn, but the cause of her discomfort had nothing to do with eating and everything to do with a big gorgeous man who made her head spin in so many ways she'd lost count. She wanted to go home, put on her flannel PJs, crawl in her little twin bed, and snuggle with her noname dog. She wanted to *not* think about Matt or the way he made her feel or the things he made her crave. She certainly didn't want to think about what was going on in that gorgeous head of his. Or why he felt compelled to kiss her socks off every time he came within an arm's length. Or why he kept pushing her away.

As she turned the corner onto Reindeer Avenue her cell rang.

"Hey girlfriend, how are things in Deer Snout?"

Josh's humor was lost on her. "Fine. The shop is ready to open."

"So who's going to man, or should I say wo*man* the place if you're busy at the bakery or when you come home?"

Home. Why was it she really didn't think of Hollywood as home anymore? "I've got several high school girls lined up." She sighed. "It'll only be open three hours a day, three days a week."

"Aw, why the gloom and doom 'tude, sweetie? You've accomplished quite a feat. Look at you providing fairy tale frocks for all those teen girls. You should be crowing from a dirty old mountaintop."

"I'm too tired to crow."

"What you need is a trip to a day spa. Want me to look one up in your area and make an appointment?"

"Josh, get real. I barely have time to blow my nose, let alone lay down for an hour while someone massages my sore muscles. Right now, I'd settle for a bottle of Cuervo, a lime, and some salt."

"Ooooh, craving the hard stuff. Not a good sign."

"Did you call for a specific reason, Josh? Or did you just feel the need to exert your snarkiness?"

"I wanted to give you an update on Inara."

"Good or bad?"

"We're talking about Inara here," Josh said.

Kate sighed again. "Okay, hit me."

"Her agent rang me when she couldn't get hold of you. She's decided to send Inara to rehab."

"I don't think the girl has a drug or alcohol problem. Just a problem with decorum."

"Exactly."

"So why would she need to go to rehab?"

"This is a different kind. Something Peggy kind of . . . invented. On the spot. Off the top of her heavily lacquered head."

"Josh?" Kate rubbed her eyes. "I'm too tired to play word games."

"Peggy is putting you in charge of rehabilitating her top client."

"What?"

"She wants *you* to take Inara under your wing and educate her the way they used to in those glamour schools."

"Wait a minute. I'm a stylist, not Emily Post."

"Peggy said Inara's career depends on it. *And* there's a six figure bonus if you can pull it off."

"Geez, no pressure." Stopped at a red light, Kate rested her forehead on the steering wheel. She was tired. She didn't want to deal with a bad mannered superstar. She didn't care about a six figure bonus. All she wanted was to make her baked goods and live life in this modest town. Her head popped up. And wow, wasn't that something she never thought she'd hear herself say. Maybe she really was just a small-town girl at heart. "Exactly when am I supposed to take on this ginormous feat?"

"She's sending Inara on a chaperoned vacation in the Bahamas until you come home," Josh said. "The most time I can buy you is a few weeks."

"A few weeks? Seriously?"

"Is that a problem?" Josh asked. "Do I sense the Silver Steamer hitting a titanic iceberg?"

Yes. Crash and burn Kate at your service. "I can't do it, Josh. Tell Peggy I'm sorry but I just can't." Kate punched *end call* and glanced down at the pup who groaned in his sleep. She slid her hand over the top of his silky head.

"We are in doo-doo, my friend. Deep, deep doo-doo."

The pup lifted his leg on a forsythia bush as Kate opened the front door. As soon as the path was clear, he trotted in the house like he owned the place. Her father, perched in his recliner, sat up and scratched the pup behind his ears as he passed on his way to the food bowl.

Kate dropped her purse and tote bag on the sofa and then flopped beside them with a sigh.

"Long day?" her dad lifted his glasses and inquired, as though the evidence wasn't obvious.

She nodded as she grabbed a pillow her mother had crocheted and hugged it to her chest. The granny squares were gold and rust—a perfect match to the trees and shrubs outside changing with the season.

"Hungry? I made some chili."

She shook her head. "Too tired to eat." Guilt slid like a noose around her conscience. *She* was supposed to be taking care of *him*. Apparently she couldn't handle that right either. "I'm sorry, Dad."

"That's okay." He hit the mute button on the TV remote. "It'll be good for leftovers."

"That's not what I mean. I'm sorry that I'm doing such a

crappy job of helping you out. I should be cooking for you, not the other way around."

"Nonsense, you're doing a fine job. More than I ever even imagined." The light from the pole lamp beside the recliner gleamed off the top of his head as he crooked his finger at her. "Come over here."

She did as he asked and found herself sitting on her daddy's lap like she did as a kid. He curled his big arm around her and she laid her head on his sturdy shoulder. His warmth surrounded her like a big fuzzy blanket.

"What's wrong, sweetheart?"

She wanted to tell him that juggling her career, the bakery, Cindi's Attic, trying to find the pup's parents, and the visits from her deceased mother were all too much for her. Not to mention Matt Ryan who insisted on driving her to the edge of Crazy Town and kicking her over the cliff. And now someone wanted her to play Dr. Decorum? Dressing people for a living was easy cheesy. But all this emotional stuff? Killer.

"I'm just tired. Nothing to worry about."

He set the recliner to a gentle rocking motion. "You know, the last time I held you like this was when you and your mom had argued about the baby raccoon you'd brought home. She was sure the thing was full of rabies and fleas and didn't want it in her house. But against her wishes you went out, found a cage, and bottle-fed that little thing until it was old enough to release back in the wild."

Kate smiled, remembering her mother's outrage when she'd brought home another stray. She hadn't had the heart to tell her mother she'd seen her cooing baby talk to the little masked bandit. Those were the days when Kate had looked for anything and everything to keep her entertained. When she thought Deer Lick was the most boring place on the planet. In fact, hadn't she thought that exact thing just a few weeks ago?

Now, she admitted silently, things didn't seem quite so lackluster. Exhausting? Oh yeah. She'd have to cut back on something before she drove herself into a coma. When she thought of the order of things to delete, she surprised herself with what she'd scratch first.

"Everything has its place in the world, Katie girl." Her dad hugged her a little closer. "Sometimes it just takes a while to figure things out."

Amen to that.

"Sweetheart?"

"Yeah, Dad?"

"Speaking of the wild . . ."

CHAPTER ELEVEN

Kate opened the door to the storeroom for the pup to curl up in his fleece bed. She flipped on the overhead lights in the bakery and the fryer and grabbed an apron off the peg.

Her father would not walk through the door today. He'd gone hunting. In the wild. Like he did every year at this time.

Who was she to prevent him from reaching out and capturing a slice of life? He deserved a break from the bakery. He deserved some time out in the woods he loved so much. He deserved a little happiness that might help him mend his broken heart.

If her mother had been able to handle the place all on her own for a week, so could she.

The day flew by with only a few lulls here and there and she managed not to think about Matt even once. Oops. Scratch that. During one of those lulls she'd managed to sneak a glazed buttermilk donut and cup of orange spiced tea over to George Crosby at the Once Again Bookstore. She'd made a deal weeks ago with the shop owner to trade donuts and tea for a chance to pluck a book or two off his dusty shelves. Kate loved to read.

And though her past tastes ran toward celebrity biographies, she now relished romance. Historicals, contemporaries, paranormal, she loved them all. Although a happy ending for her seemed to be a wasted wish, she was glad someone had the possibility. Even if they were fictional.

By six o'clock sharp she locked the doors on a fairly successful day. She couldn't wait to open her arsenal of mass deliciousness that had been delivered earlier. Her bachelor *boob* cake had been a hit and word had started to spread. On her order list for tomorrow was a divorce party cake. She guessed for some people divorce was cause for celebration. Kate thought it rather sad. If she ever found someone to love, someone who would love her back with all their heart, she wouldn't be so eager to give it up. However, for now her job was cake. Lots of cake. And she intended to give the customer what they'd asked for. Just bigger and better. Instead of a full sheet she'd made tiered rounds with a new recipe she'd concocted for spiced chocolate.

From the freezer she grabbed the layers she'd made the night before, unwound the plastic wrap and set them on the work surface. Then she grabbed the dark chocolate filling and whipped up a batch of buttercream for a dirty iced coat. Several hours later, engrossed in kneading a glob of blood red fondant, she looked up at the clock and discovered how fast time had flown. She'd been thoroughly enjoying herself, even chuckling or smiling now and again. As her design had taken shape, Kate realized she was having a blast.

She liked cake decorating.

Cakes couldn't talk back.

Cakes couldn't rip sequins off designer gowns.

Cakes couldn't put her on the worst dressed list.

Cakes rocked.

But could she ever give up her glamorous lifestyle to make cakes full time? She positioned a black rose on the top tier and chuckled. If anyone had asked her that question just a few weeks ago, she'd have laughed in their face. But now, she might just smile.

As she carefully unrolled the red fondant down the side of all the tiers she heard a tap on the front window and looked up. Maggie stood with her nose pressed against the glass. Kate waved, then went to let her friend inside.

"What are you doing here?" Kate asked as they exchanged a hug.

Maggie laughed and her apple cheeks flushed a pretty pink. "I saw the lights on and came to give you a hand."

Surprised, Kate asked, "What?"

"A little birdie told me your daddy went hunting and you might need some help."

"Was that little birdie balding on top of his distrustful little head?"

Maggie patted her on the back. "Aw, honey, don't be upset with him. He knows you can handle the place. He just feels bad that he's dumping on you."

"I don't mind."

"And neither do I," Maggie said as she walked toward the back of the bakery.

"What about the bar?" Kate followed her. "What about your husband? Your kids?"

"Are you kidding? I've got two sets of grandparents fighting over who gets to watch them. Ollie is used to me running in several different directions at once. No big deal."

Kate gave her a look.

Maggie held up her hand as though swearing in at court. "Really. I promise." She opened the freezer door and glanced at the contents. "What are those?"

Pulling out the muffin pan, Kate transferred it to the counter. She dropped her hands to her hips and looked down at the dessert only Matt had tested. And loved. "A new experiment. I meant to try them out on customers but I got so busy I forgot."

"What are they?"

"Ice cream peanut butter brownie cupcakes."

"Oh God, you're kidding me!" Maggie grabbed for one, yanked down an edge of the wrapper and bit into it. Her eyes rolled back and she moaned. A grin spread across her face. Chocolate was lodged between her teeth. "This? Is better than sex."

For some reason Matt's image slipped into Kate's overactive imagination. "Nothing is better than sex." At least not sex with one hunky stubborn ass deputy.

"Bet me." Maggie shoved the other side of the cupcake into Kate's mouth.

Kate bit off a chunk and the flavors danced across her tongue. "Mmmm, good. But better than sex?"

"Hey, I've been married for ten years, I have three kids, and I waitress at a busy bar. I've almost forgotten what sex is."

"Then, while you've got a babysitter, maybe you should grab Ollie, go home, and do some rediscovering."

"Hmmm." Maggie rolled her eyes toward the ceiling and tapped her chin as if pondering the suggestion. Then she laughed. "Are you kidding? We wouldn't even get our skivvies off before we'd fall asleep."

The lack of passion in her friend's marriage saddened Kate. "Is that what happens after you're married for awhile?"

Maggie looked at her. "No, honey. Not if you don't let it happen. Ollie and I are both to blame for letting life get in the way."

"But you love each other."

"With all our hearts," Maggie said with a whisper of sadness in her tone.

Kate hugged her friend. "I'd be happy to help you out any way I can, Mags, so you and Ollie can have some time together."

"Oh, Kate." Maggie hugged her tight. "I'm so happy you're back."

"Promise you'll call on me to babysit?" Kate said with a stern look.

"I promise."

"Soon?"

Maggie laughed. "Soon. Now . . ." She took a bite of cupcake and mumbled around a mouthful. ". . . what do you plan to do with these? Hold them hostage?"

"Help yourself," Kate said as Maggie grabbed for a second helping. "I plan to add them to the menu. Just trying to shake things up a little."

Maggie strolled over to the work counter and instantly choked. "I think you're off to a good start."

Kate joined her at the counter and grinned at her work in progress. "It's awesome, isn't it?"

"It's fantastic. The blood spilling down the side is a nice effect. The dead groom lying on the bottom tier in a pool of blood is definitely a little unexpected. Maggie leaned closer to the triple tiered anti-wedding cake. "Is the bride holding a handgun?"

"Yeah. A semiautomatic."

"Kate?"

"Hmmm?"

"What is *this*?"

"It's a *Til Death Do Us Party* cake for Maxine Waverly."

"Wow. It's . . . different."

Unsure whether Maggie had offered a compliment or not, Kate turned the revolving cake stand and asked, "But is it good?"

Looking up, Maggie grinned. "It's freaking fabulous." She grabbed Kate in a tight hug. "Oh, honey, I think you've found your calling. What else do you have up that designer sleeve?"

Kate reached into her bag of tricks and pulled out a cupcake mold in the shape of a penis. "Think this will get the town gossips going?"

Maggie screamed, then laughed so hard she doubled over. "Oh, girlfriend, you are gonna make your mama proud."

The thought made Kate smile. "I wanted to add something new to the menu. This place has been serving the same pastries for as long as those ugly tiles have been on the floor."

Maggie glanced around the bakery at the faded floor, faded silk flowers, faded wall color, and nodded in agreement. "Yeah, the place really could use a facelift. I'm sure your mom and dad worked too hard to notice its charm had washed away."

An idea grabbed hold of Kate before she could talk herself out of it. "Maybe I can change that."

Maggie looked at her the same way she had in high school

when Kate had come up with an idea that was bound to get them in trouble. "I don't like the look in those eyes, Katie Silverthorne."

Kate didn't bother to correct Maggie on the usage of her name. Because right now Kate Silver, celebrity stylist, was about to take a backseat to Katie Silverthorne, confectionary daydreamer and visionary.

She put the finishing touch on her designer cake, then grabbed her friend by the sleeve and tugged her toward the storeroom. "Come on, Mags. We've got signs to make."

"Signs?"

"We're having a bake sale."

They rushed into the storeroom and startled the pup who jumped up with a squeak, then went right back to gnawing on his sock monkey chew toy. Some watchdog.

"I don't get it. This is a bakery. Of course, you're selling the goods. So why the sudden enthusiasm?" Maggie's forehead wrinkled as she shoved the last bite of cupcake in her mouth and wiped the ice cream from her chin.

"This is a *real* bake sale. Half price for everything until it's gone. All proceeds go to Mom's favorite charity."

"Have you lost your mind?"

"Probably," Kate answered, grabbing a felt marker from the drawer and a roll of white wrapping paper. She ripped off a large sheet and thrust it and the marker toward Maggie. "Let's get started. We're putting these in the front window. And make one that says *Closed for the week*."

"An entire week? Are you sure you know what you're doing?"

Kate clamped her hand over her friend's shoulder. "Have

you ever known me to do something without going full-tilt boogie?"

Matt kneeled at the feet of a passed out high school student and frowned. He'd turned the kid over so if he vomited, he wouldn't choke.

"You figure beer or something harder?" James asked, standing beside him while they waited for the paramedics to arrive.

"By the smell of him, something 80 proof."

"Were we ever that bad?" James asked, folding his arms across his chest.

"*You* were."

James gave him a sideways glance. "I know what you're thinking, *mi amigo*."

"I doubt it."

"Yeah, you're thinking if you become sheriff you can change all this. Make it stop happening. That's an awfully big objective, Matt. You can't save the world."

Matt looked at him through the darkness of the city park. "I can try."

"Yeah, you can. But don't you think a guy your age should be focusing more on life? Chasing some hot women? Having a good time?" James scratched his chest. "Why don't you throw out all your ridiculous lists and learn how to enjoy yourself for a change? Let go. Raise a little hell."

"I did enough of that in my early twenties." Matt wasn't about to tell his friend that he couldn't allow himself to let go. Because once he did, he knew exactly where he'd go to find that good time. Or at least *who* he'd go to.

He needed to focus. On getting his campaign signs posted around town. On making a difference in the hometown he loved. On finding the right woman to marry. Though their first date had been a little wobbly, he'd set up a second date with Emma. This time, he planned to take her somewhere she didn't feel she had to dress up or ask for help to look pretty.

A movie sounded about right. Someplace dark where they wouldn't have to force a conversation. Someplace dark where he could discover if they had any chemistry. Someplace dark where he wouldn't have to look at her and imagine Kate sitting across from him.

When he'd dropped Emma at her front door, he'd kissed her goodnight. It had been a chaste kiss on the cheek. He knew she'd expected more, but if he aimed to find a respectable woman to marry, he intended to treat her with respect. Of course, after his little detour to Kate's dress shop, he'd gone home and climbed into bed. His head hadn't been filled with visions of sugar plums or sweet little schoolteachers. Nope. A certain sexy redhead haunted his dreams. And no matter how hard he tried, he couldn't force her out.

"Good evening, gentlemen."

Matt stood and turned at the voice behind him.

His rival for the sheriff position, Dave Johnson, tipped his straw Resistol as he stepped away from a gunmetal gray Silverado 4x4, so new not even a parking lot ding marred the polished surface. His Wranglers were starched with knife-sharp creases. His boots were custom made. He might be a small-town deputy, but family wealth gave him the look of a big-city boy.

He stepped between Matt and James and looked down at the intoxicated teen as the boy groaned. "He looks pretty wasted."

Johnson used the same tone with which someone would shout *Eureka*.

"That might be the understatement of the year," Matt said, while the siren of the paramedics grew closer.

"You call his folks?"

Matt nodded. "Too drunk to come get him."

The older man looked Matt over with narrowed eyes. "Expect he's just following in their shoes. Probably always will."

Matt's head came up. "He's a kid, Johnson. He's got a chance."

"Unfortunately, Deputy Ryan, kids like him usually take their one chance and throw it to the wind."

He'd been a kid like that. Then everything changed. It could happen for this boy too. "I plan to work on that when I'm elected," Matt said.

"Don't tell me you're one of those who thinks he can save the world." Johnson frowned. "It never works, you know."

Wrong, asshole. Matt lifted his chin. "I aim to try."

Johnson shook his head. "Good luck with that."

"You trying to make a point?" Matt asked.

James stepped between them, thrusting his palm against Matt's chest. "I'm sure he didn't mean anything, partner." James turned to Johnson. "You got business here? Or are you just trying to stir up a hornet's nest?"

Johnson shrugged. "Just trying to get a feel of the place. Election's only a couple of months away."

As the paramedics rolled to a stop, Johnson tipped his hat and walked toward his pickup.

"Can't say I care for that man," James grumbled. "I hope to hell you beat his ass in the election."

"Me too," Matt said as Johnson's truck pulled away from the curb.

The EMTs rolled the gurney from the back of the unit and up over the lawn. Determined to help, Matt kneeled on the cold, damp grass beside the teen curled up in the fetal position. All the kid needed was someone to care. A grownup who gave an honest shit about him. An adult who wanted to see him make something of himself.

That's what Matt had found in Kate's parents.

Grownups who cared.

Grownups who had made him feel as if he'd mattered.

Grownups who made him feel as though he belonged.

After thirty-two years, Matt finally felt like a part of something. His heart squeezed the breath from his lungs. There wasn't a doubt in his mind that the people in this town needed him as much as he needed them.

At five o'clock the following day, Kate locked the bakery door and headed toward her car. The pup wiggled up onto the seat and sat with his tongue lolling happily out the side of his mouth as he stuck his head out the open window and let the wind flap his ears.

The bake sale had been a huge success. Once word got around that the goods were half price and the money went to Letty Silverthorne's favorite charity, the town had stepped up.

Maxine Waverly had about danced on the ceiling when Kate delivered the divorce cake. The woman's enthusiasm had been just what Kate had hoped for. She had no doubt the word-of-mouth advertising would spread enough praise and curiosity to keep Kate in designer cake orders for as long as she chose to create them. She'd left Maxine's house with a huge smile and a feeling of accomplishment equal to sending a client out on the red carpet.

So maybe she could be happy making cakes for the rest of her life.

As she'd jumped up into the driver's seat of the delivery van, she decided to call her additions to the menu *Kate's Red Carpet Cakes.* Hokey, yes. But living in a town called Deer Lick with street names like Reindeer Road, she was learning to embrace hokey.

Most of the day she'd been questioned about the bakery's weeklong closure. Even when she explained that her father had gone hunting and she didn't quite have the knowledge to keep the place open while he was away, their concern for her father cracked the fragile shell around her heart. The people of Deer Lick genuinely cared. She'd seen that for herself with those gathered for her mother's funeral. Maybe she'd known it all along. At least she should have.

Now, as she turned the car toward home, Kate looked over at the pup with his ears flapping in the breeze. She rolled down her own window and felt like sticking her head out too. The air whispered crisp and cool against her cheeks. Maple leaves had turned flame red and the gold aspen leaves quaked like shiny coins. A rush of exhilaration tingled down Kate's spine. She'd always loved this time of year—the scent of burning leaves, the crackle in the air, the chance to slip on a pair of flannel PJs and read a romance beside the woodstove. Mmmm, and hot apple cider stirred with a cinnamon stick.

Just like the four seasons, things changed. And now the Sugar Shack was about to be given a new life.

Kate mentally reviewed her plan of attack. She'd made the necessary calls, placed orders, and tomorrow morning she'd hit the hardware store for paint and supplies. If HGTVs *Design on a Dime* could achieve a room makeover in one day, she could certainly make the bakery renovations in a week. The TV show might have a crew, but she had enough in her bank account to hire most of what she needed to accomplish. Some she planned to do herself. She'd never been very good at micromanaging, but she rocked at multitasking.

The pup pulled his head in the window and whined.

Kate pulled him over and petted his head. "What's up, pup? Got a bug in your eye?"

"You still haven't named that poor little guy?"

Kate glanced up to the rearview mirror. As usual, no sign of Mom, but her glow shimmered as bright as a Christmas bulb. "What? No theme song intro?"

"The radio's off, in case you haven't noticed. Are you trying to get rid of me?" her mother asked.

"*Moi?* What would even prompt you to ask such a thing?"

"Maybe that bite of sarcasm you can't seem to hide."

Kate smiled and the pup looked up at her like she might have lost her mind. She wasn't sure she hadn't. "So what brings you to earth today?"

"What are you doing to my bakery?"

"Ah, so you saw the signs."

"And the empty shelves. We can't afford to close down for an entire week, Katherine. Your father and I aren't wealthy. We're just common folk who work hard for what they have."

"I understand," Kate said, turning the Buick toward home. "We'll make up the lost revenue. I promise. I just saw an opportunity and I'm running with it."

"What? To sell the place out from under your dad?"

"How could I possibly do that? I don't own it."

"Yes. You do. Or at least you're part owner with your brother and sister."

"Seriously? Why would you do that?"

"Because it's all we have to give you, Katherine. Your father and I have spent our entire married life building up that place, working together. Every day brought us happiness, brought us together. We want that for you, Dean, and Kelly too."

Her parent's generosity sent a warm tingle through her heart. "I don't know what to say except . . . I promise we'll take care of it."

"Just don't ever sell it."

Anxiety weighed heavy in her mother's words and Kate wanted to calm her fears. "We won't, Mom. I promise that too."

Her mother seemed to give a sigh of relief. Then she leaned forward. "So tell me about this bright idea you have."

Kate managed a hesitant smile. "I'm updating the bakery. Paint, floors, menu, you name it." She waited for her mother's outrage to kick in. Waited to hear her say there was nothing wrong with the place the way it stood. She waited for the criticism she'd heard her entire life.

"That's a great idea, honey. I've wanted to slap a new coat of paint on those walls for years. Just never had the time or energy."

A surprised breath strangled in her chest. "So . . . you don't mind?"

"Only if you plan to paint it purple and black or some outrageous color that will scare customers away."

"I'm going with a pink, brown, and white theme."

"Then I approve. In fact, why don't you turn this beast around and head to the hardware store right now. Old Emmett Proctor's got a paint sale going on and it ends tomorrow."

"How do you know all these things?"

Her mother hooted a laugh. "Just because I'm dead doesn't mean I can't keep my finger on the pulse of the town. Now get on over to Emmett's before he closes. And for Pete's sake, give that poor dog a name."

At Emmett's Nuts and Bolts Hardware, Kate stood in the paint aisle examining color chips. Making a selection was more difficult than putting together a silk Dolce and Gabbana blouse with satin Versace pants.

The pup sat in the kid seat of the shopping cart, cocking his head when she'd show him a collection of possible paint colors. He wasn't much help in the decision. She couldn't make up her mind between Gumball Pink or Strawberry Shake. English Toffee or Irish Cream. Root Beer Float or Milk Chocolate. But she was getting hungry.

As she reached for a color chip of Sassy Pink Panties, the air shifted. She didn't need to turn to know who stood behind her creating a human wall. Heat radiated from him like a woodstove on a winter night.

"Now there's a color I can get into."

She cast a quick glance over her shoulder.

A smile curled his mouth. The collar of his blue plaid flannel had been pulled up so only a wedge of skin showed between his dark finger-combed hair and the fabric. His scent was clean and woodsy and all male. He filled her senses. He'd told her to stay the hell away from him because he couldn't stay away from her. And here he was, so close she could feel the brush of his jacket against the back of her sweater.

"Yes, I'm sure you've seen your share of panties," she said and pushed her cart further down the aisle. "No need to advertise it to the world."

"Who's your friend?" His husky voice asked as he reached around and petted the pup on the head. The traitorous dog wagged his tail and his long pink tongue rolled out to lick the palm of Matt's big hand.

"A stray." She pulled a can of primer from the shelf and dropped it into the cart. "I'm trying to find his parents."

"His *parents*? That's an interesting term. Why don't you just say owners?"

She grabbed another can of primer and then pushed the cart down to the selection of brushes hanging from a peg board nailed to the wall. "Because I don't believe an animal should be owned."

"Why—"

She stopped, turned, and looked up into his eyes. "Why are you talking to me, Matt? You told me to stay the hell out of your life."

He had the nerve to smile. "That might be impossible as long as we're in the same town."

"Don't worry," she said. "I'll be out of here soon and you can have the place all to yourself."

"Might not be as much fun without you around to torture."

He reached beside her head, grabbed a brush from one side and a roll of masking tape from the other, effectively trapping her between his arms. "So if you're leaving, what's with all the supplies, Hollywood? What's with closing down the bakery? What's with the dress shop?"

"What's with all the questions?" she snapped.

He leaned closer, his chest brushed against her breasts. Aroused, the tips tightened and sent a signal down to parts that were tired of being ignored. Seriously tired.

"Careful, deputy, or I'll sic my dog on you."

He didn't bother to give the pup a glance. Instead his gaze moved over her face. Her breath caught in her chest when his blue on blue eyes locked with hers and that teasing smile returned. "If you're so eager to get out of Deer Lick, why are you working so hard to make it better?" he asked.

"I'm bored. Why do you care?"

He leaned closer and his warm breath tickled her skin. "You smell like sugar frosting."

She tilted her head away while her mind told her to run like hell. Obstinacy held her in place. "And what are you? The big bad wolf whose going to gobble me up?"

He chuckled. "Is that an invitation?"

"Sorry, Bucko." She ducked beneath his arm and stepped a safe distance away. "I've never been a do-it-in-the-paint-aisle kind of girl. You'll have to choose another one of the women on your ridiculous list."

"Whoever said you were on the list?" His expression darkened. "You're not."

The reality of his words shouldn't have stung. But they did. And Kate honestly didn't know what was wrong with her that she'd care in the least. But there wasn't a chance in hell she'd let him know.

She straightened her shoulders, clasped her hands over the shopping cart handle, and strode away. "Just more proof there is a God."

M att paid for his purchases and left the store in a cloud of confusion. When he'd seen her mother's car parked in front of the hardware store, he should have kept his foot on the accelerator. But nooooo. There was definitely something wrong with him. Something that made his common sense blow a fuse and made him believe it was okay to practically dry-hump Kate in the middle of the damned hardware store. True, old Emmett had been the only one in the place, but Emmett also had one of those trick mirrors that allowed him to see down every aisle in the store. He didn't need the old man spreading tales.

Hell, *he* didn't need to be starting them.

He shoved the gear shift into drive and pulled away from the curb. Tomorrow his campaign signs would be posted all around town. His reputation needed to remain rock-solid. He didn't know why he had this fascination with Kate. He'd never been good enough for her. She didn't plan to stick around and make Deer Lick her home. He should have learned his lesson long ago.

Kate Silver was caviar.

He needed cream of wheat.

As he parked his SUV in Emma's driveway, he rubbed his eyes. He was so damned tired—tired of fighting his alter ego who apparently believed he still had feelings for Kate and should act on them. His alter ego had a nut loose. In the future he'd have to be more guarded when around her. And he'd have to make sure he was around her as little as possible. Everything he'd worked for, everything he'd dreamed of, was riding on the fact that he could get it together and keep it together.

Emma opened her door and stepped out onto her front porch with a smile and a wave. She wore a zippered sweatshirt, jeans, and white tennis shoes. That was more like it. Her sweet curves were hidden, not jumping out and doing a pole dance in front of his face.

Smiling, he opened the car door and stepped out onto the gravel driveway. "Looks like you're ready to go," he said.

"I just need to grab my purse." She disappeared into the house and within seconds was walking toward him. They exchanged a hug and when she looked up at him with her blue eyes, anticipation danced in their depths. "What movie are we going to see?"

"How about a Hitchcock film fest?"

"That sounds wonderful. Where's it playing?"

"In my living room. If that's okay. I've got microwave popcorn and I bought a jumbo box of Junior Mints."

She nodded. "Sounds perfect."

Matt returned her smile and dug down deep to gather the enthusiasm to go with it. Hand-in-hand, they walked to the passenger side of his SUV and he opened the door. He'd wanted someplace dark and maybe a little romantic to discover whether Emma Hart was the one. Somewhere he wouldn't be distracted with thoughts of Kate.

If he couldn't manage that, he wasn't going to wait around for her to run again. He would personally escort her to the city limits and give her sexy behind the boot.

The sun had set by the time Kate pulled the Buick into a parking space in back of the bakery. Her car was loaded with paint and supplies. She'd finally chosen a tasty palette of Strawberry Shake and Irish Cream for the walls and Milk Chocolate for the trim. The Java Teak laminate flooring she'd ordered for the front of the bakery would be delivered and installed tomorrow while simultaneously the prep area concrete floor would be acid stained with earthen umber. She had no choice but to get the walls painted tonight.

Just as she had no choice but to erase Matt Ryan from her *need it, want it, gotta have it* list.

"You shouldn't be so hard on the boy."

Ah, Letty Silverthorne had arrived.

The pup startled awake. He jumped up and put his paws on the back of the front seat. His little tail whipped back and forth so quick his furry fanny wagged.

"Hello, sweetheart," her mother cooed. "Did mean old Katherine give you a name yet?"

What happened to "I love you, Kate?" Kate sighed and turned in her seat to look at her troublemaking backseat driver. "I'm not mean but he's not my dog. I'm sure he's already got a name."

Her mother shook her head. "You think you're sure of a lot of things. Some I'm a little concerned about."

Kate reached down and grabbed up the bag of paint brushes and drop cloths from the floorboard. "I'm not even going to ask what you're talking about, because I know you'll only be too happy to tell me."

"You don't have to ask, dear, I'd love to share."

"I was afraid you would." She crumpled the plastic bag in

her lap and leaned her head back. The pup crawled on top of the bag and used her thighs as a perch to the window. "Go ahead."

"You're so sure that little guy sitting on your lap belongs to someone else you won't open your heart enough to realize he belongs to you."

As if on cue, the pup licked Kate's chin. "Hey, no fair siding with the enemy." To her mother she said, "It's not that I don't have a heart, Mom. It wouldn't be fair to him. He'd be locked up in my condo all day every day. I'd have to put him in a kennel every time I flew to New York, which is often. He needs a home with someone who will love him and take care of him."

"Exactly."

"So why are you pushing me to keep him?"

"Because you're *that* person, Katherine. You just don't realize it. Who's going to love him more than you?"

"Mom. Seriously. I'm the kind of person who eats takeout while I sit on the floor to make clothing alterations. I don't think my clients would appreciate dog hair clinging to their chiffon. Besides, I can barely keep up with my own life let alone this cute little guy." She rubbed her hand briskly between his ears.

Her mother shouted, "Exactly" the same way she'd shout **Bingo**.

"If you agree with me, then I have no idea the point you're trying to make."

"Listen to your own words, sweetheart. *You can barely keep up with your life.*"

"Yeah, so?"

"So why have you been living a life you can barely keep up with? Believe me when I tell you life is much too short to waste.

You're young. You're beautiful. You should be living a life that makes you happy, that makes you happy to be alive. There's nothing wrong with changing course. You'll be a success no matter what you do."

Kate opened her mouth to argue and then snapped it shut. Something pinched deep in her heart and stole her breath. How could she argue when her mother was right? She didn't need to keep up a pretense. Especially with her mother. Lately she had been thinking twice about her chosen career and life. Or lack of. Besides, who would her mother have to tell?

"Am I making sense?" her mother asked.

"Yes."

"I'm glad." The smile accenting her mother's words was unmistakable. "You're a good girl, Katherine. And you're smart. I was wrong to rain on your parade when you received that scholarship. I should have treated it exactly the same as I had when Dean received his scholarship to USC and Kelly received hers to Stanford. I was wrong to say the things I said."

A lump slid up Kate's throat. She was stunned. An apology? From her mother? "What did you say?"

"I said I was wrong. And I'm sorry."

The cold air in the car shifted and Kate felt an icy breath on the back of her neck. She turned to find her mother perched at the edge of the seat, anxiously leaning forward. She looked into her mother's face, at the regret in her eyes, and suddenly wished she could hug away her pain.

"I'm sorry too, Mom. I know you were worried and—"

Her mother lifted her hand. "You have nothing to be sorry for. I love you, daughter. Never doubt that."

As Kate nodded, along with the tears came relief. Maybe

they wouldn't always get along, but her mother loved her. And *that* was something she hadn't been sure of for a very long time. "Well, I guess I'd best get to painting those walls." Kate gathered her things and opened the car door.

"Sweetheart? One more thing."

Kate leaned back into the car. "What's that?"

"I wish . . . you wouldn't be so hard on Matt. He's a good boy. Well, I guess he's really not a boy any longer. And he really was there when your daddy and I needed him."

There was that *needed* word again. Kate shrugged, shook her head. "He hasn't been all that nice to me either."

"I'm sure he doesn't mean to be . . . difficult. He has . . ."

Issues was the word that jumped to Kate's mind.

Her mother's glow escalated to the point that Kate had to squint at the intensity. ". . . well, there's something I never told you. Something I think you need to know."

"Wow. Really?" Her mother had actually held something back? "Then please, don't make me wait any longer."

"If I tell you, I'll be breaking a promise."

"Who's going to know?"

"Believe me, if you can't keep this buttoned up, and I'm sure you won't, it's going to get messy." Her mother looked skyward and mumbled "Oh Lord, forgive me for this."

"Mom!"

"Fine. Just a few days before you left home, Matt asked your daddy and me for permission to marry you."

The bag dropped from Kate's hand as everything she thought she knew, thought she believed, imploded.

CHAPTER TWELVE

His second date with Emma had been a friggin' disaster.

Matt flattened his palms against the tumbled tile and ducked his head beneath the shower. Hot water sluiced down his back and loosened his tight neck muscles.

He thought he'd prepared a nice evening. He'd made a nice fire in the fireplace. He'd rented two Hitchcock classics, opting to give Emma the choice on her preference. He'd bought two nice bottles of wine and lit candles all around the room. He'd done everything possible to assure that the date would go nicely.

Apparently *nice* and him didn't belong in the same sentence.

The popcorn burned and stank up the house. The Junior Mints, sitting on the table near the fireplace, melted. And when Emma had told him she preferred hot chocolate to wine, he'd made her a cup. She'd burned her tongue, then spilled the hot liquid on her jeans, which seeped down to her skin and burned her there as well. The DVD player took a dump and they'd been left with nothing to do but sit and talk. There'd been no romance, no getting to know each other.

Halfway through their stilted conversation a dire realization hit Matt like a shovel to the face. He remembered standing in the dress shop and Kate asking, "How are you going to live with someone if you're not in love with them?"

He grabbed the container of shampoo and turned it upside down over his head. Empty. Damn. He couldn't force himself to love someone any more than he could wring a drop of shampoo from an empty bottle.

Love shouldn't be so damned difficult.

It hadn't always been. He recalled a long ago memory of lying next to Kate in the bed of his pickup on a chilly autumn night, much like the one outside. The sky had been clear with a million stars overhead. Her skin had been warm beneath the plaid blanket. And they'd talked for hours. Nonstop. About subjects that ranged from gossip that the man-eater Gretchen Wilkes was banging Lester Evans, their married mailman, to their favorite movies that year—hers had been *Jerry Maguire*, his had been *Twister*. There had never been a lull in the conversation that had been interspersed with kisses and laughter.

The memory seized him by the throat and sent an ache so deep into his heart he couldn't breathe.

When he'd taken Emma home, he found himself relieved when she informed him she didn't think they should see each other again. Emma Hart was an attractive, intelligent woman with a lot to offer a man. But he wasn't in love with her. And he never would be. She deserved a man who would cherish her. He wasn't that guy. He realized now that his search for a wife had never been about winning the election. He wanted marriage. He just didn't want an empty marriage. He wanted to be in love with the woman he would make his wife and he wanted her to love him back. He just didn't know if that would ever be possible. At least not while there was one specific woman he couldn't seem to erase from his heart.

And right now, she'd locked herself up behind a papered bakery window doing God knew what. He snapped off the faucet.

Maybe he'd just go find out.

Surrounded by gallons of primer, paint, and painter's cloths, Kate removed the bakery's faded confection artwork from the walls with her phone headset stuffed in her ear.

"Holy shit. How'd you find out?" Kelly verified the truth from her end of the line in Chicago when Kate called for confirmation of her mother's bombshell.

She could hardly tell Kelly their mother had spilled the beans. "I overheard someone at the market."

"You swear you really never knew? Because there have been times during our visits when we'd do the whole gossip-in-our-jammies thing and you've eluded to—"

"What, are you deaf? Did you not just hear me say I didn't know?" Kate said, scooting the pup and his two pink paws away from the obviously enticing tray of Strawberry Shake paint. For his own safety, she tucked him in the office and closed the door.

"I know, but I can't believe you didn't know. Everybody knew. He had a ring. Bought it right there at Happy Heart Jewelers, the same place you bought your class ring."

"How the heck did *everybody* know?"

"Have you forgotten our mother had her own version of Morse Code?"

Kate sighed. "But I was only twenty. How could he believe I'd know how to be a wife? Or would even want to at that age?"

"Look, little sister, when has logic ever played into life when love's involved? Haven't you ever heard the terms crazy in love? Madly in love? Wildly in love? Love at first sight? Show me where reason fits in."

It certainly hadn't when she'd been in the first grade and big bad third-grader Matt Ryan had challenged her to a race on the monkey bars. He'd won, of course, and she'd been smitten by his strength and smile and those unique blue eyes. That he'd been an *older man* hadn't hurt either.

But Matt hadn't truly noticed her until her sophomore year in Mr. Dodson's biology class. Sentenced to retake the class, Matt had laughed his muscular football-playing ass off when she'd passed out at the soles of his black Converse high tops the day they dissected frogs. She blamed the formaldehyde. He blamed her hot crush on him. A week later they were a couple. Matt had told her he'd fallen in love when she turned as green as the frog. A licensed psychologist might consider that slightly sick. Still, who was she to turn down the most gorgeous guy in school?

But love? Did any sixteen-year-old girl know what love meant?

Infatuation? Check.

Lust? Double check.

But love? The real melt-your-heart-can't-live-without-him kind of love?

For years she'd sat one seat behind him in different classes, staring at his wide shoulders, watching the way his dark hair curled at the nape of his neck when it got too long. She'd been sure he thought she had some kind of asthma condition because she constantly leaned toward him and breathed deeply to catch a whiff of his sexy male scent. Yeah, so maybe she was a little whacked. But to her, Matt Ryan smelled of clean mountain air, crisp leaves, and pine trees. To a teenage girl that was better than a gallon of Jovan Musk.

"Despite Mom and Dad telling him you'd received the scholarship, he was certain you'd run because you'd found out he wanted to marry you."

Kate's cheeks burned. A hollow ache settled next to her heart. "God, no wonder he hates me."

"He doesn't hate you."

Kate gave a cynical laugh. "Seriously? He told me to stay the hell out of his life."

"Well, then he probably just dislikes you."

He had plenty of reason to.

But what was it with him popping up everywhere? Grilling her dinner? Trapping her against walls and pressing his big body into hers? There were at least parts of him that didn't hate her. Long, hard, swollen, throbbing parts. And what was up with him kissing her? Not once, like he might have been drunk off his ass and not have known what he was doing, but several times when he'd been stone-cold sober?

"I'm pretty sure he doesn't dislike my body though," she accidentally said out loud.

"Yeah, well, you are pretty hot," Kelly said with a chuckle. "And heaven knows those flannel PJs you wear are soooo sexy."

"Shut up. You wear flannel too."

"Doesn't quite beat a warm body, does it?"

"Nope." Kate sighed, honestly not remembering the last time a warm body had laid next to hers. With the exception of the puppy, of course. "I know we don't agree on much, but I miss you, Kel."

"Miss you too."

"Promise we'll get together more than once or twice a year."

"I promise. So what are you going to do?" Kelly asked.

"About?"

"Duh. Your former *almost* fiancée?"

Kate leaned against the wall and slid down to the floor. Something spiraled inside her that she couldn't identify, but it felt a whole lot like butterflies flapping inside her heart. She held out her hand and looked at her naked ring finger imagining a glittering diamond there—one she hadn't bought for herself or rented for a client.

Her dreams may have never taken her down the path of June Cleaver or Carol Brady or even Lucy Ricardo. But something inside her heart knew that one day, at least, she'd like to have a man beside her who filled in all those empty places rambling around her life. Unfortunately for her, most men didn't like to be put on hold.

"I'm not going to do anything, Kel. He's got his life planned out and I've already got mine in motion. We're on two different interstates. He told me to stay the hell out of his life. So I'm out." Before the conversation could move in any more uncomfortable directions, she glanced up at the clock and said, "Hey, I'm sure you've got court early in the morning. I don't want to keep you."

"Kate? I know I've been too busy to call. But I promise I will get back there just as soon as this trial is over."

It was that moment Kate realized she'd been so busy she hadn't even noticed that neither of her siblings had checked in and updated her on their dad watch status. "Yeah, I know. So how is your big case going?" Kate asked.

"I can already hear the rope swinging."

Kate heard the satisfaction in her sister's voice. "Put an extra knot in it for me."

"I will. In the meantime, do me a favor?"

She hardly had time to tie her shoes anymore and her sister wanted to pile on more? Was she trying to kill her? "Sure."

"Promise me."

"Does it have to do with dressing in clown clothes or jumping off Mt. Rushmore?"

Kelly laughed. "Not even close."

"Tap dancing on top of the Grange in a tutu?"

"Where do you get these ideas?"

"I live in Hollywood."

"No tap dancing," Kelly confirmed.

"Fine." Kate sighed. "I promise."

"Give it a chance."

The phone clicked in Kate's ear. She didn't have her silly sister super decoder ring handy, but this time she didn't need it. Kelly hadn't meant to say *it*, she'd meant to say *him*.

Her sister didn't understand that Matt Ryan didn't want a chance. He'd written her off with the bus ticket she'd bought to L.A.

Two hours later while Kate battled with the paint extension pole, she also struggled with the reality that once upon a time she'd broken Matt's heart.

She hated guilt and that gnawing feeling it left in your stomach. Though she lived and worked in Fantasyland, she tried to be realistic and level-headed. Which is why she'd long ago made up her mind that her career left little to no time for a serious relationship. And she had to be equally honest that she could never be the kind of girl who followed in her mother's house slippers. She didn't even own any slippers. But during brief moments of insanity something about Matt Ryan made her want to at least try on a pair. Something about him made her think of marriage and babies and growing old beside him.

She looked up to the half-painted ceiling and groaned. Her brain, not to mention her arm muscles, were tired. She glanced at her watch. It was getting late, but still too early to call it quits for the day. She pushed the air from her lungs and stuck the roller in the tray of Irish Cream, lifted the pole over her head and was in mid-stroke when the back door creaked open. A gust of wind blew through the opening and a scatter of autumn leaves rustled in along with the man who'd been on her mind all night.

"What are you doing here, Hollywood?" He stood just inside the door, one hand tucked in the pocket of a brown duck Carhartt jacket, the other gripping the doorknob. Worn and frayed jeans encased his long legs and cupped his generous package like a gentle glove. His hair was windblown and slightly damp. His cheeks were flushed from the cold.

Her stomach twisted and she blinked, thinking he was

just an illusion created from her overindulgent imagination. But when her eyes opened again, he was standing much closer. The scent of soap clung to him and Kate imagined him in the shower, wet and naked.

"What are *you* doing here?" she asked.

"Just driving by. Saw the light on behind the paper covering the window. Cop instincts kicked in. I wanted to make sure no one was robbing the place." Matt's gaze darted around the room, then his eyes returned to hers. "What's going on?"

"Painting. Or at least trying to." She eyed the evil extension pole. "First, I have to find a way to finish the ceiling. When I look up for too long, I get dizzy."

He took the pole from her hand, adjusted the knob and the tool extended another two feet. "The trick is not to stand directly under it," he said, dipping the roller in the paint and demonstrating the proper technique.

"Oh. I guess I should have read the instructions first."

He gave her half a smile that curled one side of his mouth. "What prompted this sudden . . . transformation?"

She lifted a shoulder. "I don't know. I just looked around and everything seemed so old and faded. It's my job to make people look their best. I figured I could do the same for the bakery. Since Dad went hunting, it seemed the perfect time for this place to get a facelift."

His gaze stroked over her. "Did you ever think your dad might not want to change the bakery? That maybe the way it was decorated reminded him of your mother?"

Panic dove deep and Kate froze. "Oh my God. I never even considered—" Her palms went to her cheeks as she looked at the holes in the wall where the photo of her parents on their opening day thirty odd years ago had once been displayed. "Do you think he'll hate it?" Or *her*, she worried.

Matt studied her and then glanced around the shop. "Because *you* did it, I'm pretty sure he'll love it."

"You swear?" Relief swept through her with the energy of an ocean wave.

He nodded. "I'm going to have to be careful."

"About?"

"You. And my ever-changing opinion. Between the dress shop, the bakery makeover, and all the extra favors you're doing for people like offering to babysit for Ollie and Maggie, I might start thinking you're nice."

She laughed. "Heaven forbid."

"So what exactly are you trying to accomplish at this late hour?" he asked, gripping the pole in his large hand.

She considered the almost impossible task she'd set for herself. "Tomorrow a new laminate floor and canned ceiling lights will be installed. I need to finish painting the ceiling and the walls tonight."

"That's a big order." He looked at her as if she'd asked him to eat a bug. Then he handed her the pole.

She fully expected him to walk out of there as fast as his worn cowboy boots would carry him. And who would blame him? He'd already put in a full day behind the badge. But as he had a tendency to do these days, he surprised her by shrugging off his jacket and tossing it on the counter. He turned toward her, hand extended.

"Let's get to work," he said.

She stared at him. Or rather she stared at his wide, smooth chest and narrow waist hidden just beneath the soft, thin cotton of his light gray T-shirt. She remembered the tall lanky boy he'd been with muscles hard and tight beneath her fingertips. Now he was a grown man and she couldn't help but wonder what he looked like beneath all that fabric.

"Hel-lo?" He snapped his fingers in front of her face.

"Uh—" Kate shook her head. "What?"

He chuckled. "I said we'd better get to work."

She looked up into his eyes. "You're going to help me?"

His shoulders lifted. "Why not?"

"It's late. Don't you have something better to do?"

He took the extension pole from her hands, turned his back to her, and dipped the roller into the paint tray. "Probably. So, if you don't get over there and pick up that brush, I might change my mind." He raised his arms and began to roll on the ceiling paint.

Mesmerized, Kate watched the play of muscles flex his back and arms. She studied the way those softly worn jeans cupped his perfect rear end and she sighed.

"Kate?"

Sensibility returned with the gruff tone in his deep voice. "Right. I'm on it." She picked up the smaller roller and dabbed it in the pink paint, sponging off the excess. On the wall she raised and lowered the tool in neat straight lines. From the radio Carrie Underwood sang about love being all that mattered, and a companionable silence drifted between her and the man she'd cared for enough to give him her virginity. The man who'd planned to ask her to marry him. Even if she was interested, she'd missed the boat. She wasn't on his list. His stupid, ridiculous Kate-excluding list.

"So, no hot dates tonight?" she asked, stroking the paint on another aged section of wall while he worked toward a corner in the opposite direction.

The only response she received was the sound of the paint sloshing onto the ceiling.

"How's that list thing working for you?" she prodded.

He didn't even bother to shoot her a dirty look.

"I guess I have to give you credit." She shook her head, turned back toward the wall and lifted the roller again. "I mean, you know what you want and you're going after it. In a weird way I kind of admire that you care so much about this town that you'd be willing to—"

"You're doing that wrong," he said on a warm breath that tickled her ear and sent a shiver dancing down her spine. His heat radiated against her back. His silent approach had startled her—a talent he must have picked up from chasing bad guys. She glanced at him across her shoulder as he slid his big palm over the top of her hand and guided the direction of the roller on the wall. The warmth of his touch went way down deep.

"You make a big W," he said as he demonstrated. "That way you don't leave lines."

"Oh."

"You ever paint before?"

The deep timber of his voice rumbled against her back and sent shockwaves through her heart. Her head got a little lighter as she breathed him in. "No."

"Why am I not surprised?"

"But I'm good at a lot of other things."

He leaned closer and whispered, "Do tell, Hollywood."

A tingling sensation settled low in her abdomen as his free hand slipped around her waist and drew her back against him.

His erection pressed against her as his hot mouth found the sensitive curve of her neck.

"You've got my full attention," he said against her skin.

Yeah, no kidding. "Hey, don't forget I'm not on your list." She tried to duck away. "You don't want me."

He caught her and turned her in his arms. He lifted his hands to cup her face and looked down into her eyes. "You're all I've ever wanted, Kate. Whatever this is between us, I can't deny it anymore." He lowered his head and captured her mouth with his own.

His lips lightly brushed over hers and he kissed her with such tenderness it stripped her soul bare. His firm, determined mouth coaxed and teased. Her knees dissolved. Her heart thundered in her ears.

She meant to do as he'd asked that night in her dress shop. To push him away. Instead when his tongue slipped inside her mouth—wet, hot, and hungry—she welcomed him in. Her tongue met his while dizzying pleasure whipped through her body. The paint roller dropped from her grasp. She lifted her hands to his strong, solid shoulders and clung to him as he consumed the last of her resistance.

While his mouth worshipped her, crazy mad desire hummed through her veins. His long fingers plunged into her hair and he tilted her head for a better angle in which to devour her. A moan stuck in her throat, then broke free as the kiss ignited an electrical charge in her body. When he wrapped his arms around her and brought her firmly against him, she plunged into the passion thumping in her chest, burning across her skin, and pooling between her thighs.

She tangled her fingers in the silky hair at his nape and

her nipples rose to hard points against his solid chest. His big hands slid down her spine, then slipped beneath the edge of her sweater. Her skin tingled when his calloused fingers caressed the small of her bare back, then dipped lower to pull her tight against the long hard bulge straining against his zipper.

His fingers slipped up her side and cupped her just beneath her breast. As his thumb brushed across her nipple in a lazy motion, she leaned into him.

"This probably isn't a good idea," she whispered.

"There's no probably about it," he murmured low and sexy.

The musky scent of his male arousal filled her head. She wanted to climb his strong, hard body, wrap her legs around him and let him sweep her away on a tide of endless passion.

"You said you wanted me to stay away from you."

He kissed the side of her throat. "I lied."

There were a million reasons she should push him away and only one she shouldn't.

"Oh, what the hell." She kicked sanity to the curb, grabbed hold of his T-shirt and tugged it over his head. When the fabric sailed to the floor and she slid her hands down his chest to his flat, muscled belly, he gave her a smile she hadn't seen since that night ten years ago.

Heightened awareness brightened his eyes. "My turn." He lifted off her sweater, flicked the clasp on her bra, and tossed the contraption aside.

Then he held her away and just looked at her. The more he looked, the more her nipples hardened, and the more desperate she became to feel the heat of him surrounding her and filling her deep inside.

"You are so beautiful," he murmured, smoothing his palms

down the curves of her body. "You've always been beautiful to me, Kate." Then he drew her against him.

The way he looked at her made her feel desirable. Valuable. Necessary.

When their bare flesh met, she almost melted at the keen sensitivity of her nipples against the silky texture of the light covering of hair on his chest. She strained upward, craving more of his kiss, the warmth of his mouth. But he had other ideas.

"Mmmmm. I love the way you smell," he murmured. "Sweet . . . and sinful."

"It's sugar and vanilla."

His moist tongue skated down her neck until he reached the curve of her shoulder, then he softly sucked her flesh. "Lucky for me I've always had a sweet tooth."

Lucky *me*. Ripples of pleasure shot straight to her core. Eyes closed, her head dropped back. She slid her fingers through his hair, needing something to hold onto while his parted lips trailed to the curve of her breast.

His palms held her waist while he licked and suckled her nipples until they were wet, erect, and sensitive. Every delicious pull of his mouth sent a signal straight to the aching flesh between her thighs. She could feel the urgency in his touch as well as the tenderness in his restraint. He meant to love her, as only he could. As only he knew how. To claim her one more time.

She opened her eyes. "I want to see you. To touch you," she whispered in a husky voice she hardly recognized as her own.

He toed off his boots, looked down at her, and smiled. "Be my guest."

Her fingers were shaky and eager as they unbuttoned and unzipped his jeans. In one swift motion she pushed down the denim and the soft cotton of his boxer-briefs. He kicked them off and stood there, naked and gorgeous in the glaring overhead lights. For a moment she stood back, appreciating his incredibly smooth expanse of streamlined muscle and the line of silky hair that swirled his naval then traveled below to his full erection.

She looked up. Their eyes met.

She reached for him.

He reached for her.

They came together like rockets.

What was left of her clothing came off in a hurry. He crushed her to him, slashed his mouth across hers in a blistering kiss that tasted like heaven and became a voracious feeding frenzy of lips and tongues and red hot desire.

His hand slid into her hair. Her hand slid to his cock. It pulsed as he pushed into her grasp and the skin stretched tight. The heat and weight of it in her palm sent her heart racing. She wanted to taste him, lick him, devour him but the need to have him inside her was greater. "I can't wait any longer."

"Me either," he murmured against the side of her throat while his rough fingertips played with her sensitive nipples.

She burned with desire and ached with emptiness. She needed him to fill her with pleasure and she wasn't beyond begging. When his teeth nipped her earlobe and his warm breath brushed her cheek, her words escaped on a breathless plea. "Now. Please."

Impatient, she pushed him to a painter's cloth on the floor and crawled on top of him, planting her knees astride his lean hips. The plump head of his hot erection nudged her slick opening and she moaned her pleasure.

"Wait." His breath was ragged as he clasped her hips and lifted her off of him.

Desperation grabbed her by the heart. She wanted this man. Needed him more than she needed to breathe. He couldn't stop now. Just as panic began to invade the erotic haze wrapped around her, he grabbed his jeans, produced a condom, and rolled it on.

A huge sigh of relief pushed from her lungs. "I thought you changed your mind."

He grinned up at her, sliding his fingers into her moist flesh, slowly caressing her where she was hot and swollen and incredibly responsive. "Not a chance."

Feeling herself propelled toward orgasm with each skillful stroke, she closed her eyes and groaned. "Thank God."

Even as wonderful as his fingers felt, they weren't enough to feed her hunger. She needed *him*. All of him. She curled her fingers around his pulsing flesh and lowered herself. The thick, hard penetration was deep, complete, and powerful.

She braced her hands on his shoulders, pressed her mouth to his, raised her hips and withdrew. He sucked air into his lungs. His hands moved to her hips and guided her as she plunged down on him again. His uneven breath whispered across her temple as she moved up and down, increasing the rhythm. Friction built. Heat engulfed. Her heart beat in her ears as she rose and descended, as intense pleasure grabbed her and turned her inside out. She rocked against him while he whispered her name.

Then she was on her back and his remarkable body pushed

her into the floor while he thrust into her deeper and harder, pushing her faster and faster toward release. The sound of his passion filled her ears and her heart. She wrapped her legs around his waist.

There was nothing slow or easy about the powerful sensations that rolled through her like an earthquake. Tremors rippled across her flesh and robbed her of breath. Her muscles contracted, gripping him tight inside her as wave after wave of delicious release washed over her. A deep groan rumbled in his chest. With his head thrown back like he'd given her all of him, body and soul, he thrust into her one last time.

When his breathing slowed, he rolled to his side taking her with him. Kate relaxed with her head on his chest, his arms wrapped around her, his warmth surrounding her. His sigh of contentment nestled in her soul. The scent of their lovemaking on his skin filled her senses. The thu-thump of his heart beat beneath her ear.

Slowly the haze of satisfaction dissipated, but the question burning in her mind would not stop. Kate shifted her head to his shoulder and looked up at him. "Why didn't you tell me?"

Eyes closed he glided his calloused palm down her arm. "Tell you what?"

She exhaled a nervous breath. "That you planned to ask me to marry you."

His body instantly stiffened. And not in a good way. "How about we not dig up old rumors?"

"If it's just an old rumor, what are you afraid of?"

For a moment he laid there still as a summer night, and then he sat up. As he looked down into her face, the tips of his fingers touched her cheek. Slowly he lowered his head and pressed his mouth to hers. He kissed her once, then lingered with a second kiss that left her lips tingling and her heart bursting.

He pulled back. "I'm not afraid of anything, Hollywood." But even as the words left his gorgeous mouth he moved away, grabbed up his jeans, and stood. "Give me a second and I'll take you home."

She sat up and watched him walk away, naked, to the restroom at the back of the shop. She pulled the painter's cloth around her. A minute later he returned with his jeans on. Eyes shadowed and guarded, he reached for the gray T-shirt lying on the floor and pulled it over his head. "You coming?" He jammed his feet into his cowboy boots, then held his hand out to her.

She shook her head and his hand dropped against his thigh.

"Matt?" Her heart stuttered in her chest. "Talk to me."

His eyes stared into hers. "Let it go, Kate." He grabbed his jacket, shoved his arms through the sleeves, and headed toward the back door.

"In case you haven't noticed," she shouted, "I'm not the one running this time." When the door banged shut behind him, Kate swallowed her pride, embraced regret, and reached for her sweater. "Me and my big mouth."

CHAPTER THIRTEEN

Days passed. Matt's campaign posters popped up all over town. There were signs of him everywhere, but Kate had caught no sign of the actual living, breathing man since the night in the bakery.

She'd tried to accept that all he'd really wanted from her was sex and closure. What better way for him to get that than to make her melt in his arms and then for *him* to walk away?

Yeah, that theory would work great, except with that logic Kate would have felt used. She didn't. Quite the opposite had happened and no one had been more surprised than she.

In his arms she'd felt loved.

Who knew?

When he'd walked out that door, Kate had wanted to run after him. To make him stay and take her in his arms again. And why hadn't she? If *her* pride had stung when he'd walked away from her that night, she couldn't imagine how he'd felt when she'd left him ten years ago. Especially for something, at the time, *she'd* considered better. God, she'd been an idiot. Scratch that. No sense talking past tense.

She stood in the middle of the bakery looking at the walls that had been completely painted that night after she'd scooped up her dignity and went home. Apparently he'd come back and finished the job he'd started. But why? And would she ever have the chance to thank him?

She glanced at the floor where the ancient tiles had been covered with shiny new wood laminate, erasing any reminders of the night they'd shared together. Well, except for the big giant ache rambling around in her heart. For weeks she'd wondered what he wanted from her. She didn't believe it was just sex. And it hadn't been just the sex that made her realize what she wanted from him either.

Matt made her feel something she hadn't felt before—that she was exactly where she belonged. The thought both scared her and filled her with pleasure. She could do one of two things with that information . . . run or embrace it.

A knock rapped on the front window and she opened the door for Maggie who bustled in from the cold grinning like a kid on a treasure hunt.

"I love the awning over the door," Maggie said, shrugging off her wool coat and dumping it on one of the new bistro chairs Kate had integrated into the new design. "Might as well give people a place to sit and visit while they sample the new menu."

"I'm so glad you went with a polka-dot design. It reminds me of the Dippin' Dots ice cream we got at the hockey game in Boise last year."

Kate sighed. "I just hope my dad will like it."

"Are you kidding? He'll love it."

"I don't know." Doubt splintered Kate's conviction. "What

if in doing this makeover, I've taken away his memories of my mom?"

"Oh, honey, don't you know you can never take away his memories?" Maggie gave her a hug. "They're too embedded in his heart. True love is like that. And your mom and dad were definitely soul mates."

There was that term again. "Is that what you and Oliver are?"

Maggie laughed. Her apple cheeks dimpled. "We didn't start out that way. But yeah, we are. He was a cute guy who turned into a hell of a man. He takes care of us and he loves me unconditionally. Even when I never lost the baby weight, he didn't care." She gave a little smile and sigh. "I can't imagine my life without him."

The spark of utter amazement in Maggie's voice intrigued Kate. And she had to admit, it ignited a smidge of envy, too.

Then Maggie clapped her hands together. "Okay, let's get moving. You reopen in a few days. So what's on the agenda for today?"

Kate's wandering thoughts of soul mates and true love slipped back into her box of crazy but valuable ideas and she locked them away. "Well, I ordered arborvitae in these awesome ceramic urns for each side of the door and a planter box with Mom's favorite mums for in front of the window. They should arrive this afternoon as should the glass apothecaries we'll use to display highlighted pastries."

"So that leaves us to . . ."

"Try out some new recipes to put on the menu."

"Oh God," Maggie groaned, "If they taste anything like those ice cream cupcakes, I'm in big trouble."

Kate laughed and guided her friend to the prep area. "I promise you can have a free lifetime membership in the treat-of-the-month-club."

"Good thing Ollie doesn't mind a little cottage cheese with these thighs."

Kate grabbed a stainless steel bowl and mixing spoon and slid it across the counter to her friend. Yes, men like Ollie were definitely in the few or don't exist category. At least in Hollywood, where men spent a fortune on spas and product and expected their women to remain forever ageless via Botox and collagen. Men like her father and Maggie's husband were different. They liked women with substance instead of perfect thighs.

"What are we making first?" Maggie asked, doing a little dance with her bowl and spoon to the Brooks & Dunn tune on the radio.

"New York–style cheesecake with blackberry coulis."

Maggie's brows lifted. "What the heck is that?"

"Don't worry. You'll love it." Kate pulled a springform pan from the shelf, set it on the counter, and wondered if Matt Ryan would be different, too. Was he the soul mate type? Was he the kind of man who would give unconditional love even if his woman had a little extra junk in her trunk?

The man was a walking contradiction. One minute he was trying to select a wife from a grocery list; the next minute he was on the floor with her making love with so much passion it made her heart hurt.

She opened the refrigerator door, grabbed the packages of cream cheese, and slapped them down on the counter. Her initial reaction when he'd walked out that door had been that he wanted her body but he didn't want *her*. She could have kept thinking that if it hadn't been for the look in his eyes when she'd mentioned his *almost* proposal. It had been apparent she'd brought back unwelcome memories of heartache and pain.

Her instincts told her to let it go. Walk away. The problem remained that her instincts, along with her good intentions, always sucked. She didn't want to walk away. She felt something for him, something deep inside where hope raised its annoying little head and made her realize she wanted different things now than she'd wanted at twenty years old. Heck, wanted something different than she had just a few weeks ago.

She wanted it all.

And maybe, if she played her cards right, she could have it all.

His list was ridiculous. She knew it. Deep inside he had to know it too. For his sake maybe she should leave him be and let him move on with his life.

But until she knew exactly what was in his heart, leaving him alone was impossible.

With the Sugar Shack's grand reopening looming, Kate set the tray of her pastry samples on the back floorboard of the Buick and shut the door. She'd never realized how much satisfaction could be gained from slapping a little sugar and flour together. But as she'd arranged the treats on the tray, she'd been filled with pride. In Hollywood she made a living taking someone else's creations and putting them together. But her

pastries were all her, made from scratch, her heart, and imagination.

Hopefully they tasted as tempting as they smelled. The
combination of raspberries baked in perfectly puffed phyllo,
blackberry cheesecake squares, buttermilk pecan tarts, and
amaretto chocolate swirl fudge would surely appeal to a certain sexy bachelor. If not, the chilled bottle of Moët should do
the trick.

Whatever that little something was in the back of her mind
that nagged to leave Matt alone, Kate ignored. Obviously their
attraction to each other was a two-way street. But somewhere
since she'd stepped foot on hallowed Deer Lick dirt and now,
old feelings had raised their head and new feelings were spurn-
ing her on.

In her business she had to be a huge "what if" person—as
in *what if* she put the black Alberta Ferretti with the Cesare
Paciotti T-strap heels? Or *what if* she paired the criss-crossed
Marchesa with the sparkly Louboutin peep-toe sling backs?

What ifs were what pushed her toward the edge and dared
her to leap. They were what had made her successful. They
were what drove her to try new things even when the possibility of failure was waiting with open arms.

What if she knocked on her former boyfriend's door, forced
him to face the feelings he'd had for her ten years ago and he
slammed the door in her face? She didn't particularly like rejection.

But *what if* he didn't reject her?

The Buick rolled to a stop in the gravel driveway by the lake and Kate cut the engine. She studied the house to see if there was life inside or if she'd need to take her treats and go home. Only a flickering glow illuminated the pleated shades in the front window. Puffs of gray smoke spiraled from the chimney and confirmed a fire was burning in the fireplace.

She seriously hoped Matt wasn't entertaining one of his potential June Cleavers.

She gathered up her goodies and whistled to the pup to follow. Like the good boy he was, he lifted his leg on a nearby bush before they climbed the steps to the front door. From within the house she heard music—soft, romantic music.

Crap.

Matt probably did have someone inside and she was about to be a party crasher. She tried to peer through the shades with no luck. And as she stood on his front porch with tasty treats, delicious champagne, and, just in case, wearing her sexiest matching bra and panties, she knew she had to make a decision. Did she risk humiliating herself? Then again, the reason she was there had nothing to do with personal pride and everything to do with matters of the heart.

The cold air stung her cheeks as she looked down to the pup by her side. "What do you think?"

His cheerful brown eyes looked up at her and he sneezed.

"Are you sure?"

He sneezed again.

"Okay, but if I look like an ass, it's going to be your fault."

She took a deep breath, raised her fist, and rapped hard on the rustic pine door.

A few seconds later, the door swung open and Matt stood there in threadbare jeans that hung low on his lean hips. A red plaid flannel hung from his broad shoulders, unbuttoned to reveal smooth taut skin over a perfect set of abs. His feet were bare. His hair was mussed. And he looked at her as if she had antennas growing out of the back of her head.

Uh-oh.

"Am I . . . interrupting?" she asked in a tone purposely oozing with sweetness while she balanced the tray in one hand and grasped the champagne bottle in the other.

His ice blue eyes narrowed and he stared at her from behind a thick fringe of dark lashes. His chiseled jawline clenched. "What do you want, Hollywood?" His acerbic tone bit into the moniker she'd strangely become accustomed to him calling her.

"Like I said, am I interrupting?"

He folded his arms across that perfect naked chest and rocked back on his heels. "Depends."

Obviously he wouldn't be of any help. She rose to the balls of her feet and peered over his shoulder. When she didn't see any apron-wearing prospective brides, she went with her gut. Not that her intuition had ever led her in the right direction before. Still, she could always hope for a first time.

She edged past him and strolled into the living room like she owned the place. "Come on, pup." A flash of golden fur made a beeline for the rug in front of a huge stone fireplace that showcased a roaring fire. He curled up and laid his head on his front paws, watching her as though he knew she was about to make a total fool of herself.

Kate glanced around the room to find the place sparsely decorated in an Adirondack style without the typical bear or moose motif. Just comfortable furniture, warm earthy colors and rustic wood. "Nice place."

Matt stood in the doorway as though debating whether to toss her out or lock her in. Finally he closed the door and the icy draft retreated. A little.

"What the hell do you think you're doing?" he asked, making his way toward her—step by intimidating step.

Heart thumping, she set the dessert tray down on the coffee table, listened to the song playing on the stereo and grinned up at him. "Never thought of you as a Bublé kind of guy, Deputy Ryan."

A frown furrowed the smooth skin between his dark brows. "I like all kinds of music."

"Uh-huh." She brushed past him, went into the kitchen, and searched the cupboards for champagne glasses. "You just seem more like the Lynyrd Skynyrd type to me."

"What's wrong with Michael Bublé?"

"Nothing. He's great."

"You know him?"

She shrugged, pulled down two wine glasses from a middle shelf, and set them on the granite counter. "We've met a time or two."

"Shit." He stalked to the stereo and snapped off the CD.

"You didn't have to turn him off," she said, grabbing the Moët and peeling off the foil cover. "I love his voice."

"I'm sure you do since you know him up close and personal."

His sharp tone sent a shiver through her heart. "Oooh, do I detect a note of jealousy?"

"What the hell are you doing here, Kate?" he demanded instead of owning up to the truth.

"I need to use you."

His eyes widened. "Pardon me?"

"I brought a peace offering to thank you for finishing the paint job at the Shack. I didn't expect that. It was a very nice gesture."

"It was no big deal."

She locked eyes with him. "It was a big deal to me. You saved me a lot of work. So thank you." She nodded toward the tray. "And to repay you for your random act of kindness, I brought you some samples of desserts I'm adding to the Sugar Shack's menu. I needed an impartial opinion. Maggie taste-tested everything several times but she's no help. If it contains anything that resembles sugar, she gives it an instant thumb's-up."

She twisted the wire muzzle to release the champagne cork but before it could pop Matt asked, "What's with that?"

"Everything tastes better with champagne."

He glanced at the label and then at her. "I'm not into your fancy stuff, Hollywood. I'm more of a beer kind of guy. Regardless of whose music I listen to."

She gave the wire a final twist. "And you feel totally secure with your masculinity."

"Absofuckinglutely."

"Do you have someone upstairs?" she blurted out, then cringed at her less than composed delivery.

His hesitation raised the hair on the back of her neck. Her chest tightened.

"No," he finally admitted.

Kate had to catch herself when relief pushed from her lungs. At that moment, her thumbs dislodged the cork. It rocketed from the bottle and bounced off the ceiling. She winced. "Oops."

He didn't bother to look up and check for damage. Instead his eyes remained glued on her, on every move she made, on every breath she took. She filled the two glasses and handed one to him on her way into the living room. "Pretend it's Budweiser."

He stood in the kitchen a minute, obviously contemplating his choices. Then she heard a manly sigh. Or was that an exasperated groan?

She gave the pup a stroke between his ears before she plopped down on a studded leather armchair next to the fireplace. The heat radiated and made her feel warm and toasty. Matt kept his distance by sitting across from her on the sofa. He grabbed a woolen print pillow and tucked it in his lap as though it would protect him. From her.

Or maybe he was hiding something.

She could only hope.

"You name that dog yet?" he asked in a gruff tone.

"He's not mine to name."

"How long has he *not* been yours?"

"Ummmm, a while?"

"Yeah. He's yours."

Had he been conspiring with her mother? "There's no way I can keep him. I live in a condo in L.A. and I sublet an apartment in Manhattan. I'm never home. It wouldn't be fair."

"Since when is life fair?"

The innuendo couldn't be more clear. Ignoring the squeak in the leather, she eased forward in the chair and sipped her champagne. The fire snapped and crackled while she worked up the courage to ask the question he'd dodged the other night. When she found it, she looked him square in the eye. "I need to know, Matt."

The firelight reflected in his pale blue eyes as he watched her from across the room.

"The truth," she said quietly, "About what you were going to ask me before I left."

"So the desserts and the champagne were all a setup?"

"No. I genuinely wanted to thank you." She set her glass down on a sandstone coaster. "And I genuinely wanted your opinion. But I also want to know what you were going to ask."

"Why rehash what you already know? Hell, that's why you ran, isn't it? And do *not* try to tell me you just found out."

The pained expression on his face made her stomach queasy. "I just found out."

"Bullshit."

She slowly shook her head. "The truth, Matt. Please."

"Why does it matter?"

"It just does."

He stared into her eyes before he answered. His chest lifted on a sharp intake of air. "Yes. I wanted to marry you. Yes. I asked for your parents' permission. Yes. I bought a ring."

An ache twisted her heart as she pictured in her mind how he must have felt the day he'd discovered her gone. She pictured all the passion she'd missed from this man who had so much to give. A man who would do anything to protect the ones he loved. Who would even protect her from embarrassing herself when she did stupid things. Matt Ryan was a man who would be a friend and lover like she'd never known. Who would have laughed with her. Cried with her. And trusted her with his heart.

She hadn't appreciated that when she'd been a young inexperienced girl, but as a woman she appreciated that a man like him was priceless.

"We were only kids, Matt." she said, trying in vain to keep the tremble from her voice.

"I'd been legal to buy alcohol for over a year. Hardly a kid." He shot from the sofa and stormed to the big window overlooking the lake. He turned his back to her and downed his glass of champagne. "You don't get it, do you?"

The tension in his shoulders gave away what his quiet words did not. And there was no way she would force him to say the words that were obviously too painful for him to speak.

I loved you.

She went to him. "I didn't leave town because I heard you wanted to marry me. I honestly had no idea until the other day." She stood behind him, inhaling that fresh-from-the-shower manly clean. Their reflections looked back from the glass. She regretted her actions a decade ago. She'd hurt more of those she cared about than she even knew.

Her heart gave a painful twist. "I was selfish. I'd been waiting and waiting for that scholarship. When it finally arrived, I'd expected everyone to be excited for me. But they weren't. At least my mother wasn't. We had a horrible argument. Just . . . horrible." She shook her head to rid herself of the sorrow that night had left deep in her soul. "And I regret the awful things that were said that night."

"What was said, Kate?" He didn't turn. Didn't look at her. "What was so horrible that you would leave without a word to anyone who cared about you?"

The words her mother had screamed that night meant nothing now. She knew what was in her mother's heart. But Matt needed to know. For them to move forward with any kind of relationship, even just a friendship, she needed him to let go of the terrible way they'd parted.

"We argued for hours," she explained. My dad tried to stop us but my mother wouldn't let it go until she'd had the last word. Things escalated to name calling and she told me . . . I was a worthless dreamer who'd never amount to anything."

He looked at her over his shoulder and the understanding in his eyes nearly brought her to her knees.

"She should never have said that."

She shrugged. "She got the last word after all."

"You must have been devastated."

She glanced down at the floor and shook her head. "Beyond. I was young. Vulnerable. And I couldn't believe the one person I thought I could trust most would think so little of me."

"I'm sorry for what she said."

"Not your apology to make, Matt. But now you know why I left the way I did, without a word to anyone. So no one would stop me. I left because I needed to discover who I was. Not who I was in comparison to Dean or Kelly or who my mother thought I should be." She filled her lungs with air and let it out slowly. "I should have said good-bye. It breaks my heart that . . . all these years you thought I left because of you."

He shrugged one broad shoulder. "It happened a long time ago. No big deal."

"It's a big deal to me." She wrapped her arms around his waist and rested her head against the back of his soft flannel shirt. A skitter of nerves rippled down his back and fluttered against her cheek. "I'm not what you think I am, Matt. I'm not who you think I am."

He turned and her hands slid to his arms. He looked down into her eyes and she felt his gaze warm her soul.

"Then who are you, Kate?"

It was then she knew she had to stop fooling herself.

I'm a woman who could very easily fall in love with you.

"I would never have left without saying good-bye had I known how you felt," she said. "Never."

"I told you."

She shook her head, ran her hand up his arm to cup the back of his head. Her fingers curled in his short dark hair. "If you had, I might have stayed."

She drew his head down and whispered against his mouth. "Give me a reason to stay now."

CHAPTER FOURTEEN

Her sweet warm breath swept across his mouth and Matt knew he did not have the power to push her away.

He'd loved her for as long as he could remember. The stubborn girl who'd never cry uncle. The thoughtful girl who worked hard to help her community. The tender-hearted girl who'd find homes for lost pets.

The woman in his arms was the same.

The knowledge that she hadn't run because of him opened up his soul and he was willing to let her in. This was what he'd wanted for so long. For her to come to him. To want him as much as he wanted her.

Her free hand wandered between the open buttons on his shirt and the touch of her cool fingers against his bare flesh lit him on fire. Her lips brushed his while her fingertips traced lazy circles across his chest.

Passion raged through him but he didn't just want a good time between the sheets. He wanted more. He wanted to hold her and kiss her and take his time loving her.

"Forgive me?" A little moan rumbled in her chest and she

pressed herself against him. "Please, Matt. I promise I'll make things right."

She looked up at him with that familiar pleading in her eyes. *Please kiss me, Matt. Please touch me. Please love me.*

Had she forgotten those were the same words she'd said to him years ago—the night he'd made love to her that first time? Had she forgotten how potent the word *please* became when she used it in conjunction with his name?

"Don't make promises you can't keep, Kate."

She looked deep into his eyes. "I won't."

He slipped his hands beneath her worn leather coat, slid it from her shoulders, and tossed it on a nearby chair. Then he took her by the hand and led her up the stairs to his bedroom.

That morning he hadn't bothered to toss his dirty uniform in the hamper or straighten his sheets. Tonight he didn't care. Because right now, all he could think about was getting her into his bed, wrapping himself around her and holding her close.

The curtains over the French doors were open and muted moonlight shone through the glass. Fat glistening snowflakes had begun to fall and gather on the rail of the deck outside the doors. He didn't turn on a light. He'd seen Kate's beautiful body in the stark overhead fluorescents at the bakery. Tonight he wanted to see her bathed in nature's light. Just as he'd seen her that long ago night and so many times in his dreams.

Drawing her against him, he cupped her face in his hands and kissed her with passion and hope, tenderness and pleasure. He craved her body and wanted to touch her soul. He wanted to feed his hunger for her and bury himself in all that he remembered she could be, in all they had once been together.

"Tell me what you want, Kate."

"I want you," she said, handing him the words he'd waited ten years to hear. She leaned into him, rose to her toes and in a husky, needful voice whispered across his lips. "All of you. I want to kiss you all over."

Lost in her sweet beckoning scent and the need surging through his blood, he slid his fingers into her silky hair and moved his mouth down the graceful column of her neck. "Me first."

Her head dropped back, allowing him access and he gently sucked the flesh at the curve of her throat. Her pulse throbbed beneath his tongue and he slid his hand beneath her velvety sweater. His fingertips tingled to life when they met her warm skin. He unbuttoned her top and tossed it aside as he stood there, looking at her bathed in moonlight in a light blue bra that lifted her breasts and formed perfect mounds above the lace edge. His thumb traced slow erotic circles across the satiny material and her nipple pebbled beneath his touch. Then he undid the front clasp and eased the straps down her arms.

Her silky hair fell across her bare shoulders and tickled the crests of her plump breasts. "So beautiful," he murmured as he trailed his fingers slowly down the smooth skin between those perfect peaks. His body pulsed, his erection throbbed. He lowered his head, sucked a rosy tip into his mouth, and circled it with his tongue. Her throaty moan shuddered through him.

She arched against him. When what he really wanted was to strip her of the rest of her clothes and plunge himself into her hot, slick body, he forced his hands to be gentle as they slid down her curves. He knelt before her, removed her boots and unzipped her jeans. Then he slid the fabric down her legs until she stood before him in nothing but tiny blue panties. He drew her against him and pressed his mouth against the little lace triangle that kept him from what he wanted.

He could feel her moist heat through the thin fabric.

She wanted him too.

The knowledge turned him on more than anything he could remember. As his tongue licked and teased along the outline of the lace, his hands slid up the backs of her silky thighs. He tucked his fingers into the elastic and drew the fabric down her legs. Then gently grasping her firm behind, he brought her to his mouth. He pressed his lips to the apex of her thighs and swept his tongue between the parted folds of her flesh.

"Oh!" Her head dropped back, her knees buckled, and he grasped her behind to hold her in place.

Slowly, methodically, and hungrily, he alternated loving her as though he had all day and as though he had only seconds. She gripped his hair in her hands. A shudder rippled through her body and she cried out, "Oh. God. Matt."

He stayed with her until she let go a deep, satisfied moan and slumped against him. He smiled as he kissed his way up her belly to her mouth.

Between hot, feeding kisses, his name broke from her lips on a sigh. "Matt. I need you inside me." She pushed away his shirt and reached for the button on his jeans. "Right now."

Tangled up with powerful feelings of possessiveness and tenderness, hope and desire, his good intentions snapped. She pushed the denim and his boxer-briefs down his legs. He'd barely kicked away the material trapping his ankles before she took his hard length into her hand. He closed his eyes and a low groan of pleasure rushed from his throat as her grip tightened around him.

Deep in his chest his heart raced and he knew he could come just like that with her hand curled around him. But that wasn't what he wanted.

"And I need you," he said with a low growl. "Right now." He reached for her hands and wrapped them around his neck. He lifted her onto the bed and followed her down. Then he kissed her. Nibbled at her. Drew her lower lip into his mouth and deepened the kiss with unyielding broad sweeps of his tongue. She responded with eager hands pulling him closer, racing down his sides to his butt. His knee nudged her legs apart and he poised himself intimately against her heat. She arched against him.

When he covered her with his body, she gasped. He buried his face in her neck, breathed in her sugar cookie scent, and basked in the reeling awareness floating through his head.

"Love me, Matt. Please. Please. Please. Love me now."

"Let me in," he whispered but thought *I'll love you always.*

She opened her legs while he rolled on a condom. When he slid into her, she completely gave herself up to him and the giant ache in his heart disappeared.

The clock struck midnight as Kate straddled Matt's lean hips and fed him another bite of amaretto chocolate swirl fudge. Neither of them wore a stitch and she was amazed at how comfortable she suddenly felt in her own skin. Of course, that might have something to do with the warm masculine skin pressed against hers. Between talking and laughing, they'd made love twice. Three times if you counted the fooling around they'd done in the shower just now. She couldn't get enough of him and she never wanted to leave this cozy cocoon they'd made in the warmth of his bed.

"Do you like this one?" she asked while the delicacy melted in his mouth.

He smiled and drew her down against his chest. "I like you."

She laughed and laid her head against his shoulder. "Since when? Before I took my clothes off or after?"

His warm palm caressed her naked back in slow, hypnotizing strokes and his deep voice rumbled against her breast. "Always."

"I'll bet you say that to all the girls."

"There are no *all the girls*."

That got her attention. "What about your list?"

He lifted one shoulder in a shrug. "Stupid idea."

"Seriously stupid. Thank God you're such a smart man." She kissed him and the taste of the sweet chocolate on his tongue swept through her mouth. Their hearts beat together, swift and uneasy like butterflies trapped in a box. And she had to admit what she'd felt for quite some time. She framed his handsome face between her hands and looked down into his eyes. "I like you too." She kissed him again. "I like the way you smile at crotchety old ladies and make them feel young again. I like the way you took a falling-down cabin and made it a home. I definitely like the way you grill a trout. And maybe I even like the fact that you're probably the most honest person I know. Even when that honesty is directed at me and it hurts like hell."

His hand slid down the curve of her spine and he smiled. "Are you buttering me up for a reason?"

"Mmmmmm, only so I can do this." She kissed her way

down his chest, paying as close attention to his hard nipples as he'd paid to hers. While he slid his fingers into her hair, she ran her tongue down his flat belly to the line of fine hair below his belly button and his very serious erection. "And . . . this."

She swirled the swollen head with her tongue and looked up into his lust-heavy eyes. "Especially this." She took him into her mouth, deepening the suction and then easing back to tease him with just the tip of her tongue. As she lightly scraped her teeth across the head he gave a long, sighing moan.

"Do you like that?" she asked.

He drew her up against him, rolled her over and eased into her warmth. "What do you think?"

An intense pleasure filled her and curled around her heart like a woolen mitten. At that moment, Kate knew that in Matt Ryan's arms was exactly where she wanted to be.

Maybe even forever.

Morning filtered through the French doors on pale light and Matt lifted his head off the pillow. Judging by the several inches of white powder that lined the deck rail, snow had fallen all during the night. Naked, Kate was pressed to his side with her head on his shoulder. Her no-name dog had curved himself around their feet at the bottom of the bed. And Matt sank into his favorite fantasy of waking every day with Kate curled up to him just like this.

Last night had been unexpected and yet more than he ever could have imagined. They'd consumed her champagne and between making love and feasting on each other, they devoured her treats. It didn't take long for him to realize the woman he'd imagined for so many years was more than just a fantasy. He'd waited so long for her to come back he could hardly believe she was lying in his arms. His heart pounded. She fit perfectly. As sure as the snow fell outside his window, he knew Kate was exactly where she belonged—in his bed and in his life.

But how to convince her of that was another matter.

As if she could read his mind, she stirred in his arms, lifted her chin, and gave him a sleepy smile with lips still flushed from his kisses. He bent his head and kissed them again.

"Morning." She stretched and the puppy lifted his head with a *don't disturb me* look in his big brown eyes.

"Thanks for not sneaking out," Matt murmured.

"What? And leave all this coziness to go out in the cold? I don't think so."

He laughed. "Well, thank God you didn't stay because of me. That would have been awkward."

"Mmmmm." She trailed her finger across his chest. "I have to admit, you are much better than a silk comforter."

"And you've given me a huge appetite." He lifted her finger to his lips and kissed it. "How about some breakfast?"

"It's Sunday." She rolled on top of him and pressed her sweet, warm breasts into his chest. "How about we stay right here and I worship your body a little while longer?"

Sometimes it was just best to let a woman have her way.

Icy wind whipped across the shield of the helmet stuck on Kate's head as she clung to Matt from the back of his snowmo-bile. At a brisk speed they glided across the blanketed valley until they reached an ungroomed trail that wound through the forest thick with snow-dusted pines. As the incline increased, Kate snuggled closer to Matt. He let go of the handlebar long enough to gently squeeze the hand she had tucked into the pocket of his coat.

She breathed in a lung full of clean mountain air. This was a hell of a way to travel for breakfast.

Having the chance to wrap your arms around the most gorgeous man in Montana? Stellar. Add in the scenery? Unbelievable. Kate had forgotten about the beauty of the backcountry. She'd forgotten the benefits of having nature's playground in your own backyard. In L.A. the only wilderness to be found was Griffith Park, which, for the most part, was usually loaded up with picnickers and tourists.

Here, they were completely alone.

The snowmobile fishtailed as they rounded a curve up to a stunning vista where rugged mountain peaks continued to rise above the snow-covered valley floor. When Matt slowed the machine to a stop and turned off the engine, Kate jumped off the back, pulled the helmet from her head, and wearing a too big pair of his snow pants, slogged through the snow to the rocky edge of the rise.

Several hundred feet below, the lake sparkled sapphire in the sun. Overhead, fluffy white clouds drifted across a turquoise sky. The whole scene looked like a Currier and Ives postcard.

"Wow! This . . . is amazing." She did a slow spin to view the panorama, then turned to find Matt still straddling the snowmobile, watching her from behind the visor of his black helmet. "Aren't you going to come look? The scenery is beautiful."

He lifted off the helmet and smiled at her. "I'll say."

Her cheeks flushed. But maybe that was only from the cold. "You're not looking at the scenery."

"I'm looking at the best thing I've seen in years." He swung his leg over the seat and walked toward her. He pulled the gloves from his hands and brushed the backs of his fingers across her cheeks before cupping her face and lowering his head.

His lips were cool. His tongue warm. And as he kissed her slow and sweet, Kate's heart swelled. Foreheads together, they looked into each other's eyes. She slid her hands up the smooth fabric of his down jacket. "Thank you for bringing me here."

He grinned. "Best place in Montana for breakfast."

"I don't see a restaurant."

"I've got something better." He kissed her fingers before he released her to grab a pack from the snowmobile.

She watched him walk away, admiring his long legs and confident carriage. "Yes, you do, Deputy Ryan."

He turned and caught her smiling. "Are you checking me out?"

She lifted an eyebrow and nodded. Laughing, he turned his back. Temptation proved too much. She scooped up a handful of snow, patted it into a ball, and let it fly. It landed with a splat on the back of his coat. "Oops."

When he faced her, humor lit up those already bright eyes. "So that's the way you want to play, huh?" In a blink he was after her. She squeaked, laughed, and dodged him as he made a grab. But the pants she'd borrowed were way too big and way too long and her efforts were wasted. She went down. Hooking her hands in his coat, she pulled him with her. With a *whoof* they landed in the snow. Him on top. Her loving every second.

Their laughter stopped when they looked into each other's

eyes. Hearts pounding their lips met. When they came up for air he asked, "Hungry?"

"Starving." Though she wasn't at all sure she was talking about food.

He got to his feet, pulled her up, and dusted the snow off her backside. Then he went to the snowmobile, unzipped some kind of backpack and withdrew an insulated bag, thermos, and two travel mugs. "While you were taking a shower, I made some coffee and breakfast burritos."

"Wow. Handsome and can cook too. Got any sweetener in there?"

He held up a ziplock bag containing small packets. "This is the only time you'll see me carrying pink."

She laughed. "You are a saint."

"Nah, I just didn't want to hear you whining. Come on over here." His long legs carried him over to a grouping of rocks where he proceeded to brush off the snow and lay a folded blanket for her to sit.

"What about you?" She asked, perching herself on the warm wool cushion. "Won't your butt freeze?"

"Will you warm me up if I do?"

"Yes."

"Then I hate to admit that with these snow pants I won't feel the cold at all." He sat on a rock behind her, took the aluminum-wrapped burritos from the bag and handed one to her.

Kate pulled her gloves from her hands and peeled away the foil. Steam rose from the egg, cheese, and sausage concoction and she took a bite. "Either I really am starving or this is excellent."

"Well, we did work up an appetite before we got out of bed."

"Mmmmm. Great way to start a morning."

"The best," he said. "I'm glad you agreed to come here with me."

"I am too. I'd forgotten there's more to see around here than just beautiful downtown Deer Lick."

"Then I'm sure you've forgotten the hot springs and how much you liked going there after dark."

"I remember loving the hot springs and how much *you* liked going there after dark because I wouldn't wear a bathing suit."

He sipped at his coffee and chuckled. "You can hardly blame me."

"Yeah, well you weren't the only one who got a free peek. And may I say you certainly lived up to the advertisement."

He laughed. "I'll take that as a compliment."

"Please do." She finished the last bite of egg burrito and wadded up the foil.

"Kate?"

"Hmm?"

"I missed you when you left."

"I know." And with all honesty she said, "I missed you too."

As they gazed out across the wonder of the Montana wilderness, she leaned back against him. He slid his arms around her, locked their fingers together, and rested his chin on top of her head.

Kate had been to Hollywood, New York, Paris, and Rome, but nowhere was more wonderful than sitting on a mountaintop wrapped in Matt Ryan's arms.

Chapter Fifteen

Almost a week had passed since Kate had flung herself on the mercy of Matt's doorstep, hauling sugar-laden desserts and fine champagne as backup bribery. And every night since, after she'd worked to finish up the bakery makeover, she'd locked the doors and put her mother's cruise ship on auto pilot to his house.

Today as she finished up restocking the display cases and the lunch supplies he walked through the door and toward her take-out counter. While his long muscular legs carried him closer, she imagined him sans clothes and aviators. Mmmm, maybe he could leave the sunglasses on. They did add a little mystery to his already sexy appeal.

"Good afternoon, Deputy Ryan. What can I do for you today?"

He leaned his big hand on the counter, pretending to peruse the new menu above her head. But not even the aviators perched on his slightly imperfect nose could hide where those pale blue eyes were really fixated.

A slow, seductive smile curled his lips. "How about a tuna

sub. A repeat of this morning. No tomato. A repeat of last night. An iced tea. And something new for when you come home tonight."

Home. Hmmm. She liked the sound of that. "And would you like mayo? Black panties or white?"

His smile broke into a grin. "I'm in a dark mood today."

"Then black it is." She flashed him a wink, spun on the toe of her Chucks, and since they were alone, went about making his tuna sub in the most erotic fashion possible. He removed the sunglasses and hooked them in the pocket of his shirt. The intense way he watched her made her feel beautiful and desired and way, way hungry for him.

She wrapped his sandwich, added chips, and tossed in a few brownies. Then she slid the order across the counter. "Deputy?" She slid her hand over the top of his when he reached for the bag. "I wonder if you wouldn't mind helping me in the stock room." She batted her eyelashes to sufficiently put Scarlet O'Hara to shame. "I need some sugar and it's just too much for little old me to reach alone." Ah, God, she loved the fun and games that came with a comfortable relationship.

His blue eyes brightened. "Why certainly, ma'am." He tipped two fingers to the brim of his Stetson. "I'd be happy to help."

He followed her to the stock room and with every step, excitement fluttered from Kate's heart to the tips of her breasts and way, way lower. She could not get enough of this man.

The moment they were both inside the storage room he kicked the door shut and pressed her against the wall. He leaned in, his clean-shaven face brushed against her cheek.

His clean, sexy male scent wrapped around her like the best of birthday presents.

"Where do I find the sugar, Kate?" he whispered against her mouth. "Is it here?" He kissed her forehead. "Or here?" His lips brushed the tip of her nose. "Or maybe . . . it's right here."

Bull's-eye.

His mouth covered hers and he kissed her in a deliberate, tender, and incredibly intense way that made her knees go weak and her heart pound. His lips were warm and soft as his tongue coaxed, caressed, and promised a heaven Kate knew he could deliver.

She moaned, threw her arms around his neck and his soft feeding kisses turned to unrestrained hunger. His hand shot up beneath her white apron and cupped her breast through her sweater. His palm molded against her and the hot caress sent zaps of electricity down into her jeans. When she thought she could take no more until she got her hands on his warm skin, he slid his big hands down to her bottom and lifted. She gave up all hope of decorum and wrapped her legs around him.

He leaned his big body into hers and she pressed herself against the swollen crest of his erection. His satisfaction groaned deep in his chest. With both of his hands on her butt, holding her tight against his very proper uniform khakis, he murmured, "Too bad you're wearing jeans. Or I could slide your panties down your legs and have my way with you right now."

"I can take them off fast." She panted like she'd run a mile at the high school track. "I swear." He responded by sliding his hot mouth down the sensitive curve of her neck and gently sucking. Desperate to feel him deep inside her, she reached for her zipper.

The radio transmitter attached to his shoulder squawked and crackled. Then dispatch called out a series of numbers and Matt pulled back.

Wham! Reality intruded and left them both gasping for air.

"That's for me," he said.

When her senses floated back to earth, Kate giggled. "Busted."

Matt leaned his forehead against hers, pressed his erection into her one last time and groaned a sad sound. "Not the first time that's happened."

"Sad but true." Reluctantly she unwound her legs and he lowered her feet to the floor. She dropped her head back against the wall and breathed deep to steady her heart.

He leaned in and kissed her again. "If you promise to be a good girl, we can finish what we started after we get off work."

She wound her arms around his neck and gave him a kiss she hoped would make him think of good things to come. "It's a date."

After a few moments of readjusting, rearranging, and getting it together, Matt followed her to the front of the shop. Before he walked around the counter, she grabbed his lunch bag and tossed it to him. "You might want to use that to cover up so you don't give any little old ladies strolling down the street a heart attack."

He didn't bother looking down. He just gave her a private smile, grabbed his iced tea, and headed toward the door.

"Thanks for your help, Deputy Ryan."

He turned and lifted a dark brow. "Gotta go, beautiful."

Through the front window she watched him open the door to his patrol car and slip inside. A nice little hum vibrated through her body when she thought of the naughty promises he'd just made for after they both got off work. When she went home to him. She sighed.

She was falling in love with him.

She could feel it in every breath she took. Like she was falling from a cloud, spinning and twirling through the air with nothing to catch her but those big strong arms that had held her last night while she slept.

With only a day left to wrap up the finishing touches on her bakery remodel she scooted off to the storage room. From the pocket of her apron her cell phone chimed. She glanced at the caller ID, then hit *answer*. "Hey Josh."

"OMG!" Josh's panic wailed through the phone. "You have to be in London next week!"

"What? Why?"

"Our favorite wreck of a songbird just landed a role in the new Peter Jackson film. They're doing a promo shoot and Peggy, agent tormentor of the century, insists you be there."

"What happened to Inara flying away to temporary lockdown?"

"It's off. Apparently a ten million dollar price tag tops lack of decorum. Besides, who says no to an Oscar-winning director?"

"Not anyone with common sense."

"Correct. Look, I can book you on a flight out of Deer Spit tomorrow morning to L.A. You can catch a connecting flight from there."

"I can't just go running off, Josh. My dad needs me." *And I'm in the middle of remodeling the bakery and I have the bakery grand reopening plus the grand opening of Cindi's Attic and . . . a beautiful man to go home to.*

An exaggerated sigh whooshed through the phone. "Sweetie, exactly how long is your dad going to need you?"

"You can't put a time frame on something like that and you know it."

"Fine." His snippy bitch side surfaced with a vengeance. "I didn't want to have to tell you this but you leave me no choice."

"Cut the drama and just say it."

"You *have* to come back. Peggy wasn't happy when I told her you wouldn't come back to play Miss Manners to her number one catastrophe of a client. But she said she'd let it slide. Once. When I spoke to her not ten minutes ago, she told me you already used your get-out-of-jail-free card. She reminded me in a way only Peggy can, that you signed a contract to be Inara's stylist. And this time, she's going to hold you to it."

All the happiness that had been in Kate's heart before the phone rang shriveled like a grape in the sun. Emotion tangled in her stomach and tightened in her throat. "Or?"

"She'll sue."

"Shit."

"Exactly."

"Josh, you've been my assistant for three years. You've been with me from the beginning. You deserve to take the lead. I completely trust you to make all the right decisions."

"I appreciate your confidence, Kate, but I already tried that angle. And even though you and I both know I am unbelievably fabulous Peggy wouldn't buy it. Her exact words were 'Kate signed the contract. Kate is the business. Kate better have her skinny ass in London next week or I will sue her for every pathetic rhinestone she's ever earned.'"

"Wow." Kate flinched at the tone and delivery of Peggy's message. "You remembered all that? Word for word?"

"I am nothing if not efficient."

While Josh related the rest of the not-so-nice things Peggy had proclaimed or threatened, Kate paced the length of the back room. When the admonitions ended, she stopped and dropped her forehead to the office door with a thunk. "I'm up shit creek, aren't I?"

"Without the proverbial paddle."

There were times in his life Matt could clearly identify as *a moment*. Lying in bed with Kate wrapped in his arms after making love ranked top on his list. With her head resting on his shoulder, he caressed the soft silky strands of her hair. She smelled like sugar cookies and sex and promises. And as soon as he regained his strength, he planned to love her some more.

For ten years he'd learned to live without her. He didn't think he could manage that again. When she left his bed in the mornings, he missed her. When he left the Shack after he picked up his lunch, he missed her. Hell, when she went downstairs for a glass of water, he missed her. They'd found a peace, a rhythm to being with each other. And hopefully, with enough time, they could make it permanent.

She shifted in his arms and looked up at him. "Matt?"

The way she spoke his name gave his heart an uncomfortable squeeze. "Yeah?"

"Something came up today after you left the Shack." She propped herself up on an elbow.

"What's that?" He repositioned the pillow beneath his head to see her better.

"I got a call from Josh."

"The non-boyfriend gay assistant Josh?"

She nodded but didn't laugh.

"I . . . have to leave next week," she said.

Everything inside him turned ice cold. "Leave?"

"I have to go to London."

And the fantasy ends . . . three, two, one . . . now. "Why?"

"One of my top clients just signed a ten million dollar deal and I have to be at a promo shoot."

"Your assistant can't go?"

"It's complicated."

"What's complicated? I thought he's been taking care of things for you."

"He can't this time."

"He can't or won't?"

She shook her head. "He'd love to, believe me."

"Then why doesn't he?"

"My client won't allow it."

There were so many things wrong with that statement he didn't even know where to begin. He sat up. "What do you mean they won't *allow* it?"

"I have a contract and she's threatening to sue if I'm not there."

"So basically this person can control your life?"

The lips he'd been kissing just a few minutes ago tightened

as she too sat up. "I hadn't thought of it like that but I guess that's one way to look at it."

"How many other people have you signed control over your life to?"

She shrugged one bare shoulder. "A few."

"A few meaning?"

"Maybe three or four."

"So three or four people can basically tell you what to do, where to be, and how you can live your life because they need you to *dress* them? They can tell you to walk away from your dad when he needs you?" *Or me when I need you?*

"I . . . um . . ."

"Are these the so-called clients who pay you to be their friend?"

"Matt, you don't understand." Her brows slammed together. "This isn't just all about me. I'm a business owner. I have an employee and clients to consider."

He inhaled a calming breath and nodded. "How long will you be gone?"

"I'm not sure. After I leave London I'll probably go back to L.A. and finish up some projects."

"So you're leaving next week and you don't know when or if you'll be back?"

"I'll . . . be back—"

"You don't sound very confident about that." *How had this conversation just turned into a nuclear meltdown?* "Exactly how long are these *clients* going to rule your life, Kate?"

"I don't have exact dates."

"But until your contracts are up you're at their beck and call."

"You make it sound so horrible."

Maybe it wasn't for her, but for him? Yeah. It sucked. They both sat there, silent for several breaths while he tried to still his aching heart.

"Come with me," she finally said.

"What?"

"Don't yell. It was just an idea."

"I'm not yelling and it's a shitty idea."

"Why?"

He got out of bed, grabbed his jeans from the floor and shoved his legs through. "Why?"

She drew the sheet up to cover herself. "I already said that."

He couldn't stop his eyes from rolling or the dagger of pain that stabbed him in the brain. She didn't get it. At all. Damn it. He should have known this would happen. "Because I'm running for sheriff," he said, stating the obvious. "I have signs posted all over town. Perhaps you've seen them."

Her chin lifted. "Of course I've seen them. It doesn't have to be—"

"Kate?" He planted his hands on his hips. "I don't want to just blend in like the people in L.A. I want to make a difference. I can't go running off. My life is here. I'm a part of something that means a lot to me and in just a few days I plan to stand up in front of the entire community and convince them why they should elect me to protect them, their children, and their homes. How would it look if I just took off on a whim?"

"I understand." She scooted off the bed, taking the comforter with her. "But you don't have to get so mad. It was just a suggestion."

He wrapped his fingers around her wrist to keep her from escaping. "Why would you even ask me to go?"

"I think you know why." She tugged her arm.

He tugged back. "Humor me."

She looked at the ceiling, the door, anywhere but at him. "Because I might . . . have feelings for you."

"You might? Or you do?"

"Is there a difference?"

"The fact that you even have to ask pretty much tells me everything I need to know."

"It's not like I'll be gone forever." Her palm slid down his chest. "I'm so sorry."

"Bad timing, huh?"

"I don't suppose I could interest you in a long-distance relationship?" she said, obviously trying to lighten the mood. "Maybe a little phone sex? I could even fake a British accent."

"Would *you* be happy with that?" he asked, knowing the truth even though he'd tried to erase it in the past few days. *I'm still not enough.*

"No." She turned away and slipped from his arms. "I hope you can try to understand how important this is to me."

"Then it's important for you to go." Aching to touch her again he reached for her, then thought better and dropped his hand to his side.

She bit at her bottom lip. "Matt, I—"

"I wish you well, Kate. I really do. And I hope you find what you're looking for." But he had to be honest with himself and admit that what she was looking for *wasn't* him.

Everything inside him urged him to go to her, take her in

his arms and things would work out just fine. But that was a lie and he knew it. What he wanted and what she wanted were on such different ends of the spectrum they'd never be able to meet in the middle.

An ache deep in his chest made it hard to breathe as he watched her pick her clothes up off the floor and put them on. She slipped her arms through the sleeves of her coat and clutched it together near her heart.

She looked up at him. "I don't want to say good-bye."

A heavy sigh pushed from his lungs. "Easier now than later."

She searched his face, then nodded as tears slipped from her eyes. Then she cupped his cheek in her hand and rose up onto her toes and kissed him. He kept his arms at his sides and curled his fingers into his palms to keep from grabbing her and begging her not to go.

The kiss ended way too soon and she stepped away. "Good-bye, Matt."

She whispered his name on a sob and his heart shattered into a million pieces. He forced himself to stand there and watch the woman he loved walk out the door. When he heard her footsteps on his porch, he forced himself to walk out onto the balcony and watch her drive out of his life. He forced himself to feel the pain. And when all that was left were her tire tracks in the snow, he forced himself to go back inside—to face life a lot less hopeful than just a few hours ago.

The bottle of Jack in his kitchen cabinet called his name, promising a comfortable numb to take away the pain in his heart. The emptiness in his arms. A chill ran up his bare back and he opened his dresser to grab a T-shirt. From the back corner of the drawer a small white box peeked out from behind a layer of cotton shirts. He picked it up, flipped open the cover, and looked at the ring nestled in black velvet that had been hidden for a decade. He removed the ring and held it up to the light.

Easier to say good-bye now than later?

Who the fuck had he been kidding?

K ate felt like she'd been kicked in the chest by a team of stubborn mules. She grabbed a tissue from the box between the seats of the Buick and blew her nose. Everything that had just happened was all her fault and she had no one, absolutely no one, to blame but herself. She'd fallen totally and completely in love with Matt. And yet she'd just watched every ounce of their newly formed trust fade from his eyes like the last rays of sunlight fading into night. His walls had come up and he'd shut down.

A sob burst from her throat. How had she let that happen? There had always been the very real possibility that she'd have to leave. She'd wanted the life she'd made for herself in Hollywood. She'd gone hungry for it. She'd busted her ass for it. And now it just all seemed so inconsequential.

"Honey, please slow down or you'll spin out."

With no warning, Letty Silverthorne took up her place as Kate's backseat driver. Snow had fallen all day and the plows hadn't yet reached the side streets. Deep drifts grabbed at the Buick's tires making the car go a little squirrelly around the corners. Kate looked down at the speedometer.

"I'm crawling, Mother," she said on a hiccup. "Fifteen miles an hour is hardly NASCAR speed."

"Are you okay?"

Kate tightened her hands on the steering wheel and pushed a breath from her lungs if only to control the tears that had been a constant waterfall since she left Matt's house.

"Come on. Tell Mommy dearest what's wrong."

Kate hit the brakes. The Buick slid at least twenty feet and almost took out Mrs. Gooding's cat. Kate didn't watch to see if the calico made it to the other side of the street. She whipped around in her seat and faced her mother.

"No. I am not okay. And I really don't need your advice today."

"I wouldn't give it if I thought you didn't need it."

"I *don't* need it. I've managed very well on my own for the past ten years. I can manage for another fifty."

"That's what I'm afraid of."

With a mental image of her stuffed into some retirement community playing Yahtzee with a bunch of other old maids in their flowered muumuus, Kate protested. "I'm fine with alone." She was such a liar. She'd probably never be fine again as long as she lived.

"I don't believe you."

Kate frowned. She didn't feel like going into a tit-for-tat shootout with her mother. She just wanted to go home, crawl in bed, and cry till she fell asleep. "Just goes to show how much you know me."

"I *do* know you, sweetheart. I know you wouldn't put so much of your heart and soul into a shop where teenage girls can afford beautiful ball gowns if you didn't care."

"I was bored."

"I know you wouldn't have given that bakery the facelift it so sorely needed if you didn't care."

"Maybe I just needed a design fix."

"You wouldn't have volunteered to donate a sheet cake to the bunko club every month and even offered to be a dealer at casino night at the Grange if you didn't care."

"So I like to gamble a little. No big deal."

"For years, no one has paid attention to dreary old George Crosby at the used book store. Yet every day you take him a donut and a cup of orange spice tea. And rumor has it you've signed up to participate in the town's spring cleanup in May. You wouldn't do that if you didn't care."

"I got suckered in, that's all."

"Honey, you've melded yourself into this community and you don't even realize it."

The truth of her mother's words hit a homerun. At first, she hadn't realized she'd started to get involved in things. Maybe because she'd been enjoying herself. So why was it so hard to admit out loud? Why couldn't she just say "You're right, Mother. I love this place. I love Matt Ryan. And I'm not going anywhere."

Just a few days ago she'd shown up on his doorstep and forced him to admit that he'd loved her and had wanted to marry her. Then she'd thrown herself at him. And from that moment until she'd walked out his door she'd been happier than she could ever remember.

So why had she wussed out just now? What? Was she afraid of a little lawsuit? Was she afraid of Inara's agent and her smoker's hack and dragon nails? That kind of fear had nothing to do with it. If *she* made the decision to walk away that was one thing. But someone threatening to *take* it away was another.

Or was she just all talk? Was she really just afraid to fail? Just a big old sissy because she feared she wouldn't be the person everyone thought they saw? That she wouldn't be good enough? That she'd never measure up to their expectations?

Matt had been right, in L.A. everyone blended in and she'd just become a speck in the overblown, overindulged, over-Botoxed landscape. But in Deer Lick, everyone knew what you did and they kept you in their crosshairs. They knew what kind of salad dressing you chose, if you ordered onions on your burgers. They knew how many times a year you visited the dentist and what brand of tampons you wore. And as much as she loved being a part of this community, that just plain scared the crap out of her.

She couldn't live with herself if she disappointed them. If she disappointed Matt. She couldn't live with herself if somewhere down the road he realized she was just a big giant nothing special. She couldn't live with herself if she wasn't the right woman to make him happy. She was complicated. Sometimes cranky. Often stubborn. And once in a while she was just a big chicken shit.

She should have told him how she felt.

She knew what he wanted in a relationship. And when he had started to pull back his emotions, she should have gone toe-to-toe with him. Forced him to believe they could work it out. Instead, she'd fallen back on what was safe. She'd run.

"You wouldn't be crying over Matt if you truly didn't care," her mother said.

Kate blinked away her tears and turned from the one person

who probably knew her better than anyone. She gripped the steering wheel and eased her foot down on the accelerator. "I care, Mom. But maybe . . . it's just time for me to go home."

Her mother's sigh whispered up the back of her neck and sent cold chills down into her heart.

"Oh, my darling daughter, you're already home."

The following day, with a heavy heart and a lack of sleep, Kate had no time to feel sorry for herself. Her father was on his way home. She'd asked him to stop by the Sugar Shack first and to come in the front door. He'd chuckled and asked if she'd just mopped the kitchen. "Something like that," she'd told him. Now she waited anxiously outside for his truck to appear around the corner.

The snow had been cleared from the sidewalks yet she was still careful as she turned to get an overall look at the place before he arrived. The new awning looked inviting with its chocolate background, big pastel polka dots and new script logo. The arborvitae that framed the door had been trimmed and the mums in the flower box were the burnished gold her mother loved.

Everything was perfect.

Everything except the giant ache in her heart. Last night had been the first in days when she hadn't slept in Matt's arms. She missed his warmth, his smile, the way he held her, the way he whispered her name when he was buried deep inside her. She missed his laughter, their bond, and the love that poured from his heart and soul even when he tried to keep it hidden.

He was the last person she'd ever wanted to hurt. And yet—

"Ruined the place. That's what you've done."

Kate spun to find Edna Price and her stupid moose-head walking stick hobbling up behind her. "I beg your pardon?"

Edna jerked her head toward the Sugar Shack. "Nothing was wrong with that place. But as soon as your dear sweet daddy blinked you go and bring your big-city ideas and ruin what wasn't broke!"

If it ain't broke, don't fix it.

Kate turned again and looked at the exterior of the shop her parents had built from the ground up over three decades ago. "I hardly think I ruined it, Mrs. Price. I'd like to think I re-energized it so my father wouldn't have to."

Edna's gray brows pulled together over her faded hazel eyes. "And did you think it was necessary to *re-energize* your mother's wonderful recipes too?"

"How did you—"

"I peeked through the damned window, that's how. You got the menu up there and there's hardly anything left of your mama. For your information, young lady, her pastries were what made this place successful."

Not for the first time, panic settled in Kate's chest like a ship's anchor. "I didn't—"

"Of course you didn't." Edna gave the sidewalk a whack with her cane. "Selfish. That's all you've ever been. Nothing like your mama and daddy. Nothing like your brother and sister."

"Mrs. Price, I've tried to be nice to you. I've given you extra pickles with your sandwich, free brownies . . . Why do you hate me so much?"

"Why?" Every wrinkle on the woman's face deepened. "I'll

tell you why. Because for over thirty years your mama was my best friend and for the last ten of those years I had to sit by and watch you slowly kill her. That's why."

"Kill her? Mrs. Price, you can't keep blaming me for something I had nothing to do with."

"I suppose you're going to tell me that you had no idea about the heart attack you gave her when you left."

"What?" Kate's throat tightened. "When?"

"Like you don't know."

Despair balled up in the pit of her stomach. "If I knew, I wouldn't be asking."

Her mother's friend studied her like she was a bug under an entomologist's microscope. "The first one happened just a few days after you left. She spent two weeks in the CCU in Bozeman. Your daddy knew. Your brother knew. Your sister knew. The whole damn town knew. So you can't tell me you didn't know."

Kate lifted her hand to her forehead and rubbed, trying to remember if anyone had mentioned anything at all about her mother's health. True, when she'd left home, she hadn't called for several months. But surely someone would have mentioned something so important. "Nobody said anything."

"For ten years?"

After you bailed, your folks needed me. Matt's words came rushing back at her. Is that what he'd meant? Is that why they'd needed him? Because her mother had been gravely ill? Why hadn't her father said something? Or Dean? Or Kelly? Nausea rolled through her stomach.

"I honestly didn't know," was all Kate could manage to say.

In Edna Price's eyes, she was a neglectful, worthless human being. And if what Edna was telling her was the truth, Kate couldn't agree more.

Edna speared Kate with a disbelieving glare, then hobbled off.

Kate fought back the bile rising in her throat as she watched Edna's backside retreat, her worn red wool coat, and black orthopedic shoes. Then Edna turned and Kate could feel the daggers halfway down the block.

"You ought to be ashamed, Katherine Silverthorne. There are people in this world who'd give anything to have the love that's been bestowed on you. But you . . . you just toss it away."

As the old woman turned the corner, Kate's knees wobbled. For the first time in her life she understood. Edna Price didn't hate her. Edna Price envied her.

Kate had the one thing that Edna wanted. Love.

Was she really stupid enough to throw it all away?

Kate stood back as her father stepped through the bakery door and stopped as if he'd hit a wall. His camo gear was dirty and he smelled like a man who'd been out in the woods for a week without a shower. But she'd never wanted to hug him more. She needed to find out if what Edna had said about her mother was true. But first things first.

"Daddy? Are you okay?"

Arms dangling at his sides he nodded while his head turned slowly from left to right as he scanned the interior of the shop. His shoulders lifted and dropped with a sigh. Kate came up beside him. Tears filled his eyes.

She'd failed.

"I'm so sorry, Dad. I thought—" Words clogged her throat as she tried to rush an apology, an explanation. She buried her face in her hands and a huge sob sucked the breath from her lungs.

Her father gathered her in his arms and soon they were crying together. He stroked her hair like he had when she'd been little and had crawled up on his lap to be consoled. It seemed so wrong for her to seek comfort from him when she was at fault.

For everything.

"I didn't mean to—"

"Oh, Katie girl, it's . . . beautiful."

The weight in Kate's chest lifted. She looked up at her father and the watery smile now spreading across his face. "But . . . I thought . . . you like it?"

"Honey, I love it. Your mother would love it too."

She wiped the tears from his cheeks. "Then why are you crying?"

He gave a little nod. "The picture."

Kate swung her gaze across the room to the photo of her parents on their original opening day. She'd had it restored and blown up to poster size and it was now the focal point of the entire shop.

"Your mother was a beautiful woman."

Her mother's red hair had been slicked back into a ponytail just like the one Kate now wore. Her smoky green eyes sparkled. And the smile on her face brought life to the entire photo.

"You look just like her," her father said, hugging her closer. "And you have her heart."

Wrapped in her father's arms, Kate knew she'd just been paid the highest compliment she'd ever receive. Even if she didn't deserve it.

"But, honey, why are you crying?"

"Dad? About mom's heart."

Opening day for the remodeled Sugar Shack and Cindi's Attic arrived dark and dreary. With thick pewter clouds hanging low in the sky, the sun didn't stand a chance. As Kate stepped into her Chucks, she tried to focus on getting through the day. Not the weather. Not the pressure being put on her from Josh now that he'd detected blood in the water.

And especially not the ache in her heart.

Her father had sampled the new additions to the menu and gave his stamp of approval. He'd laughed when she'd told him of her designer cakes and made her promise she wouldn't create anything too risqué. Hard to do when you wouldn't even be around. And he'd told her of her mother's heart condition and the promise her mother had made them swear to not tell Kate.

Kate swung her mother's Winnie-the-Pooh key ring around her finger and whistled to the pup. "Come on, boy. We've got a busy day ahead." He lifted his head from his favorite sleeping spot at the foot of her bed, then jumped to the floor and wagged his tail.

Kate opened the front door. "See you at the Shack, Dad."

He waved from the kitchen while he poured his coffee into a commuter mug.

There was a hesitant skip to Kate's heart as she opened the door to the Buick and helped the pup up onto the seat. She'd barely made a left turn onto Whitetail before a whisper of cold air whooshed past her head. Kate pulled to the curb and turned in her seat. Her mother's glow was a little blue today.

"So now you know."

The knot in the center of Kate's chest twisted. "Yes. I know what happened. I just don't know why you refused to tell me for ten years. Or why daddy or Dean or Kelly didn't say something."

Her mother's eyelids lowered, then she looked away all together. "Because I made them promise not to. Because it had nothing to do with you and everything to do with cream puffs and watching too many reruns of *Law & Order*. I should have eaten a salad now and then or walked to the bakery once in a while instead of riding in this heap. Life happens, Katherine. You'd made your decision." Her mother's gaze met hers again. "And despite myself, I was proud that you'd even had the nerve to get up and go. When I'd been the exact same age as you, I'd toyed with the idea of getting out. But I never had the courage. So while I was afraid to let you go . . . I was a little envious. I didn't want to do anything to screw up your chances.

"So what if I had a little heart issue. I was sure it wouldn't slow me down. And for ten years, it didn't."

"But, Mom—"

"It was *not* your fault, Katherine. Okay?"

Kate wiped away her tears and nodded.

"I'm so proud of you, honey. Whatever you decide to do with your life, wherever you decide to live, I just want you to be happy."

A warm flutter eased the knot in Kate's chest. Before she'd come back to Deer Lick, she would never have believed she'd ever hear those words. How could she? Kate knew she'd been given a gift. Another chance to make amends.

"Thank you, Mom. I'm really sorry for all the things I thought. All the things I said. Especially for calling you a big butthead."

"Shoot, if that's the worst you ever called me I'd be surprised."

They laughed and her mother's glow brightened from blue to lavender.

"Sweetheart, before I go, I want you to reach under the seat. There's something there that belongs to you."

"To me? What is it?"

"Just a little reminder in case you ever feel lost."

Kate turned but once again, her mother had Houdinied out of there. Kate looked down at the pup. He looked up at her and with a flop of his ears, sneezed.

"If I reach under there and lose a finger to a rat trap, I'm blaming you." She reached beneath her seat, grabbed hold of something, and pulled out a scrapbook. She lifted the cover and slowly flipped through the pages. Kelly had been right. Her mother had kept a memory book.

There were photos of her growing up, some with her alone, some with Dean and Kelly. There were blue, red, and white ribbons she'd won at the county fair for her 4-H projects, articles about her from fashion magazines and a few pages from entertainment rags where she'd been photographed on the red carpet in stunning gowns.

A photo of her entire family, their arms around each other in front of Sleeping Beauty's Castle in the happiest place in the world, eased the sting in her heart. She remembered that day so well. The enticing smells, the shrieks of laughter, and the complete and utter joy of being with her family.

The last photo was a slightly faded shot of her on graduation day. She wore her black gown and cap with the gold tassel. Matt held her in his arms. Her held was tilted back, her feet were kicked up in the air. And Matt was looking down at her.

She could see it now on his face. The love. The happiness.

The ache knotted in her chest lifted as she remembered back to that day. To being in his arms and loving him with every inch of her young heart.

Why had she ever wanted to leave that?

And what had she found after she'd left?

She shook her head to keep the tears at bay and turned to the back of the book. The very last page displayed a hand-embroidered handkerchief that read—*If you ever need to find your heart's desire, look in your own backyard.*

The photo of her and Matt sat like a time capsule in the pocket of Kate's apron. Several times during the day she'd taken it out and looked at it. She loved him. Period. Paragraph. Hopefully not the end of the story.

At noon she sent Chelsea over to Cindi's Attic with a tray of shortbread cookies to keep the flock of teenage girls nourished while they oohed and aahed over the array of celebrity gowns. Chelsea had informed Kate that the first to be reserved for the autumn formal was a silver sparkler donated by Taylor Swift. And while Kate couldn't be happier they'd received their first customer, she had other troubles on her mind. Like the overflow of orders for Kate's Red Carpet Cakes and how she could fill them all. By herself. And still sleep.

Maybe she could use this as an opportunity to bring Chelsea in under her wing and teach her to be a cake decorator. At least the PG-rated cakes. The business would grow and they would need the help. Might as well be someone enthusiastic.

The bell over the door chimed and Kate looked up to see James Harley strolling in. She put on a smile.

"Hello, Deputy Harley."

He glanced around and nodded. "The place looks good."

"Thank you." She proudly accepted the compliment. While he walked the length of the display case, she wiped her hands down the front of her apron and went to the new lunch counter to take his order. "Let me guess . . . two tuna subs, no tomato, and two iced teas.

James looked at her and the brown of his eyes deepened. "Just one order today."

She cocked her head. "Just one?"

He nodded, averting his gaze.

She stood there for a minute taking in what that meant. "Why?"

"Shit. I told him you'd get upset."

"You told *who*?"

"Ryan. He's . . . uh . . ."

"Taken his business elsewhere?"

His silence verified what the chill in her spine already knew

James raised his hands. "Look, Kate, I don't get into his personal business. Well, not much. He didn't say why. I didn't ask."

"Uh-huh." She glanced over his shoulder and through the

front window to the patrol car parked at the curb. The steam puffs coming from the tailpipe told her two things—it was cold outside and the car was idling. For a quick getaway no doubt.

"Is he out there?" she asked with a tilt of her head.

James looked over his shoulder. "Yep."

Matt could be as stubborn as he wanted, but she would not let him make the bakery suffer for her actions. She gritted her teeth and forced a smile to her lips. "Will you excuse me for a moment?"

A flash of humor lit up James's handsome face as Kate pushed open the bakery door. She stormed to the driver's side window, and folded her arms.

Matt looked up in mid-bite of a greasy cheeseburger from the Grizzly Claw Tavern. Surprise widened his icy eyes. Kate leaned her weight on one hip, determined not to move an inch until he rolled down the window.

Fortunately his cop skills made him good at reading body language and the window motor whirred as the glass slid down into the door.

"What?" he said.

She held her hand out, palm up.

He looked at her hand then looked into her eyes. She swiped the burger from his grasp and marched away.

"Hey! That's my lunch."

"And a heart attack waiting to happen. If you want a decent lunch, Deputy Ryan, you will get your stubborn ass out of that patrol car and get inside that bakery. Stop behaving like a child. Avoiding me will solve nothing." She turned on the heel of her Chucks and stormed back through the bakery door.

As she returned to her place behind the counter, she

threw the burger in the trash and gave James's startled face a smile. "Would you like to have a seat at one of our new tables, Deputy Harley? It's much nicer than sitting in a smelly old patrol car."

He chuckled. "Sure."

"Good. I'll have your order ready in just a few minutes." While she prepared two tuna subs, no tomato, the front door opened and Matt walked in. His hands were shoved into the pockets of his fleece-lined uniform jacket and a scowl darkened his face. He looked nothing like the boy in the photo in her pocket and everything like the man who lit her up like she was some freaking pyrotechnic. He said nothing as he joined James at one of her tiled bistro sets.

She completed their order, added a square of cheesecake for each of them, and carried the meals to their table on a tray. She set the plates in front of them.

"Dessert is on me, gentlemen." She looked at James. "If you enjoy it, I'd appreciate it if you could spread the word."

With her heart aching to kiss him until he couldn't breathe, she looked at Matt. If he truly thought they weren't meant to be together, she had to prove him wrong.

She turned her smile flirtatious and went in for the kill. "I chose the blackberry especially for you, Deputy Ryan, because I know how much you like it. The way you moaned the other night . . ." She smoothed her hand across his wide shoulder. ". . . was a dead giveaway."

He gaped like a big fish as she sauntered away. The heat of his eyes burned a hole in her backside.

Good.

If Matt Ryan wanted a war, he was messing with the wrong girl.

An occasional crackle from the scanner broke the silence in the patrol car and the sky spit wet heavy snow against the windshield as Matt ran the lake to lookout patrol. When the flames in his fireplace had become an image of Kate writhing naked on his sheets, he called the station and volunteered for the patrol no one wanted on a night like this. He needed to get Kate off his mind and out of his heart. Nothing better than driving in a white-out to regain his focus.

Wind gusts bent the tips of the pines and the moon couldn't break through the thick layer of clouds. Matt was having a hell of a time keeping the SUV straight. Halloween hadn't yet arrived and they'd already been doused with a blanket of white that wouldn't melt until the daffodils pushed up in the spring. By then the special election upon Sheriff Washburn's retirement would have been held. Before then he had plenty of work to do. He gripped the wheel and eased the SUV around a treacherous curve. There were speeches to write. Promises to make. Babies to kiss. Ex-girlfriends to forget.

The tires crunched on fresh fallen snow as he rounded the final bend and into the space that made up Deer Lick's version of Lover's Lane. His headlights swept the area.

Shit.

Through the Star Wars effect on his windshield, he saw the big brown Buick parked across the lot. With one occupant.

He cut the lights and rolled the SUV to a stop behind her.

Below and beyond her front bumper the lights of the town glowed behind a haze of white. Enough to allow him to see her right hand move and flail as if she were in a heated discussion. Before he could open his door, she flung her cell phone out the window. It landed with a splat in a mound of snow.

He grabbed his hat from the seat next to him, pushed it on his head, and zipped up his jacket. He could smell trouble a mile away. And lately she came with the scent of sugar cookies and gingersnaps.

His boots crunched against the snow as he walked to her side of the car and discovered her with her back pressed against the door. He tapped on the window but wasn't surprised when she ignored him. He noticed the door wasn't locked and yanked it open. She nearly fell out. His gloved hands caught her and not even a layer of fleece and leather could keep him from the electricity that snapped between them.

"What the hell are you doing up here?" he asked.

She righted herself and glared at him from beneath a knit cap that looked like it had braided pigtails. "It's my thinking spot."

He laughed and looked around at their solid white surroundings. "You don't have enough sense to stay home on a night like this and do your *thinking* there?"

Her smoky eyes narrowed. "Are you calling me dumb?"

"Kate. In case you haven't noticed we're having a white-out. I know in Glitter Town that might have something to do with a different kind of powder and might be considered a good time, but here in Redneckville we call it dangerous. So yes, I'm calling you dumb."

She grabbed the door handle and tried to pull it closed. He

put himself between her and the door and made that impossible.

"Go to hell, Matt."

"Already been there, Hollywood."

"I would appreciate it if you would stop calling me that."

The commonsense side of him said to run away. Fast. "Move over," he told her.

She looked up at him, tightened her lips, and then slid across the bench seat. With her arms folded across her puffy white parka she looked like a big marshmallow.

He slid in next to her, shut the door, and extended his arm across the back of the seat. Frosty breath curled from her nose like she was breathing fire. The snowfall had swallowed all sound and he could almost hear her blink.

Trying to ignore the memory of what had transpired in this place years before, he released a hard breath. "So this is your thinking spot, huh?"

She tightened her crossed arms. "Yes."

"Why?"

"Don't laugh."

"Me? Never."

"I like it because the town reminds me of Whoville from up here."

"Whoville?"

"Yes. You know the place where life is wonderful and everybody holds hands and sings." She untangled her arms and shoved a hand through her hair, knocking her pigtail cap askew, and shot him a look. "Until the Grinch shows up and ruins everything."

He laughed. "Are you calling me a Grinch?"

"You said you wouldn't laugh."

He laughed again. "Sorry."

"No, you're not."

"Yeah, you're right. Are you talking the Dr. Seuss version or the Jim Carey version? Because honestly I don't think I'm that funny."

"Pfft. No kidding."

He shook his head and pulled off his gloves. "So what is it you're sitting here thinking about? Aren't you supposed to be on your way to London by now?"

"You want to know why I'm still here?"

He shrugged. "I'll probably kick myself for asking, but sure, Kate, why are you still here?"

"Because of my dad." She turned toward him. "And the bakery. And this town I seem to want to be a part of. And I'm still here because of you, Matt."

And on her list of reasons to stay, he came dead last.

He didn't want to be last in a woman's heart. He wanted to be first.

Was that so awful?

He wanted a woman in his life. Someone permanent. He wanted a family. Love. He wanted to protect the people in the town he called home. He was a man of simple dreams. Kate had built a life on fame, fortune, and glamour. She should be proud of herself. Hell, *he* was proud of her. Sure they had chemistry—the kind that was too explosive to even fathom. But that was all they'd ever have. Had. Past tense.

It had taken him a few days but he'd finally accepted the truth. He needed to move on. She needed to move on. Before they both went crazy. "Who was on the phone?"

She lifted her head and swept a finger beneath her eye, capturing a drop of moisture. "What?"

"Who was on the phone before you tossed it out the window?"

"Doesn't matter. Just more threats of lawsuits and ruination." Through the dark she looked across the cab at him long and hard. "And none of that means jack right now." She curled her hands in the front of his jacket and pulled him toward her. She pressed a hot hungry kiss to his mouth.

Before he could respond she'd climbed onto his lap and straddled him.

The sweet taste of her filled his mouth. The delicious scent of her skin saturated his senses. He welcomed the punch of white-hot lust that twisted his insides as she knocked his hat off and plunged her fingers into his hair. A moan stuck in her throat, then broke free as the kiss turned into a carnal assault.

Then she was gone.

When he opened his eyes, she was staring into the backseat as if she'd seen a ghost.

"Not here," she rasped.

"What?"

She pushed the door open, crawled off him, and yanked him outside.

"Kate?"

She pulled him by the hand through the snow to his patrol car, opened the door, and slid inside. "Get in," she said and peeled off the marshmallow parka.

Kate watched him hesitate. Without giving him another moment to think she reached for him, dragged him into the car, and dove into the passion spreading across her skin like a summer wildfire. Held within his arms her heart swelled and the emptiness began to subside. When his hot breath brushed her cheek, her words escaped on a breathless plea. "I need you, Matt." She reached for the buttons on his shirt and closed her eyes as the eagerness to feel his warm skin, his heart beating beneath her fingers, consumed her.

His big hands manacled her wrists. "Stop."

Her eyes popped open. "What?"

"I said stop."

She leaned back to see if he was kidding. "Seriously?"

He lifted her off his lap and set her onto the seat beside him. Humiliation burned her cheeks and she scooted toward the door.

"We can't do this, Kate." His icy glare cut through the darkness. "*I* can't do this."

She tore her gaze from his and stared out the windshield at the heavy snow collecting on the glass.

He exhaled. "Honestly, in the beginning I thought it would be enough just be with you a few times. But I can't. I want more. And I can't play this game. No matter how much it tears me up inside."

She looked at him. "What if I were to tell you I plan to stay? Here. In Deer Lick."

"Why would you do that when you've got clients and employees and lawsuits and a whole other life that has nothing to do with me?" As if easing the pain he rubbed at the back of his neck.

"I want you, Kate. All of you. But I guess I'm old-fashioned. I won't settle for less. I can't base the rest of my life on someone who *plans* to stay. And I just don't think you're ready to take a leap of faith and *definitely* stay."

Everything inside of her froze and restricted in her chest as he reached for the door handle. She grabbed his arm. "Where are you going?"

"To get my hat, pull your cell phone out of the snow, and lock your car." He pulled the handle back and opened the door. Big fat snowflakes fell on the sleeve of his dark green jacket. "Then I'm taking you home and saying good-bye."

"What do you mean *good-bye?*"

"You're a smart woman. Figure it out." He gave her a look that broke her heart. "Go back to Hollywood, Kate, because you're too late. Way too fucking late."

The realization hit her like a rock-filled snowball between the eyes. He meant good-bye. Forever. Just like that, everything she really wanted but had been too wimpy to grasp had now become completely out of her reach.

CHAPTER SIXTEEN

Halloween arrived a few days later with blue skies and sunshine that turned the snow to slush. Heartaches tended to turn everything upside down and Kate hadn't slept since Matt had dropped her off at her father's house. And since she was now close to losing every ounce of remaining normal brain cells she possessed, she was desperate for a distraction. Trick or Treat night had always been one of her favorites and she decided to indulge.

Even if she did so on autopilot.

The bakery door had been swinging all day with patrons filing in for orders of spiced pumpkin cookies or black marshmallow cats. The mice she'd made of Hershey's kisses and the haunted house designer cake she'd donated to the senior citizen center were a hit. Her Little Red Riding Hood ensemble was anything but innocent, but her only other choices had been Carnal Cave Girl or Hottie Heidi the Upstairs Maid. And, okay, she looked pretty darned good. So sue her if she hoped the elusive Deputy Ryan might come by for a tuna sub.

Her father, with his offbeat sense of humor, had dressed

as Melvin the Mad Butcher. Though with their brisk business, she didn't imagine the hatchet sticking from his head would deter many from sampling the new menu.

From the back room she grabbed a few fresh towels from the shelf. The click of toenails came up behind her. "What's up, my little pimp?"

Togged up in his very own costume, the dog looked up at her with utter humiliation in his big brown eyes. Kate squatted down and cupped her hands around his adorable mug. "Who's the cutest widdle doggie in the world?" She pressed her nose against his and kissed the top of his head. If the purple velour and cheetah print jacket and pimped-out fedora—green feather included—weren't enough, the poor little guy had to endure her baby talk too.

She washed her hands and returned to the counter. As she slid a bat-shaped cake into an oversized pastry box for Irene Neilson's book club party, the bell over the door chimed. With moose-head cane leading the way, Edna Price hobbled inside. The collar of her worn red coat had been pulled up and her usual thick beige hose had been replaced with a pair she'd obviously hand-dyed orange. Her idea of a Halloween costume, Kate assumed.

When the older woman peered into the display case, mentally selecting the perfect chunk of brownie, Kate grinned and reached beneath the counter to retrieve the special treat she'd made for her sparring cohort. Kate hoped the small token of apology would soften the woman's bitterness.

"I have something special for you today, Mrs. Price."

Edna looked up and peered at her suspiciously. "Why?"

"Because it's Halloween and I thought you might like something a little different but equally as delicious as those plain old brownies." Kate pushed the white box bearing the Sugar Shack logo across the counter.

An extra wrinkle or two creased Edna's forehead as she lifted the lid and looked inside. "Is this supposed to be funny?"

"Funny?"

Edna's faded eyes narrowed. "Are you trying to insult me?"

"I wouldn't do that, Mrs. Price. I don't know what you're talking about."

"I'm talking about you calling me a witch." Edna shoved the box at her across the counter, turned, and hobbled toward the door.

"What?" Kate lifted the box lid and groaned when she realized she'd grabbed Felicity Houtman's witch cake instead of the happy pumpkin brownie she'd decorated especially for Edna. "Mrs. Price! Wait!" But all that remained of Mrs. Price was a flash of her red coat as she turned the corner.

Seconds later, as Kate stood there with her gut burning from her stupid mistake; James Harley strolled in with one of his famous woman-eating grins.

"Afternoon, Red."

Kate glanced down at the black lace-up corset and red skirt wishing her basket of goodies for grandma included a magic mirror to disappear through.

"Why the gloomy face?" James asked. "I'd have thought with business booming you'd be overjoyed enough to accept a date."

Kate glanced around the bustling shop, then looked back at James. "Business has been great."

He shrugged. "I figured it would with all the folks Ryan has been boasting to about the new menu."

"*Matt?*"

"Yeah, he's promoting this place like he owns stock or something."

Go figure. The man wanted nothing to do with *her* yet he'd brag about her treats to send people to her door. It might not have been quite a shocker when he'd told her she was too late. No, make that way too effing late. If she'd figured things out and spoken up sooner, she wouldn't have had to hear those words coming from his gorgeous mouth. Her fault. Not his.

That night after he'd taken her home, she stopped playing games with herself. She knew it didn't matter if she walked away from her business or if someone took it away. She simply didn't care anymore. She'd built a life here. She loved this town. She loved her cakes. And she loved Matt Ryan. Not necessarily in that order.

She knew she was a good person, most days, and she deserved to be loved as much as anybody else. It was long past time she did something about it. And for once, she planned to make her intentions perfectly clear. Scratch that. Matt didn't like the word *plan*. Too iffy. She'd *definitely* make her intentions clear.

"Well, thank him for me, will you?" she told James.

"Sure thing." He grinned and a dimple appeared deep in his right cheek. "Now about that date?"

"Two tuna subs, no tomato?" she asked, evading the question with a smile.

"I'll take that as a hell no," James said. "Sorry, Red, just one order today. Ryan took the day off. Something about an important date."

"An important date?" *Please Deputy Harley, tell me more.*

"Yep." James tucked his hands in his jacket pockets. "I drove by him earlier. He had a woman in the car. Must be serious. That boy rarely takes a day off."

A woman? Kate's heart climbed into her throat. Maybe that's what he'd meant when he'd said she was way too late. He'd agreed his list was stupid, but maybe he'd found someone else. True it had only been a few days since they'd parted but . . . "Well, he is looking for the right woman to marry," she said.

James's dark eyes captured her gaze and held. "Yeah. And I think he found her."

Kate swallowed the jealousy rising like acid in her throat. She grabbed a picnic roll from the tray, shoved the serrated knife through the center, and sawed away like she was Leatherface in *Texas Chainsaw Massacre.*

The moon floated high above Deer Lick and the Trick or Treaters were winding down their great candy caper. The line at the Grange's annual haunted house had dwindled and Kate had to juggle her purse and her pimped-out puppy while she unlocked the bakery's back door. In a hurry to unload the remainder of the Halloween-shaped cookies on the senior center, she'd left her coat behind. The temperature had dipped below thirty degrees and no one in their right mind would be caught outside in a tiny skirt, a thin red hood, and some severely mangled fishnet stockings. Puppy claws were deadly to a good pair of hose—which was not to say the pair on her legs were good to begin with.

She set the pup down inside, closed the door, then did a walk-through to make sure everything was locked down and turned off for the night. As she passed the lunch counter, the pastry box on the shelf below the register caught her eye. She pulled it out, set it on the counter, and lifted the lid.

Edna's happy pumpkin brownie stared up at her.

How had she managed to screw up so badly? She'd been trying to make amends. Instead she'd sent the poor old woman scurrying away as though she'd been poked with a cattle prod.

Kate closed the lid and sighed. She ran her fingers over the imprinted Sugar Shack logo, then turned and looked down at the pup who was trying to dislodge the green feather from his purple fedora.

If she was going to make her good intentions clear, now was a good time to start.

"Feel like taking a ride?" she asked him.

He responded with a sneeze.

"You sure? We might get the door slammed in our faces."

Another sneeze. "Okay, but if she turns a fire hose on us, it's going to be your fault."

Kate grabbed her coat off the hook and shoved her arms through the sleeves. Then she leaned down and removed the fedora from the pup's head. "I've tortured you enough for one day, little man." He looked up at her and his tail swept happily across the floor. "Fine, I'll take off the jacket too. But don't tell me you didn't have fun playing dress-up."

He sneezed, then rubbed a paw over his nose.

"Yeah, that's what all you dogs say. But deep inside I know you really love it."

Kate parked her mother's boat in front of a quaint little cabin with a jack-o-lantern grinning out from the front porch. Smoke curled from the chimney and only a single light glowed from behind the white curtain. She grabbed the box from the backseat and told the pup to stay before she closed the door. He put his paws on the window ledge and whined as she walked up the path to Edna's front door.

She tugged down her skirt trying for a little more modesty, but nothing would make her look any less slutty in Edna's eyes. Kate didn't even know why she bothered. She raised her hand and rapped twice on a door that could use a good coat of wood sealer.

The door swung open and Edna stood there in a poufy pumpkin suit with her hand-dyed orange stockings. On top of her head she wore a green Leprechaun hat. At her feet a strawberry blonde Pekinese yipped and tapped its small feet. Edna held a purple and black bat-shaped bowl half full with packets of plain and peanut M&M's. Her eyes widened.

"What the hell do you want?" she growled.

"Now is that any way for a pumpkin to talk?" Kate asked and held out the pastry box.

Edna's faded eyes zeroed in. "What's that?"

"*This* is the special treat I made for you. *This* is the treat meant to hand you earlier. Not Felicity Houtman's witch cake."

Kate's nerves were grinding as she waited for the door to

slam in her face. Instead Edna surprised her by setting the bat bowl on a chair near the door and taking the box from Kate's hands. Her mother's dearest friend lifted the lid, looked inside, and for a moment was completely silent. Then she looked up into Kate's eyes and something passed between them. It wasn't exactly a truce, but more like someone had come along and sprinkled water on the fire that always sparked between them.

"You made this? Just for me?"

Kate nodded.

A large intake of breath lifted the eyes on Edna's pumpkin suit. "Well . . . it looks . . ."

Delicious. Please say it looks delicious.

"It looks . . . better than anything your mom ever made for me," she said as her face crackled with a small smile.

Kate didn't know why but the compliment Edna Price had just bestowed on her felt better than any red carpet mention she'd ever received. "Thank you, Mrs. Price. That means a lot. I'm really very sorry about the mix-up earlier." Kate glanced at a trio of teenaged witches skipping down the sidewalk. "Could I . . . um . . . talk to you a minute?"

"About?"

"My mother. Her heart. And a few things that might completely surprise you."

Edna stepped back. "Why don't you come on in and have a brownie?"

"Oh. Well . . . I've got the puppy in the car and—"

"Well, bring him in. I've got some kibble. Skipper won't mind sharing."

"Are you sure?"

Edna grinned. "I've got hot cocoa too."

Kate smiled back. Who was she to turn down a double dose of chocolate? "I'll be right back."

She trotted down the path as fast as her Loubitan's would allow her to go and opened the car door. As she reached for the pup, a rosy glow filled the center of the backseat. Kate drew the pup into her arms and blinked. When she opened her eyes, her mother sat there in her overalls and red plaid shirt. Not a hair had gone askew in the bun on top of her head. She looked exactly the same as she had every time before.

Yet something was different.

"Mom?"

"You're a good girl, Katherine."

Kate's heart skipped.

Her mother gave her a smile and reached out her hand. Kate shifted the pup into her other arm and reached out her hand too. In the center of the Buick their hands met and Kate felt a warm tingle whisper across her palm.

"Can you feel that?"

Kate nodded as tears clogged her throat and stung her eyes. "What is it?"

"A mother's love, daughter. Even death can't take that away."

CHAPTER SEVENTEEN

Weeks of preparation had come down to this night. Matt had done everything he could to be successful, which included consulting with an expert on public speaking. He'd even taken a day off work—something he never did—to meet with the woman who'd come here to coach him on his presentation.

Win or lose he was as ready as he would ever be.

With the wind biting at his back, he walked into the Grange. Folding chairs had been set up like a church service was about to commence. He made his way through an audience of a couple hundred residents to take his place at the table set up front near the podium. With the election set for January, he scanned the crowd to see who'd shown up to hear the first sheriff's candidate debate about to take place between him and Dave Johnson.

Johnson, already seated, wore a tailored suit and a confident smile. Matt had chosen a fresh-from-the-laundry uniform. The same type of uniform he wore every day to protect those sitting in this building. No one would be elected on whether their clothes had a designer label or not. They would be elected on what they were willing and able to do for the community.

Matt noticed those in attendance were a true reflection on Deer Lick—farmers, ranchers, small business owners, parents, and other hard-working citizens interested in the future of their town. Kate's father, in the middle of the crowd, gave him a smile and a thumb's-up. From the front row, Buddy Hutchins glared and Matt hoped he wouldn't have to toss Buddy and his uncle in a cell tonight. James and the rest of Matt's coworkers who weren't on duty sat in a group to the side. He felt their support in the collective nodding of heads as he glanced their way. Any qualms he might have had disintegrated.

He glanced over the crowd one more time but knew he was searching in vain. Chances were she'd already skipped town and was dining on champagne in merry old England.

Matt knew he was completely prepared for tonight's debate. But he'd been completely unprepared for the ravaging ache left in his heart after he'd forced himself to walk away from the woman he loved.

Sheriff Washburn caught him halfway up the aisle and clamped his beefy hand over Matt's shoulder. The sheriff's belly strained against the buttons on his shirt and draped over the top of his belt. His brows were gray and bushy. And there was no question why he'd been chosen year after year to play Santa at the Christmas Eve festivities.

"You know where my loyalties lay, Matt. I know you've worked hard to learn the ropes." He chuckled. "And somehow you haven't managed to hang yourself."

"Came close a couple of times."

"Well, we won't tell anyone about that." The sheriff smiled.

"Just wanted to make sure you were prepared for this. Lots of folks are going to think you're too young. Too inexperienced."

Not to mention too unmarried *and* the son of a drunk. "Don't worry, sir." Matt patted the sheriff's shoulder. "This is only the first of three debates. I'll reel them in like you did that derby winner last year. Real slow and easy."

"Atta boy." The sheriff took a step, then turned back. "And Ryan?"

"Yes, sir?"

"You make sure you've got good hooks, because I don't want Johnson running my town."

"Yes, sir."

Matt continued to the podium and extended his hand to Johnson who looked up at him as if this was where the debate started—to be cordial or not. The hesitation gave Matt a burst of confidence. When Johnson finally accepted the handshake, Matt noted that it was weak.

Mayor Remington had been chosen to moderate and once he quieted the crowd, he introduced Matt's accomplishments and endorsers. Then with a welcoming response from the crowd, the mayor called Matt to the podium.

Matt approached the microphone and knocked the butterflies swarming his stomach aside. The message he needed to deliver was more important than the fact that he had never won a single argument while on the high school debate team. As the public speaking coach had instructed him, he just needed to speak from his heart.

He pulled air into his lungs and looked up.

That's when she walked in.

And everything turned upside down.

Her shiny hair hung straight down the back of her marsh-mallow parka. Her boots were silent as she took an empty seat near the back next to Edna Price. When the two women hugged, he couldn't have been more surprised. Then again, he didn't figure it would take long for a smart woman like Kate to figure out that Mrs. Price had one of the kindest hearts in the state of Montana. She just had a big bark to go along with it.

When Kate turned her smoky eyes on him, he could feel their intensity all the way across the room. She gave him a smile and a nod of silent encouragement.

She hadn't run.

She was here.

Matt realized at that moment everything he wanted was in one room. And it was all up for grabs.

"Thank you, everyone, for coming tonight," he said, clamp-ing his hands on the podium. "Before we get started, I want to thank the women's auxiliary for putting this debate together and the mayor for offering to moderate. I promise to try not to bore you, but just in case, any of you who want to grab a cup of coffee first, feel free."

The audience chuckled. Kate's eyes remained glued on him.

For ten long minutes Matt spoke of working his way from the ground up, his tactics on the budget, and his priorities, which included education on drug and alcohol abuse and adding more patrol to the streets. "I'm very proud of the sup-port and endorsements I've received from my fellow deputies as well as the volunteer firefighters. I'm hopeful that the person they choose to lead them will mean something to you. I believe Deer Lick needs a leader who will set the tone. A leader who shares your vision of what Deer Lick can be." Matt looked over the crowd. His gaze lingered on Kate. "I, for one, know exactly what I want." Several heartbeats later he glanced over the crowd again. "To keep Deer Lick safe. And I'll do whatever it takes to meet that goal."

He received a standing ovation for his efforts, but Matt knew anything could happen in the next couple of months. People were fickle. They wanted to be on the winner's side. If the polls turned against him, the good people of Deer Lick would jump ship faster than mice with their tails on fire.

"And now," Matt said, "I'd be happy to answer your questions."

Audrey Lambert, the Baptist church's organist asked about his intentions for the devil's playground. Meaning, would he try to close down the bars? Hank Wilburn wanted to know if Matt intended to ask the mayor for tax increases. And then Buddy Hutchins stood. He gave Matt that same bully sneer he'd used all during high school. Matt hadn't been intimidated then, nor was he now. Though Buddy despised him, Matt knew he had nothing to hide.

"I got a question for you, Deputy Ryan."

Though the man basically spat out his name, Matt gave him a polite nod.

"That was a mighty pretty speech you gave there. Full of promises and all." Then Buddy turned to the audience. "But how is it you plan to accomplish all that when you spend most of your time jumping from bed to bed with the women in this town?"

"I'm not sure what you mean, Buddy."

"Sure you do. I've been watching you real close, see. And I lost count of all the women you've been hooking up with."

Anger flashed through his system and Matt took a step toward his lifelong antagonist. Before he could move any further, James was there holding him back.

Buddy turned toward the audience and used that time to throw more dirt on Matt's career aspirations. "If any of you wondered what was going on behind the papered windows during the renovations of the local bakery, I can tell you that Deputy Ryan took it upon himself to instruct a certain local pastry chef on the finer points of . . . *stuffing the donut hole*."

Oh shit. James's hands dug tighter into Matt's shirt while Matt's gaze shot out over the murmurs and gasps and pinpointed Kate by the flush creeping up her creamy complexion. Her eyes darted around the room as she slowly rose from her chair.

When Matt was sure she'd run, she pointed her finger at their accuser.

"Shame on you, Buddy Hutchins. Shame on you for letting your overinflated ego get in the way of common sense. Don't you think it's time you moved past a silly high school grudge to what's really important? Deputy Ryan is willing to put everything on the line to protect the people in this town. What are you doing, Buddy? Drinking the bars dry?"

Buddy's face turned three angry shades of pink and it took Matt a moment to realize Kate was defending him.

"I know some of you might not think very highly of me," she said to the crowd, "and that's okay. But please don't hold my bad behavior against Deputy Ryan. What can I say? He's an incredible, healthy, *single* man who has the right to date or sleep with whom he desires."

She turned that smoky gaze on Matt and he felt it all the

way to the soles of his feet. Then she addressed the housewives and farmers and humble citizens surrounding her. "There shouldn't be a question in your mind on what's most important to Matt Ryan—to protect this town and the people in it. The same way he protected my parents when I didn't have the courage to stay. And I never even thanked him."

A cold chill ran up Matt's back. Why hadn't she just said this to him in private? She could have, probably would have, but he hadn't wanted to hear her excuses and he'd pushed her away. He'd been too busy bouncing between the fear that she'd leave again and the fantasy that she'd stay. He'd been so damned wrapped up in his own imagination that he'd been afraid of reality. Afraid she wouldn't say *exactly* what he wanted to hear.

He shouldn't have been so demanding.

And he shouldn't have been such a pansy ass.

If he'd listened, if he'd given her a chance, they could have been tearing each other's clothes off the past few days instead of dodging each other.

"I'm sure Mr. Johnson is a nice enough man," Kate continued, "but he doesn't love this town. He doesn't have it in his blood. If you all can't see that Matt Ryan is the right person to replace Sheriff Washburn, then you deserve what you get. I'm betting you'll do what's right. Personally, I look forward to the optimism Matt Ryan has for this town. I grew up here and I had a wonderful childhood. I know Matt wants to keep this community just as amazing for future generations."

Surrounded by silence, Edna Price reached up and squeezed Kate's hand in a show of support. "He has my vote." Kate took in a big breath and with a wobbly smile, pushed it from her lungs. "Now if you'll excuse me, I have cookies in the oven." Avoiding Matt's gaze, she and her marshmallow parka slipped through the crowd and pushed open the big steel doors.

"Kate." He lunged to follow her. When he didn't budge, he looked down and discovered that James still had his iron fists curled into the front of his shirt.

"Let her go," James said. "Whatever you do right now, whatever you say, remember your entire future is on the line."

"Bullshit. My future is walking out the door."

Somewhere in the back of his whirling mind, Matt heard amplified laughter.

"There you go, folks," Buddy said into the microphone, "Deputy Ryan's focus is clearly dirtied by trashy celebusluts and not—"

Matt didn't wait for him to finish. He drew back his arm and felt a shock of pure pleasure when his fist caught Buddy square on the chin.

"Shit!" The rocky parking lot poked the bottoms of Kate's boots as she charged toward her mother's car. "Shit. Shit. Shit!" She yanked open the door and twisted the key in the ignition. Gravel shot out from beneath the tires as she sped off before anyone could follow.

"Shit!" She pounded her fist on the steering wheel as tears spilled over her bottom lashes.

"Katherine?"

"Oh God, Mom, not now."

"Honey, please slow down. I don't need any company up here."

"Did you see what just happened?" Kate couldn't control

the hysteria leaking through her voice. "I should never have come back here. Everything is so . . . fucked up! And please don't chastise me on my potty mouth!"

"I wouldn't dream of it. I just don't understand why you're so upset."

"Because that jerk Buddy Hutchins just told everybody I had sex with Matt on the bakery floor!"

"TMI, Katherine."

"Sorry."

"So, Buddy told everyone about your extracurricular activities. Why do you care what the town thinks of you?"

Kate pulled the car to the curb. The seat squeaked as she turned around. "Mom, don't you get it? I'm not worried about me. I could care less about me. I care about Matt. I care that I just ruined his chances to fulfill his dream. Buddy is trying to turn the community against him." Kate slumped in the seat. "I should have kept my mouth shut and denied everything instead of bull-horning the truth to the entire Grange."

"Sounds like you've got some strong feelings for Matt."

Kate stared through the windshield at the stars twinkling back at her. Her chest lifted on a long intake of breath. "Of course I do. I'm crazy about him."

"Do you love him?"

"Yes!"

"Then what are you going to do about it?"

"Mom. Seriously? I tossed him away once and now I've gut shot his entire future. Do you honestly think he'd ever give me another chance?" She shook her head. "It's too late. He said so himself."

"It's never too late," her mother, corrected her softly. "Just look at me. Who'd have ever thought you and I could have a second chance? Now, what can I do to help?"

Kate smiled and reached out her hand to cover her mother's transparent one. "I love you, Mom, but this is something I need to handle on my own. I screwed up. I've got to make it right."

Chapter Eighteen

She'd vanished.

In a town the size of a peanut, it seemed Matt had kept two steps behind her. He'd stopped at the bar and Maggie had told him he'd just missed her. He'd gone to her house and her dad had said he hadn't seen her since she tore out of the Grange. He'd driven down Main Street hoping to spot her mother's old bomber parked at the burger joint or at the Gas and Grub. He'd driven through the back alley at the bakery but no Kate. He'd searched the entire town at least twice. But he'd had no more success than the last time he'd spun a Las Vegas roulette wheel.

At midnight Matt found himself steering the patrol car up the hill, past the rock formations and sweeping cottonwoods. Now bare of leaves, patches of snow garlanded between the long branches. He rolled to a stop at the plateau and stepped out of the car. The sweet scent of earth and pine rose up to greet him in Kate's thinking spot.

He walked to the edge and looked down over the town.

Whoville, she'd called it. A place where life was wonderful and everybody held hands and sang. A place he wanted to protect. A place he wanted to raise his children and grow old with the woman he loved by his side. He watched smoke curl up from the chimneys of homes filled with families. Homes filled with love. Homes filled with everyday life that went on without him because he hadn't stepped up and told Kate that he loved her.

He'd blamed her when it had been him who'd been unwilling to risk it all.

He'd convinced himself that she'd never be willing to give up her career, her goals, her ambitions—for him. When what he really should have done was to figure out how they could make both their careers, goals, and ambitions work together.

He'd taken what she'd given because he couldn't not take. With her in his arms he'd been living his fantasy. But when he'd asked her to stay, she'd hesitated. He'd panicked and pushed her away. He'd pushed her away and yet she still stood up to Buddy and the entire town on his behalf.

Somewhere in his muddled brain he'd thought if he could push her all the way back to Hollywood, she'd be out of his life and out of his head. But even if he pushed her all the way to Egypt, he'd never be able to erase her from his heart.

He knew her now to be a woman who worked hard, who made her dreams a reality, who came back home and in the face of adversity made a town fall in love with her. She was a woman who loved her family, who was still rescuing strays, and who had the guts to stand up for him so he could follow his own dreams.

Making love with her had been incredible, indescribable, but he didn't just crave her, he needed her . . . in his heart, in his arms, in his life. And he'd do whatever it took to have her there.

Once upon a time he'd vowed to let her go.

Well, forget that.

If she went, he was going with her.

Perched on an icy picnic bench on a snow-covered deck over-looking the frozen waters of the lake she'd once fished, Kate buried her cold nose in the sleeve of her parka. At the same time she buried the life she'd once lived.

The woman she was now was no comparison to the one a few months ago who'd boarded a plane to go bury her mother.

Everything had changed. Once she'd thought she'd been satisfied with work, work, and more work. Now she wanted it all—a man who loved her, babies, and a career working along-side her father in the bakery he'd built beside the woman he'd loved.

She knew where she belonged.

And it wasn't Hollywood.

Her mother had been right. And while it had taken Kate a decade, she finally figured it out too. Small-town life pumped through her blood. And while the big city and bright lights had been intriguing for a while, she really was a small-town girl at heart.

If she left now, she'd miss her dad, her dog, her friends. She'd miss the faces that greeted her every day with a smile and a wave. Faces that knew her name instead of calling her *dar-ing* because they couldn't remember. Faces that were genuine and filled with character when they smiled, not so frozen with Botox they barely moved.

Most of all she'd miss the man she loved—the promise in his kiss, the warmth of his soul, and the way he made her feel so complete.

If he didn't love her back . . . well, she'd have to find a way to change his mind.

She closed her eyes and waited. Surely he'd come home before she turned into a Popsicle.

"Why did you leave?"

Kate's head jerked up to find Matt walking toward her. Moonlight dusted his dark hair while her tail-wagging pup wiggled in his arms. He looked like all her dreams come true and he simply stole her breath. "I figured I'd done enough damage for one night."

"You didn't do any damage."

"What about what Buddy said? He was trying to turn everyone against you."

"Yeah, well, he didn't have much to say when I cold-cocked him right after you walked out the door."

She stifled a laugh. "You did?"

He stopped an arm's length away and nodded slowly while his big hand stroked the pup's golden ears. "I didn't like what he said about you."

"I didn't like what he said about *you*."

His pale eyes searched hers. "Why are you here, Kate?"

"We need to talk."

"Good. Because I've got things to say. Things I should have said a long time ago," he said. "Things you need to hear whether you want to or not."

"Okay." The word rushed out on a whisper and she felt herself shake all the way down to her boots. She wasn't sure what he was about to tell her. And the dark expression on his face was definitely sending out a mixed message. "You first."

Matt set the pup down and ran his free hand through the side of his hair, mussing it just a bit from its unusually perfect style. "Ten years ago I let you run away. I didn't ask why and I assumed wrong. I loved you when you almost threw up on my shoes in biology class. I loved you the day you walked out of my life. I loved you when you were a thousand miles away living a life I couldn't even fathom."

He wrapped her in his arms and held her against his chest. "I know I've been an ass lately, but I've spent my whole life loving you, Kate. And I don't want to be without you ever again."

Incredible warmth stole through her body and pushed her lips up into a smile. "You don't?"

"No."

"Can I say something now?"

He lifted his hand. "Not finished."

"Oh."

"I know you have your career," he said, "and I know how important it is for you to be in L.A. so—"

She shook her head. "Matt, I—"

"I thought I could apply for a position with the L.A. County Sheriff."

"You what?"

"If you don't want to stay here, then I'll move to be with you. I'll go wherever you are, Kate. Hollywood. London. Egypt. It doesn't matter because I love you."

Her heart did all kinds of crazy leaps in her chest and her hand trembled as she lifted it to her mouth. "Oh, Matt—"

He lifted a dark brow. "Not done yet."

"Sorry."

"I was a fool to think I could just choose someone off a list of names to spend the rest of my life with. I want someone special, someone who loves me, someone who wants to wake up in my arms every day, someone who wants to have my babies and grow old with me. And I want that someone to be you."

"I can do that."

He tilted his head. "Are you sure?"

She nodded. "No more running. I swear."

"Your turn," he said, his chest expelling a hard breath.

"Finally." Fifty pounds of guilt and anxiety lifted from her shoulders. "I never thought you weren't good enough for me. I know I'm stubborn, and sometimes I don't make any sense, and sometimes it takes me a while to figure things out. But there's one thing I'm absolutely sure of."

"What's that?"

"I'm sure that I love you, Matt. And I'm sure that we are one hundred percent perfect for each other."

"Well that's a relief."

He looked at her for a few seconds but instead of taking her into his arms, he walked away. The pup lifted his head and whined as the soles of Matt's boots crunched against the snow covered deck.

Panic slithered up Kate's spine. "What are you doing?" she shouted as he opened his front door and disappeared into his house. "Why are you walking away?"

"Hold that thought," he shouted back.

A thousand glass half-empty ramblings scrambled through Kate's mind while she stood there digging the toe of her boot into the snow. When the bedroom light beyond the French doors came on, she thought maybe he'd changed his mind and didn't want her after all.

"Well, too bad for him," she told the pup who sneezed in response. "I'm not running this time and neither is he." She took two steps toward the door when he came back outside and walked right up to her.

"What was that all about?" she asked. "I was in the middle of ooey-gooey how-I-plan-to-spend-the-rest-of-my-life land and you just walk away?"

He smiled, reached in his pocket and withdrew a white box. Kate gasped even before she saw what was inside. Then he lowered himself to one knee in the snow, took her hand in his, and flipped open the lid. Against a bed of black velvet sat a beautiful solitaire diamond.

"This is the ring I bought for you ten years ago."

"And you've kept it ever since?"

He nodded. "It's kind of small. If you don't like it, I can buy you a bigger one."

"Don't you dare. It's beautiful."

He smiled. "You're beautiful."

She smiled back. "You're not so bad yourself."

"I'd planned to ask you to marry me ten years ago. Obviously I never got around to it. I love you, Kate. I've always loved you. I waited ten years hoping you'd come back."

She didn't wait for him to pull the ring out of the box and place it on her finger. She dropped to her knees in the snow, wrapped her arms around his neck, and pressed her face against his cheek. As she inhaled the scent of his aftershave, as his warmth surrounded her on the cool November night, she knew exactly what her mother had been talking about. Soul mates. That's exactly what Matt was. He was her once-in-a-lifetime love.

"I love you, Matt. So much." He lowered his head and kissed her. As they came up for air, she said, "But I don't want you to give up your dream. It's too important."

He shook his head, "I can't ask you to give up everything you've worked for. I know Hollywood is important to you."

"You don't have to ask me to give up anything. I have no ties there. Not anymore."

"What about the lawsuits?"

"I made a few calls to my clients and personally explained the situation to them. Once they heard the truth, they were all very understanding. Even Inara's dragon lady agent. Apparently Josh had been playing the drama queen to the hilt and hadn't been quite forthcoming as to the reasons I'd left or the reasons I'd stayed. I can't blame him. I did dump an awful lot of responsibility on him." She ran her hand down the sleeve of his jacket. "While I was making calls, I found a buyer for my couture collection and put my condo up on the market."

"You've been a busy girl."

"I don't belong there anymore, Matt. I belong with you, in Deer Lick or planet Mars or wherever you plan to be."

"I'll be right here." He wrapped his arms around her. "With you."

"You know, I wasn't going to leave. At least not without fighting Sarah or Diane or whatever her name is for you."

"Are you kidding?"

"No." She leaned her forehead against his. "And whatever her name was would have been sorry, too. I've taken kickboxing."

He threw his head back and laughed. "Now that would have been a sight to see."

"Could have led to a frisk. And handcuffs."

"I think I can accommodate you there." He hugged her tighter. "You do know there was never any competition, don't you?"

She smiled. "I do now."

"Do you remember the wish I made that night?"

"You wished that I would love you forever," she said.

He nodded.

"I'll love you forever and then some," she promised. Knowing that loving someone beyond their time on earth was entirely possible.

"Will you marry me, Kate? Will you be my wife?"

"I was your first love, Matt, and I want to be your last. So yes. Absolutely. Without a doubt. I want to be your wife."

He smiled, took her hand in his, and slid the ring on her finger. The diamond flashed in the moonlight. "A perfect fit," she said, not even trying to hold back the grin that broke across her face.

"Yeah," he kissed her again. "We are. By the way, what did you wish for that night? You know, the one a long time—"

"I remember."

"So?"

"I wished that my Prince Charming would be patient enough to wait for me."

"Thank God for second chances."

She laughed. "You have no idea."

"Maybe it's time to make another wish," he said.

"I've already got everything I want."

"Everything?"

"Mmmm. What else have you got in mind?"

He lowered his forehead to hers. "That's a loaded question."

Having had enough of being ignored, the pup barked. Kate laughed, cupped her hands around his silky ears, and rubbed her nose against his.

"Are you finally willing to admit that he belongs to you just as much as I do?" Matt asked with a grin.

The pup wagged his tail and slurped his tongue up her chin.

"Yes. I guess I really didn't try very hard to find him a home for a reason."

"Then don't you think it's about time you gave him a name?"

"Probably." She looked into the pup's big brown eyes. "What do you think?"

He looked up at her and sneezed.

"Are you sure?" she asked him.

He sneezed again.

Matt laughed. "Are you seriously asking the dog what he wants you to call him?"

Kate wrapped her arms around Matt's neck. "Uh-huh. You got a problem with that?"

He lifted his hands. "Not me. Unless you plan to open an animal psychic business."

"I think I'll have enough to do with the Sugar Shack, Cindi's Attic, and getting you elected sheriff."

"And planning a wedding."

Her heart burst with happiness. "Definitely planning a wedding."

"Then what does he want you to call him?"

She reached down and pulled the pup into her arms. "He wants me to call him . . . Happy."

Matt smiled and pressed a kiss against her lips. "You can call me that too."

On Thanksgiving Day, Kate set aside her empty dessert plate. She'd eaten far too much and was tempted to unbutton her jeans. She couldn't have been more satisfied than being snuggled on the sofa next to Matt while Happy lay across her lap. On the TV they watched her brother throw a touchdown pass.

"God, his arm is like a rocket," Matt said in awe.

From his recliner, her dad laughed. "Well, don't tell Mr. Perfect that. His ego can hardly fit in the door as it is."

Edna, sitting in her mother's recliner chirped in, "Mr. Perfect. Ha! He's gotten too big for his own britches." She waved her moose-head cane at the TV. "He needs to get home and shovel some manure. Nothing like shoveling crap to make you eat a little humble pie."

They all laughed. Kate stroked Happy's fur. "I wish Dean and Kel could have been here today. I hate to think of them having turkey dinner all alone."

"Judging from the magazine cover I saw at the Gas and Grub yesterday," Matt said, "I hardly think your brother needs to worry about being lonely."

"Yes, but can the supermodel du jour bake a melt-in-your-mouth pumpkin swirl cheesecake?"

"It only matters that you can," Matt said with a kiss on her forehead.

"I think I'll call Kelly. Just to see if she's okay."

"Make sure she's coming to the wedding," Edna said.

"She has no choice. She's my maid of honor."

Their upcoming nuptials had barely made a splash in the Hollywood tabloids, but it had created a whirlwind of excitement in Deer Lick. The Grange had been rented for their reception. Ollie would bartend. Maggie would serve as a bridesmaid. And her father would make their cake. Kate had put Edna in charge of decorations. God knew what she'd come up with. It was hard to tell with a woman who dyed her own stockings and wore a pumpkin suit on Halloween. But to Kate it didn't matter if her newfound friend used tumbleweeds and saw grass.

She only wished her mother could be there.

An ache floated around her heart and she nudged Happy from her lap and stood. "I left my cell in the car. I'll be right back."

"Hurry up, sweetheart," her dad said between bites of a turkey sandwich. How he could eat so soon after their enormous feast, she had no idea. "You don't want to miss the last five minutes of the game."

"I'll be right back." Kate knew her phone was in her purse in the bedroom and she'd already talked to her sister earlier. But there was one person she'd yet to wish a Happy Thanksgiving.

She opened the car door and slid inside, shivering at the crispy cold air. "Mom?"

For several minutes there was no response. She'd been about to give up when suddenly, without a key in the ignition, James Brown screamed from the radio "I feel good!"

Kate shook her head and laughed. "Another theme song?"

"Couldn't find one that said *I told you so.*"

Kate turned in the driver's seat. Her mother was riding shotgun. "You sound pretty pleased with yourself."

"Eh, I'll take all the credit I can get. That's one hell of a man you've got."

"I know."

"You better never run out on him again."

"I promise I won't." She couldn't imagine being without him.

"No regrets?"

"Not a one. Will you be at the wedding?"

Her mother chuckled. "Wouldn't miss it for anything."

Kate sighed. "Mom? Thank you. For everything. But especially for loving me when I wasn't so easy to love. And for never giving up."

Her mother laid her hand on top of Kate's. A tingle traveled up Kate's arm and into her heart.

"I told you, sweetheart, nothing can stop a mother's love. Not even death." A grin swept across her face. "It can't stop one from meddling either."

The tingle in Kate's heart turned to dismay. "So is this it? The end of your mission?"

"What? With a perfect matchmaking record you think I'm just going to give up and go hang out on some boring cloud?"

"Nah, not your style." Kate smiled. "So who's your next target?"

"Guess you'll just have to wait and see." Her mother shrugged. "One kid down, two to go."

"Will I still be able to see you?"

"I'll be there on the day you marry. I'll be there when your children are born."

Kate's eyes widened. "*Children?* As in plural?"

"Oh yeah. I'll be there for each and every one. Angels couldn't drag me away. And believe me, they've tried. Oops. Gotta go."

Kate blinked and her mother was gone. A knock on the car window made her jump. She looked up to find Matt standing there with snowflakes in his beautiful dark hair. She opened the door and he slid in next to her.

"Hi," he said, pressing his lips against hers.

"Hi."

"You okay?"

"I'm . . . great."

"Who were you talking to?"

Did she dare tell him? "It's kind of a long story," she said tentatively.

He drew her onto his lap and grinned while he slipped his hands beneath her sweatshirt. "I've got all night."

Kate laughed as he hugged her close. She brushed his mouth with hers. "Then I can think of better things to do with that mouth than talk." Everything inside her melted into a puddle of love and need. "You've got exactly five minutes to take me home and make love to me."

He gripped her bottom and she ended up flat on her back on the bench seat with him on top of her. "Who needs five minutes?" His warm breath whispered against the side of her neck.

Kate moaned as his hand covered her breast and he kissed her soft and sweet. She knew how lucky she'd been to find her way home again and into the arms of a man she could trust with her heart. And she certainly didn't plan on leaving anytime soon.

She'd found exactly what she'd been looking for when she hadn't even been looking.

Welcome back to the Sugar Shack with the second book in Candis Terry's fabulous, sweet and sexy small town series . . .

A career-ending injury sends NFL Quarterback Dean Silverthorne home to Deer Lick, Montana, with a chip on his wounded shoulder and no idea what to do with the rest of his life. Accustomed to living large on and off the field—often with an actress or model *du jour* on his arm, Dean's none too pleased to be in his backwater hometown . . . even if he loves his ridiculous, bakery-running family. But with a little motherly advice from beyond the grave and an instant attraction to a tenderhearted but feisty kindergarten teacher, Dean learns that there's more to love than life between the goal posts.

On sale November 2011

Candis Terry was born and raised near the sunny beaches of Southern California and now makes her home on an Idaho farm. She's experienced life in such diverse ways as working in a Hollywood recording studio to scooping up road apples left by her daughter's rodeo queening horse to working as a graphic designer. Only one thing has remained constant: Candis' passion for writing stories about relationships, the push and pull in the search for love, and the security one finds in their own happily ever after. Though her stories are set in small towns, Candis' wish is to give each of her characters a great big memorable love story rich with quirky characters, tons of fun, and a happy ending. For more, please visit *www.candisterry.com*.